Christel's Sunrise

The fourth book in the Twelve Dancing Princesses Series

Christine Young

ISBN: 978-1-62420-657-3

Credits
Cover Artist: Designs by Ms G
Editor: Christie L. Kraemer

Printed in the United States of America

Chapter One

London 1817

"Goliath, stop that!" Christel set the bow on the ground along with the arrow she was about to let fly at the target in front of her.

Ryder MacLaren watched Christel McLellan. He noticed her the first time he saw her and he'd inexplicably been drawn to her. The Duchess had sent him to the lake to find her and bring her to the recital. His father had been a good friend of the duke when he was alive. He'd stopped by to see how The Duchess was doing, something he always did when he was in the city.

Inwardly, Ryder grinned. Christel's hair had fallen in a few fanciful wisps around her shoulders, the sun catching the golden blond tresses and highlighting them. She was the most beautiful woman he'd ever seen and she had a way of captivating him to the point he couldn't stop thinking of her.

"Goliath..." The dog, the biggest wolfhound Ryder had ever seen, dropped a ball in front of her then sat back on his haunches, tail wagging and tongue lolling.

"All right then." She grabbed the ball and tossed it for the dog. He gave chase, picking it up in his huge mouth then tossing it into the air and catching it.

Ryder's breath caught in the back of his throat. He didn't move. The scene seemed so dreamlike and enchanting he could barely breathe, and for a moment he felt as if he intruded on something private.

Goliath tossed the ball in the air again but didn't catch it. The ball rolled toward the lake, then with a plop sent ripples flowing and water droplets flying.

"See what you've done." Christel placed fists on her hips and looked at the dog as if he could answer her. The dog sauntered toward her and with a bounce, placed his front paws on her shoulder.

The huge animal was taller than Christel, and now her light pink dress sported paw prints. Getting her to the recital in this condition would mortify The Duchess. But it appeared the lady in question didn't care if she arrived at the gathering.

"Go get it." She pushed the dog away and pointed to the lake. Goliath sat and grinned, shaking his head as if to say, make me.

"Go on." Christel pointed her finger toward the ball again as if trying to urge him forward.

"Goliath, you threw it in the lake. Do you expect me to get it for you? Well, of course you do."

Goliath wagged his shaggy tail, seeming to grin at his mistress.

Christel breathed in deep before looking at the lake and the ball. She found a large rock close to the ball and stepped on it. She kneeled, pulling the water in front of the ball with her hand.

It inched closer.

She tried again, stretching—stretching. Then, with just the slightest waver, she fell stomach first into the water.

He couldn't stop the roar of laughter that followed her drenching. She rose from the lake, hair dripping, gown molded to her hourglass figure. At the sight, his body tightened with need. *My God, Christel, you've turned into a beautiful woman. It seemed he could see every curve and what wasn't apparent he imagined.*

Somewhere in the back of his mind he recalled a visit from the Clan McLellan to his home at MacLaren castle. She'd been a precocious child back then. Blond ringlets bouncing around her shoulders while she played in the courtyard with some of the children.

He was at least five years older at the time, and he didn't pay much attention to her and her younger siblings.

Having seen her several times during the season, she'd even been part of a wager between Damian Andrews, Aric Lakeland and himself. Now her cousins were married. He didn't understand why, but during that time he'd kept his distance.

At that moment, Goliath chose to join Christel in the lake. He grabbed his ball, racing away only to return and drop his ball at Ryder's feet

"So, you want me to play too." Ryder picked up the ball just as Goliath shook, water droplets spraying everywhere. "Well, I didn't see that coming. Don't know why though." Laughing, Ryder wiped moisture from his face.

"He's incorrigible." Christel rose from the water and held her hand out to Ryder. "Just when you think he's going to behave, he does whatever he wants."

Just like his owner, I presume. "Christel McLellan?" he questioned, knowing exactly who she was. "The Duchess sent me..."

"To bring me to the recital?" she finished for him. "Well, I'm not going in this condition. Couldn't have planned it better if I'd tried, but I didn't—try, that is. And I don't believe I know who you are."

"Ryder MacLaren." Disappointed she didn't remember him, he accepted her hand and helped her from the lake. "You're right. The Duchess wanted me to bring you to the recital." He let go of her hand when she reached land and stepped onto the grass. "You can't go like that."

She smirked, trying to look solemn before she shrugged. "I know. Like I said, couldn't have planned this scenario better."

"I'm at a loss for words."

"No one wants to hear me play or sing. When it's my turn, the good people of the ton either leave the room or cover their ears. I screech like an alley cat when I sing, and my fingers are all thumbs when I play."

"That bad?" He chuckled, thinking about all the horrible ones he'd attended. "I don't like recitals either but for far different reasons."

"Let me guess. The good mothers parade their daughters for your inspection. That's why I'm going to become a nun."

"Really?" *The poor convent would be in an uproar from sunrise to sunset.*

"It's true."

"Tell The Duchess how you feel." Ryder shrugged out of his

3

jacket and wrapped it around Christel whose body shook from the cold. When he touched her, untamed energy swept through him as if a bolt of lightning had slammed into his chest. He cleared his throat, unsure of what to say next.

"I have told her. Thank you for the jacket." She adjusted it around her shoulders. "She has a mind of her own and thinks she knows what is best for me, but she doesn't."

"You've goose bumps on your arms. We need to get you back to the house." Ryder wondered if The Duchess would make her change and go to the recital.

"Whatever for? I can't make it on time and I'm not going late." She set off towards her discarded bow and quiver of arrows. "Could you get the target for me?" She shivered, rubbing her arms.

"Sure."

A few seconds later, he returned to her side, the target and four arrows in hand. "You're a great shot." Ryder admired her ability. Most women had no talents such as this.

"You sound surprised. All my sisters are good archers." She pushed wet hair behind her head then wrapped it around her hand, squeezing water from it and watching it drip onto the ground.

"I am, truthfully. Most ladies don't spend their time at target practice or retrieving balls for their dog."

"And falling into lakes? In case you haven't noticed, I'm no lady and I don't want to be either." Her back stiffened and her hands fisted. "Parading me in front of appropriate suitors will not create one, a lady."

He focused on her, thinking how wrong she was and wondered how she would describe a lady. "From my viewpoint, you are very much a lady. Why would you say you're not?"

"I'm not like them. I'm not searching for the most eligible man to wed. I don't want to marry and find myself beholden to some man's whims. While I might want children someday, I'd like to decide when and how many."

His laughter rolled across the lake and his regard for her grew. "Once again you surprise me. If not a wealthy husband, what do you want in life?" His strides slowed to match hers as they walked to The Duchess's home.

"I don't know yet. I just know I'm not meant for marriage—at least not to a man. I desire more from life, something fulfilling."

He coughed, trying to keep back the words. "I see." Who was she meant to be married to, a woman?

"No, I don't think you do. Even though my sisters Aidan, Eveleen, and Allura, have spent half of their lives trying to deter me, I'm meant to be a nun, married to the church. But they've left me wondering if my life long ambition is really what I want. So for now, I'm going to wait and see what the next few years brings my way."

"A good plan I'm sure." Truly perplexed now, he wasn't sure what to say to this woman who he was suddenly focused on and who drew his attention like no other. Pursuing this conversation as well as the lady interested him more than he cared to admit. She had been his focal point since she arrived in London. Business had taken him away for a while, but now he was back.

They walked in silence for a few minutes, the townhouse now looming in front of her. They stopped. Brief thoughts of holding her in his arms and kissing her swept his body with a swift intense heat.

"I hope The Duchess isn't too angry. Think I'll run up the back stairs."

"And leave me to explain everything that has transpired to her? I don't think so." He was usually pretty calm about such matters, but this incident was not of the ordinary variety. The Duchess was a formidable lady who had most the ton cowering in their shoes when she vented her anger their way or called in her favors. The Duchess held compromising information on most.

"Please." She smiled at him, and lightly touched him on the shoulder. "I'll change as fast as I can. You won't be alone with her for very long. I promise."

His heart melted and for the first time in his life, he couldn't figure out how to say no. "Very well." Bloody hell, what would he tell The Duchess? Her charge fell into the water while she was chasing her dog's ball?

Ryder's mind raced with a myriad of stories and false

explanations. He didn't think anyone would believe the truth unless they'd seen it first hand. But perhaps The Duchess knew who she dealt with. This couldn't be the first or the last scrape Christel McLellan would undergo.

He inhaled a long and very deep breath, praying for courage to confront the legendary woman with the facts. This was a formidable lady. He looked up just in time to see the back door to the townhouse close. Well, in for a penny in for a pound.

He strode up the steps and knocked on the door. Scarlet, The Duchess's maid and companion, stood in the opening tapping one foot.

"Ryder?" Scarlett asked. "Where's Milady Christel? You best make sure she is alright and not a hair on her pretty head has been hurt, or The Duchess will have your hide."

Well, that was blunt and to the point. He couldn't tell her she was in her room hiding for a few minutes. He cleared his throat, running a finger around his collar. "Well..."

"She's done it again, hasn't she?" Scarlett motioned for him to step inside. "Now the truth; out with it. We all know it's not your fault. What has she done this time? Would you like tea? Or some lemon bars?"

"I don't think she's going to be ready in time for the recital." He peered around the corner to see if The Duchess was waiting for them.

Come in and sit down. I'll pour you a glass of brandy or scotch. Oh, I forgot I asked if you wanted tea." Scarlet bustled around him then pointed to a seat, clearly distracted by the events.

He sat down, still holding the target and the arrows. "Scotch, please." This was not at all what he'd expected, but then The Duchess wasn't in the room yet.

"I see Miss Christel was out shooting that bloody bow and arrow again. Can't get her to practice the piano or go to her voice lessons. Just doesn't have any interest in ladylike things."

Ryder wasn't sure how to tell her that learning to use a bow and arrow where the McLellans lived could save her life or someone she cared about which was something playing the piano could never do. He cleared his throat several times in an attempt to speak.

"Here it is." Scarlet handed him the drink.

"Well, did you find her?" The Duchess, leaning on a cane and appearing uncharacteristically fragile walked into the room. "I suspect you did and she's found a way to escape her responsibilities."

Last time he'd seen the lady, she'd not used anything for support and that was only about an hour ago. "She's..." He cleared his throat once more wishing he didn't feel so tongue-tied.

"I'm here," Christel flounced into the parlor with an amazing smile just in time to keep him from explaining what had happened.

"You're late. Again." The Duchess, a stern expression on her face, tapped her cane on the carpeted floor.

"I'm sorry, but I fell in the pond trying to retrieve Goliath's ball. Ryder," she nodded his way, her wet hair dampening her dress, making it cling tightly to her body, "was so kind. He pulled me from the water without thinking about himself. He's a hero." She stopped to draw in a deep breath and slanted him a wicked grin.

Ryder almost laughed outright. Christel McLellan was a little devil in an angel's disguise. He could almost see the halo. The Duchess was wrapped around Christel's little finger, and he didn't think either of them knew it.

The Duchess turned his way. He nodded and shrugged his shoulders, trying to look nonchalant, yet he couldn't keep the grin off his face. "Happened just as she said. Wasn't a whole lot I could do about it."

"Darling child, you can't keep on this way. You have to at least pretend to like these things. Scarlett, pour me a glass of brandy, please." She took a moment, "Are there any lemon bars around?"

"Balls, recitals and the never-ending stream of suitors? Why would I pretend to appreciate events that make me feel self-conscious and awkward?" Christel picked up a strawberry tart and plopped it in her mouth. "I like to shoot and take long walks. I like to play with Goliath, not on the piano."

"Of course, and Lord Rathen, you should really answer some of his letters to you. He's interested and politeness is important."

"Why?" Ryder and Christel questioned in unison, both staring at the other. Ryder knew exactly who Lord Rathen was and what he wanted from Christel. His gut tightened.

"Sorry, none of my business," Ryder said but noticed the grin on The Duchess's face then watched the smile change to a look of concern.

"Because he's a cad. He believes I have some sort of trust fund or inheritance. I've told him several times I don't have a penny to my name and that I have to find a wealthy man to marry or none at all, but he won't be dissuaded."

"He is wealthy," The Duchess said.

"He's gambled away his entire inheritance plus some in IOUs." Ryder needed to clear the air and tell The Duchess the truth. Then he stood, "If I'm no longer needed to take Christel to the recital, I'll be on my way." He didn't want to leave, but he was beginning to feel like an intruder in this conversation.

"Please stay for dinner," The Duchess invited him, once more a grin on her weathered face no longer seeming as fragile as she had when she entered the room.

"That won't be necessary." Ryder pulled at his neckcloth, wishing to be anywhere but here, suddenly feeling as if The Duchess played matchmaker with him. Settling down with a debutante, even one as fetching and intriguing as Christel, was not on his list but still, there was something about her that called to him. What he really needed was to find another sunrise in some other land. He sorely needed a distraction.

"Of course it's not necessary. Relax, please. It's just my way of saying thank you. We would appreciate your company."

"Auntie Charlotte, he probably has somewhere else to go. I'm sure the MacLaren is a busy man. He doesn't have time to waste with the likes of me." Christel smiled sweetly, appearing to be as weary of The Duchess' intentions as he was.

"Pshaw," The Duchess waved her hand in the air. "A man has to eat. You must stay and tell us all about your travels. I've heard via the grapevine you've been most everywhere in the world and learned a few different tricks along the way."

Goliath stood at the top of the stairs, barking and seeming to punctuate the invitation before turning and racing down the hallway.

"The source of my troubles." Christel watched the dog go then turned to her aunt.

Ryder stepped toward the door. "Really, I must be on my way." He turned to Christel, wondering if he'd ever get the picture of her rising from the lake, clothes plastered to her as if they were a second skin from his mind.

"Will I see you again?" Christel asked, seeming to be unexpectedly interested in him.

If I have any say...

But Ryder cleared his throat. "I'm leaving town for a couple of days, perhaps when I return next week."

The smile on her face turned to a tiny frown, her eyebrows furrowing together. "It's that way? All right. I don't care at all." She picked up her skirts and headed back up the steps. Before she reached the top, she turned. "Perhaps Richy Rathen will take me for a carriage ride in Hyde Park."

~ * ~

Why did she say that? No way in hell would she go on a carriage ride or anything else with the cad. Yet she appreciated the look on Ryder's face when she'd mentioned Richy. Perhaps the desired result was achieved.

"Duchess." Scarlett entered the room. "Lord Richy Rathen is here to see Miss Christel."

Her stomach lurched as her body quivered, despising the man. *No.* She looked at Ryder, hoping he wouldn't leave her alone with Richy, a man she detested. But Ryder didn't appear to see her fear or recognize the distress she felt.

Richy strode in, swinging a cane and whistling with a confident air. His eyes focused on her. She stood at the top of the stairs, hands clasped tightly in front of her while her skin crawled. "Lord Rathen," she nodded.

"Come down, dear," The Duchess motioned her forward. "You must be polite to your guests. All of them."

Where she came from, in Scotland, she was expected to speak her mind in a situation such as this. With a deep breath, she complied, wishing the lady wasn't so intent on finding her a husband and trying to figure out a way to get rid of Richy. She knew her auntie had been dreaming of planning big weddings for her and her cousins. Both Amorica and Ravyn had disappointed her. Amorica eloped and Ravyn's wedding was a small one in this very parlor.

Rathen bowed. "I was hoping you were at home this evening when you didn't appear at the recital." He slanted Ryder a meaningful glare, seeming to say, what are you doing here?

Rathen's red-rimmed pale blue eyes were eclipsed by his waxy appearing flesh. Beneath his shirt his stomach sagged, proclaiming the indulgences he'd partaken of throughout his life. He twirled his mustache and grinned, his gaze riveted on Christel.

"Would you care to join me for a ride?" Richy asked pleasantly. "It's a beautiful day and I'm sure everyone who is anyone will be in the park."

Christel prayed Ryder would jump in and claim her time, but the eerie silence told her that wasn't about to happen.

"I'm not really feeling well. I've a monstrous headache." She brought the back of her hand to her forehead and closed her eyes, wishing the horrible man to vanish. When she opened them, he still stood in front of her.

"Perhaps a ride would help the ache in your head. A little fresh air always works wonders." Ryder's husky voice surprised her.

He really didn't mean to encourage Lord Rathen, did he? And did she hear a hint of laughter?

"I..." she began, playing with her skirt.

Ryder had turned to Rathen. "Miss Christel has already agreed to a ride with me. The horses have been saddled and Christel was just going upstairs to change into her riding clothes and dry her hair so she doesn't catch a cold. The Duchess has asked me to stay for dinner."

Thank God Ryder had taken charge of the situation, but Richy was clearly displeased.

"Perhaps the lady should make her own decisions." Rathen cleared his throat and looked pointedly at her.

"I did. I told Ryder I would ride with him." Lord, but she'd never been so relieved. Just looking at Ryder made her head swim with thoughts of romantic sensual kisses exactly the way Amorica, her cousin, had described them.

"Then why did you claim sickness?" Richy asked her pointedly a frown on his face.

She paused, winding her fingers tightly into the fabric of her dress. "I didn't know what to say when you asked. Please accept my apologies. I guess I handled that poorly."

"Politeness is ingrained is some people." Ryder spoke up as he stepped closer to Christel who had descended the stairs during the conversation.

"I don't equate a lie with politeness," Lord Rathen said. "I will join the two of you."

"No." Christel could not allow that to happen. "The truth is, Lord Rathen, I do not like you, and I don't want to go for a ride with you. Ever. The lie was simply spoken so I wouldn't have to tell you how I feel about you."

Richy's brows drew together in a scowl, his lips pursed then twitched. He squinted his eyes and venom leapt from his words. "You will regret this." With that said, he turned and marched from the room.

Scarlett let him out before returning. "Doubt if we've seen the last of him even though I hope I'm wrong."

"Oh, Scarlett, I hope he never comes around again. That man makes me sick to my stomach." Christel looked to Ryder for confirmation.

But Ryder stared out the window, his arms behind his back, rocking on his heels. "What are you waiting for?"

"Me? I didn't think...I mean you were leaving. Are we going for a ride?" She caught her breath with a deep inhale.

Ryder turned from gazing out the window. "Changed my mind. Richy was right about one thing. It's a beautiful day and I'd like to enjoy the afternoon in your company. Everything else can wait."

Her heart fluttered and she felt the smile to the tips of her toes. "I'd love to ride with you. Give me a minute to dress."

"And dry your hair." He added with an emphasis on dry.

Good God, but his appearance was different from Lord Rathen. She met his whiskey-hued eyes, and her stomach made a little flutter, the response catching her off-guard. Surprised, she stared at his dark, furrowed brows, the well-chiseled lines of his rugged face. His black hair was tied back with a leather thong, dampened as if he'd just been doused by Goliath, a slightly off-center nose that spoke of an adventurous past. A few days' worth of razor stubble covered his throat and jaw. And his body was lean and well-muscled.

Skirt hiked, she raced up the stairs. Once inside her room, she explored her closet, tossing clothes on the floor until she found a beautiful blue riding habit—thought again. She didn't want to ride sidesaddle and somehow she didn't think Ryder would think less of her if she rode astride. Arturo hated the sidesaddle. He'd prance around as if he wanted to shake off the horrible thing.

From her trunk she pulled out a pair of riding pants and a shirt. She didn't take the time to dry her hair but wound it in a tight coif, securing it with pins to hold it in place. A few minutes later she stood at the top of the stairs, one hand resting on the banister, her heart beating a rapid staccato. She drew a deep breath and closed her eyes.

When she opened her eyes, Ryder stood at the bottom, a smile on his face. "What took you so long?"

"Couldn't decide what to wear." She made her way down the staircase, still hesitant.

"You like to ride astride?" He held out his hand for her as she reached the bottom step.

"I'm Scottish," she said as if that explained everything. Until she'd arrived in London, she'd never ridden sidesaddle. The Duchess had insisted she learn.

Christel liked to believe no self-respectable Scotswoman would ride any way but astride.

He led her through the house to the back door and on to the stable.

"Have a nice time." The Duchess stood in the doorway of her townhouse waving and grinning.

Christel turned and waved at her. Ryder nodded.

Cantering down the streets of London, Christel felt as if she were in heaven. The sky, dotted with clouds, was a brilliant shade of blue. Once they reached Hyde Park, birds sang in the trees, a soft breeze ruffled the leaves and a song in her heart helped her believe in life again.

Riding next to this handsome chivalrous man gave her second and third thoughts about giving her life to God. Perhaps her cousins were right. She wasn't cut out to be celibate. Particularly if she acknowledged the carnal thoughts racing through her mind about Ryder, the nuns would kick her out or not let her in the door.

She didn't know what to say so she swallowed the ridiculous phrase that came to mind. She felt like a schoolgirl with her first beau. She was no longer a schoolgirl, and Ryder wasn't a beau, just her savior.

"I'm worried about you." Ryder slowed his horse.

"Why?" That was a strange thing to say.

"Richy is after you for some reason. He's a wastrel and a gambler. He wants you and he's not going to stop until he gets you to the altar. He can be ruthless."

She shook her head, feeling as if Ryder was wrong. "He lost the wager and Damian won. It's done with. I won't ever marry that horrible man."

"So, you do remember me." He didn't wait for an answer and grinning continued to say, "Don't delude yourself. Rathen is not finished where you're concerned. Rumor has it he has no money and his father is about to disown him if he hasn't done so already. A respectable wife would go a long way in his relationship with his father."

Heat rose to her face. "I remember every time I saw you, talked to you." She had to clear her throat, trying to answer his every statement. "If he's after me for my money, he should know I have none. Not a penny to my name."

"No dowry?" Ryder questioned, grinning, seeming to enjoy their easy banter.

"No. I have nothing." She wondered if Ryder acted interested in her because he thought she had funds to bring to a marriage. She hoped not. If that were true, this might be the last time she would see him.

"Where Richy is concerned, perhaps that's a good thing." Ryder pointed to a squirrel scampering up a tree. "You could hope he runs from you, but first we'll have to put the word out there. Make sure he understands what you've been trying so desperately to explain to him."

"You really think he might persist in wooing me? Even after what I told him today? What kind of fool would pursue a woman who despises him?"

"One who is in dire financial straits and can think of no other way to pay back a huge sum of money." Ryder's back had stiffened.

She followed his line of sight to see Richy Rathen riding in a carriage with a lady. "Do you know her?"

Ryder shook his head. "Is he moving on to someone else, or is he trying to make you jealous?"

"He can't make me envious, so let's assume he's moving on." Relieved he didn't want her any longer and must believe she was poor as a church mouse, she urged her horse a bit faster and in the opposite direction of Richey's carriage.

"Let's enjoy the rest of the day, shall we?"

"Can we ride somewhere else?" Christel had lost her light-hearted mood. Richy had a way of bringing dark clouds whenever he appeared. He terrified her and she didn't know why.

"Where? I'm yours for the day." Ryder motioned with one arm, seeming to indicate they could ride anywhere she wanted.

"Don't know." Christel eyed the surrounding countryside. "Any suggestions?" She didn't want to be so bold as to ask to go somewhere more private.

"I believe I know just the place. Follow me."

They left Hyde Park behind them, riding farther into the country and leaving the city in the distance.

A meadow stretched in front of them. Christel looked sideways at Ryder. "Race?" She dug her heels into Arturo and he surged forward, leaving Ryder behind.

"No fair."

She heard him call out the words and grinned. Arturo flew with the wind. Her hair fell loose from the many pins that had confined the locks. Her breath raced, her heart pounding. She heard the thundering of his horse and knew he closed in fast. His stallion was larger and would win, but the exhilaration of the moment had her wondering if there was anything better than this.

He flew past her then nodded at her before slowing his horse to a walk.

"You win." She pulled up. Arturo was winded and needed a nice cool down. She slid off the horse and taking the reins, strolled to the top of the hill. Below, a small pond shimmered when sunlight danced off the ripples made from the wind.

"It's beautiful."

"Yes."

He stood beside her, hands clasped behind his back, his body so close she was sure she heard his heartbeat and felt his heat.

Leather and horse were the scent emanating from him. She wanted to reach out and touch him but she didn't dare. The thoughts in her head were bad enough, enough to condemn her in the eyes of the church.

She sat down, trying to keep her view on the water but so aware of the male strength beside her. She smoothed her trousers across her knees, which she'd tucked up in a tight ball then set her chin on top them.

"It's so peaceful." She picked a dandelion and twirled it between two fingers then plucked off a petal.

He loves me. He loves me not. Crazy, I'm going certifiably crazy.

She remembered all-too-well this saying. She'd pulled many dandelion petals from its rightful stem.

"Look." Ryder pointed to a large bird that had suddenly soared into the air, a fish hanging from its bill.

"I wish..." she began.

"What is it you want, little one?" he asked before he sat down beside her, stretching out and leaning on an elbow. He picked a piece of grass and stuck it between his teeth.

He appeared relaxed and all male. "I just wish I were home, in Scotland. I don't like London, hate the endless parties and gossip, despise that some men marry for money then keep a mistress on the side. Like they were dessert. I wish I could feel as free as that bird." Christel pointed to the bird.

"Not all men." His brows furrowed together.

"Would you keep a mistress if you were married?" She covered her mouth with one hand. "I'm sorry. It's none of my business. My horrid curiosity and my unmannerly way of blurting out my thoughts are some of the reasons my cousins and my sisters tell me I'd never make a very good nun. I'm just not pious."

"Why on earth would you give yourself to the church?"

He looked displeased for some reason she couldn't fathom.

She shrugged her shoulders, unable to really give an answer. "I'm not sure you'd understand. Sometimes I'm not sure I understand. It's just, well, I feel a calling. And I can't explain..."

"Really, a calling. Or are you afraid of men and sex?"

"Well, that was blunt."

"Touché." He smiled before bending close and tucking an errant strand of hair behind her ear. "If you are going to ask probing questions, then I believe I should be able to do the same. And to answer your questions, no, I don't believe I would keep a mistress. You see, I wouldn't marry anyone unless I cared for them a lot. And if you care for someone, you would do nothing to hurt them."

She had looked down at her toes peeking out from beneath her dress. "Was that Richy's mistress in the carriage?"

~ * ~

"I told that Richy Rathen not to come here ever again." Spittle flew from The Duchess' lips when she spoke. "I've never been so outraged. If he ever shows up on this doorstep, I'll have him thrown out." She gestured so hard tea flew from her cup.

"Calm yourself. I'll have him tossed on his arse if he ever has the audacity to darken these halls again." Scarlett took the cup from The Duchess' hand and poured her more tea. "Have a lemon bar." She pushed the plate closer to the older woman. Food will soothe your anger."

The Duchess held her hand at her throat. "I don't think my heart will ever stop racing."

"Look on the bright side, Charlotte. Ryder didn't leave and now the darling couple are out riding."

"Bright side, yes, if she hadn't chosen to wear her riding breeches. She has several lovey habits that were just made for the sidesaddle." The Duchess sipped her tea, hoping Christel and Ryder's little excursion would take them someplace a bit more private than Hyde Park. Before she died, she wanted to do something right, and she'd always known Christel and Ryder were made for each other.

She hadn't exactly failed on the first two attempts at matchmaking, but her plans had not resulted in beautiful weddings. She needed to get this one done right and maybe the proud papas of the other families would send three more girls. My goodness, she pondered, who would come next?

"You wouldn't think as much of your little niece if she gave in to womanly wiles. She likes to be herself, that one."

"She's a lot like me, but I never for one minute thought the place for me was hidden away in a convent, married to the church. No, I wouldn't give her two minutes before the kindly nuns were overwhelmed with her antics and tossed her out on her tiny backside."

"When do you expect them back?"

"Not for a couple more hours." She slanted Scarlett a sly smile.

"No!" Scarlett covered her mouth with her hands and leaned forward. "Really, you're not hoping..."

"Not what you're thinking, but maybe a first kiss would be nice, a real kiss. There is nothing at all wrong with kissing." She set her cup on the table and looked at the ceiling, remembering the first kiss the duke gave her. Ah, but how she missed him, the laughter, the quiet conversations, the sex...

"A kiss would be nice," Scarlett agreed then she waggled her finger "But nothing more until the vows are said."

"Let's not put the cart before the horse. They are not even engaged. Ryder has not courted her properly yet." But she didn't think Ryder would do anything properly.

"Are you telling me not to start planning a wedding?"

"I think we need to give the young ones some time to fall in love first."

"Or get in a wee bit over their heads," Scarlett added with a wink.

Chapter Two

Ryder slanted Christel a sideways glance, not wanting to tell her the truth about Richy but knowing she deserved the facts. "I believe the woman you saw in the carriage is his mistress, at least the one of today. It seems he changes them weekly." Ryder watched carefully for her reaction.

"Actually, that's what I thought." She smoothed the fabric of her pants then looked upward. "What would it take to fall in love?"

Ryder often wondered about that. "I'd have to really like the woman, and I'd want her to be someone I could tell my every thought." And that was what he did here. He wanted to touch Christel, smooth her hair off her shoulders. He wanted to kiss her, taste her essence.

"Me too," she said and her voice sounded a bit wistful.

"Tell your every thought?" His query had him thinking about Christel as more than just a pretty face and luscious body.

"Yes," she nodded. "I think so. I'd want to spend every waking minute with him, and I'd have to enjoy his company."

And I, my little one, would also like to spend every sleeping minute with you. "I'd not want to leave her side but would be happy to know she was in my home waiting for me when I returned from work."

"Or an adventure?"

"It would be imperative for me to have my wife by my side when I saw a new sunrise." If he loved someone, he knew that to be the truth, and the more he spent time with Christel the more he thought she might be that woman.

"I like to see new things, but if I enter a convent and become a nun, I don't suppose I'd have a lot of opportunities."

18

Ryder stiffened, her wistful expression tearing at his heart. He needed to find a way to dissuade her of those thoughts. "I think..." he paused for a moment and did take that time to move a piece of her hair behind her ear, thinking he'd like to trace the delicate pink shell with his tongue, "...you'd wither and die if you became a nun. Your spirit is wild and untamed."

She pointed a finger at him, a strange light shining in her eyes. "Why does everyone think that?"

He knew, at least for him, it was in his best interest for her to stay far away from a convent. His feelings for her were something he wanted to explore in depth and he needed time. "Because you have so much to offer the world, and I honestly don't believe you would be happy if you were confined."

"I don't know if you are right. I do want to give my life to God. Amorica says there are other ways besides entering an abbey."

"She is right, you know." He leaned closer to Christel, could smell the sweetness of her breath, the subtle fragrance that was hers alone. His heart raced with anticipation of a kiss.

Christel sighed. "I've studied the bible. I love the stories." She placed her hand on his shoulder.

"That doesn't mean you could survive living the life of a nun. Do you want children? A husband? Have you ever thought about those things?" He held his breath, waiting for the answer.

"I never really thought a husband or children were in my future, at least not until we all came to London."

He placed his hand on her cheek then gently touched her lips with his thumb. She moved her head slightly as if trying to give him better access. "I want to kiss you."

"All right."

He gently touched her lips.

He knew he had to move slowly and doing so proved to be difficult. His mouth met hers. The kiss was soft and she felt so delicate beneath his caress. He moved his hand to the back of her head but didn't need to hold her in place. She moved a tiny hand to the back of his neck as if working on instinct.

Then he pulled away, slightly, to look into sky blue eyes. "Do you like that?"

She nodded and licked her lips. Then he bent closer and kissed her again, this time tracing the seam of her lips with his tongue. He desperately wanted to taste the very essence of her life.

She met him, touched her tongue to his. He closed his eyes, knowing he'd never been quite so gentle with anyone before. But he needed her to understand how beautiful this was and sensual. He wanted to bind her to him in the most primitive ways, and he needed her to ask for more.

Her fingers wound into his hair and he reveled in the feeling of her touch. His hand slid down her back, pulling her closer. He felt the rise and fall of her breasts against his chest, and he wanted to peel her clothes off and see her but he knew that would scare her. So, he savored the moments he was able to have, knowing he would come back to her and that she meant more to him than anyone else ever had.

He drew away and looked at her. "Did you like that? The kiss?"

She nodded. "Yes." Her single word was a breathy sigh.

"Would you want to go without that—kissing—the rest of your life." She was not meant for a life of celibacy.

Christel fiddled with her fingers and the fabric of her shirt. "No." she looked away from him. "I don't think you play fair."

He leaned back and let out a deep belly laugh. "I don't, not when I want to prove a point." But he wanted so much more from her and the feelings came on fast, strong and so unexpectedly.

"I think we need to get back." The sun sat low on the western sky. "The Duchess will start to worry."

He had enjoyed his time with Christel so much he hadn't noticed the lateness of the hour. He had never thought to fall in love or how it would feel, and he didn't know if this was love, but he knew he didn't want to let her out of his sight, and he felt a strong need to protect her. He wanted to make love with her but understood he would wait. These feelings and thoughts were so new to him, he intended to take a step back and think.

An hour later, The Duchess stood at the door of the stables, tapping her foot, her back so rigid Ryder thought of a broom handle. He knew she'd be worried but he hadn't expected her to greet them before they dismounted. The Duchess' protective nature matched his.

"Oh my, she must be so worried about us. I should have paid closer attention to the time."

Ryder searched for a plausible excuse for their tardiness but could come up with nothing. *Sorry, Duchess, the time got away from me,* didn't sound very good. He knew what his imagination would come up with, and The Duchess had been married to one of London's most dangerous and notorious rakes.

"My apologies."

"Well, you should." The Duchess shook her sword cane at him, the glint in her eyes startling him.

She must want to slice and dice him for his transgressions. Surprising him, she set the cane down and slanted him a wicked smile, one that sent a lightning bolt to his core. She thought she knew what they had been doing and she was happy.

"Duchess, really we were just talking." Christel turned to Ryder. "Would you like to stay for dinner?"

Ryder wasn't sure. He glanced at The Duchess and back to Christel. Then he loosened the tie on his shirt. "I—"

Looking over her shoulder, "Of course he is going to stay." The Duchess strode across the lawn to the house. "Any man who steals a kiss from a debutant has to stay for dinner."

She blushed, confirming The Duchess' words. "You know you don't have to. If you have other more important—"

Ryder cut her off with a flourish of his hand. "I have nothing waiting for me at home." He'd planned to meet friends for a little drinking and gambling, but he realized he'd rather spend time with Christel.

Christel's smile melted his heart; all his macho vanished with the smile. His parched throat threatened to give his emotions away.

"Christel, how are you." Ravyn flew in the door and gave her cousin a big hug.

"What?" Christel turned to Ravyn for an answer.

"Ravyn and I are here for dinner. We are leaving on the morning tide. Didn't Ryder tell you?"

Ryder felt awkward. He'd forgotten they were leaving. Had forgotten everything but looking at Christel and wondering if he would find a chance to steal another kiss. He shrugged. "I didn't think to say anything. The subject never came up." And the way their marriage had played out, he wasn't positive Ravyn would follow Aric to the States.

"Are you my only surprise tonight?" Christel asked.

"I hope so. Sometimes surprises aren't nice." Ravyn's smile didn't convince Ryder she wanted to leave with Aric.

The girls sat down to chatter and gossip. Aric took Ryder aside. "When are you going to need me in the states?"

"Another few months and I think we will have the crops in. You can bring the three horses over when you come."

Ryder nodded, unsure how this would all progress. He didn't want to leave London and when he'd volunteered for the job, he didn't know Christel. He'd seen her and been mesmerized by her beauty, but he never talked to her. Today had revealed a lot about Christel. She'd stolen his breath with her smile and his heart with her sweetness.

Along with his burgeoning feelings for Christel, he was afraid for her. A determined Richy, and one who owed half of London money lost through gambling, was a dangerous man.

"I doubt if I'll stay long," Ryder told Aric, fear taking over thoughts. "Have you ever had the feeling something wasn't going to end well?" He wondered where that thought came from and once again the image of Richy Rathen stood out in his head.

~ * ~

After the men had left, Christel and Ravyn chatted in Christel's room.

"Do you love him?" Christel watched the play of expressions on Ravyn's face. Christel needed to know what love felt like.

"Yes," Ravyn answered, but the one word didn't sound convincing.

"But you're not sure."

Ravyn sighed and gathered her skirts around her. "I intended to rid myself of Dicky. And I blurted out that Aric and I were engaged. The Duchess took us one step farther and had us married before either of us could explain what I'd done. But I think I love him. We haven't really had a chance to find out."

"But you don't want to go with him." Christel cocked her head and studied her cousin.

"I'd like to stay in London. I'm not like you, Christel. I love parties and balls." She waved her arms in an outward motion. "All the festivities."

"I would be happier anywhere else. Isn't it strange how things work? You're going off to an untamed wilderness and I'm staying here."

"And what about you and the MacLaren?"

"I don't know what you mean." Christel rose and paced the room. She stopped to look out the window at the street below. She heard Ravyn laugh.

"Of course you do, silly child. Do you love him?"

"I haven't known him for all that long." She plucked at her skirts.

"But he's been around all these past months," Ravyn said.

"Off and on," Christel said. "When you and Amorica were avoiding Damian and Aric, Ryder was rarely anywhere to be seen."

"I suppose you're right. But he couldn't stop looking at you and whenever you caught his attention, he had this strange expression. I don't know how to explain it but he looked smitten."

"Even if I were in love with him, he's not a man to settle down. Everyone knows that. He chases sunrises and adventures." Christel felt a wave of sadness sweep through her. She touched her lips, remembering the kisses between them and the heat that pooled low in her gut. She closed her eyes and relived the moments.

"You are in love with him."

"I think he's the kindest, most gentle man I've ever met. He makes my heart race when I look at him, and I could tell him anything. If that is love, then yes, I'm in love with him."

"Then we are both a sorry lot, aren't we? Aric is racing off to America to make a home in the backwoods, and Ryder is a man who never sits still. He'll be in the states in a few months."

"The states..." Christel murmured, knowing her thoughts about Ryder were true, but she held out hope that perhaps he'd love her enough to ask her to go with him. Unlike Raven, she wouldn't care if there were no balls to dress for or recitals to attend.

"You didn't know."

Christel shook her head. "Why would I? He has no ties to me. We went for a ride today and he stayed for dinner. In truth, he rescued me from Richy, nothing more."

"Don't fool yourself."

"I'm being realistic." Christel turned from the window. "I've heard a lot about Ryder. All the debutants talk about him as if he's the catch of the day. But he doesn't show interest in anyone."

"Except you."

"Very little. He stepped in today when Richy wanted to take me for a carriage ride in the park, that's all. He's chivalrous."

"Men like Ryder don't do anything they don't want to do."

"Really, not even to be nice?" Christel thought Ravyn was right, but that put a new spin on what had happened. She touched her lips again.

"He kissed you." Ravyn rose and gave Christel a big hug. "See, I'm right. He loves you."

"Ravyn, one kiss does not mean a man is in love." Christel swallowed back the tears that formed in her throat.

"No, but it means something."

Christel's tears turned to laughter at her cousin's crazy thoughts. "You are the foolish one if you think to turn one kiss into love."

"But you don't want to become a nun any longer," Ravyn shot back. "He's changed your mind."

"Maybe." Christel had come to the conclusion she wasn't suited for life in a convent a long time ago. She just didn't know what to make of her future. She couldn't live with her aunt Charlotte forever, and she certainly didn't want to be in the marriage market for another month.

Ravyn clapped her hands together. "I'm so happy for you."

"Ravyn." A knock on the door startled Christel. "It's time to go." Aric stood outside.

Ravyn gave Christel another hug.

"Be careful."

"I will, and I will hope for only the best for you." Ravyn left Christel with her thoughts.

Christel knew she had to find a way to go home. She didn't belong in London, and if Ryder were leaving, she would return to the McLellan estate. Convincing Aunt Charlotte would be difficult, but she had to get as far away from Richy as possible.

Chapter Three

A few months later Ryder paced the floor of his loft apartment. His path had never been clearer, but the ultimate destination would have to be put on hold for a few months. He wasn't sure how to broach this to Christel or even if he could convince her to wait for him. The last few months he'd spent as much time as possible with Christel. While he didn't know if love was something real, what he did know was that he wanted to spend the rest of his life with her.

So engrossed in his thoughts, the knock at the door startled him.

"Abbot, you're right on time." Ryder ushered him through the door then offered him a drink. Ryder hoped Abbot could help him with everything. He had written out some musts that would have to happen for him to be secure with leaving London and Christel.

"You said it was urgent." Abbot sipped the Scotch then sat down by Ryder's desk.

"I have a long list we need to go over." Ryder picked up the paper he'd been working on prior to Abbot's appearance and handed it to him.

"Well, let's see what I can do." Abbot sat back, setting his glass on a nearby table then he took his glasses from his pocket and slipped them on. "I see. Yes, that would be good. Let's start with the McLellan lass."

"She needs twenty-four-hour protection." Ryder's gut churned. He'd heard conversation. Richy was desperate, and while the name was never mentioned, he knew Richy's intent was to kidnap Christel and take her to Gretna Green. He couldn't allow that to happen.

"May I ask why?"

"Lord Rathen has designs on her." Ryder fisted his hands.

Speaking the words made it more real. He searched for a way to stay behind but found none. The cargo he was taking across the ocean was expensive and needed his care. Plus, he'd promised.

"I've heard the talk. He's lost at the gaming tables and the horses. His father, the earl, has cut him off. So, he thinks Miss McLellan and a marriage will provide him with new funding for his habits."

"Apparently so," Ryder stood and walked to the window, taking solace in the setting sun and the fact he would see Christel tonight at the ball. Yet telling her he was leaving and asking her for her hand in marriage in the same second seemed counterproductive.

"I will arrange for men to guard her."

Ryder turned. "She can't know. Discretion is important here. I don't want The Duchess or Christel to be fearful."

"I will tell my men. This will cost."

"Spend whatever is necessary." Ryder needed to know Christel would be in London and safe when he returned.

"When do you want the men to start?"

"As soon as possible. This moment if I could arrange it, but I understand you will have some leg work to do."

"I'm sure I can have this set up by tomorrow morning. Will that do?" Abbot asked.

"Could you get them on duty tonight? There is a ball and I will be there, but after that I will be onboard the ship."

"I'll do my best. What's next?"

"I have a shipment coming in from China."

The men talked for several hours before all arrangements for Ryder's life the next few months were put in order.

After Abbot left, Ryder breathed in a sigh. The fear for Christel had not vanished, but he knew he'd done all he could. Now he needed to dress for the evening and put his other proposition in action. The thought of asking her to travel with him flitted through his mind, but he dismissed the notion. With all the arrangements he made, she would be safer here.

He slipped a small box from his pocket. It held the beautiful emerald ring he meant to give Christel tonight. He'd spent hours picking it out and he hoped she liked it. He knew green was her favorite color.

Lighthearted was exactly how he felt because a weight had been lifted from his shoulders.

He decided to walk instead of calling for a carriage. His conversation with Abbot was in the forefront of his mind. He wondered just how the man was going to keep Christel and The Duchess from discovering his ruse. Would Christel be angry with him?

He didn't want that but came to the conclusion her anger with him really didn't matter if she was kept away from Rathen and any plans the man might have concerning her.

Tonight, a crescent moon hung in a clear sky dotted with stars. Thoughts of dancing with Christel and twirling her onto a balcony for a kiss made him smile and have hope for the future.

What if she said no to his proposal? He hadn't thought of that. Despite the small breeze and the cool evening air, sweat beaded on his forehead. Confidence evaporated with each step, nausea rolling through his belly.

At the townhouse he stopped at the steps. Music floated from the ballroom on the third floor.

He swallowed hard and was greeted by the butler then ushered up the stairs. Inside, he searched the room for Christel and The Duchess.

"Surprised to see you here." Richy walked up behind him. "Lookin' for a wife?"

Revulsion snaked down Ryder's spine. "Heard you were disowned."

"That's none of your business." The bravado vanished from Richy's tone. "I'm looking for Christel McLellan. Have you seen her?"

Wouldn't tell you if I had. "Nope." Ryder rocked back on his heels, his hands clasped behind his back, still searching for Christel.

"Heard you were taking horses to Baltimore. You going to race them?"

"No, but I think Damian is planning on breeding them. He might have a trainer lined up. Don't really know. I'm just the transportation."

"Sounds like a lot of work to me."

"A foreign thought to you, isn't it, Rathen? Work." Ryder caught sight of The Duchess and Christel stood behind her, looking as if this were the last place she wanted to be. He laughed softly. What would she think of his proposal?

"Ah, I see a game starting. Care to join me?"

"I've got better things to do." Ryder watched Richy wander away and wished he could put him on a ship to keep him away while he was gone.

Ah, but shanghaiing a man was against the law. Ryder turned his attention to Christel who had managed to disappear. He guessed she'd found a corner where she could hide. He picked up two glasses of champagne and strode around the ballroom, peeking into each corner.

Frustration ate at him, thoughts of turning around and fleeing crossed his mind. It was just like Christel to walk through the front door, decide she didn't like what she saw and ask for a carriage home.

He knew she was safe from Richy, at least for the night. Richy had found a game and until he was booted from it, he'd find a way to remain at the table.

The sight of her stole his breath. He'd been right. She'd found a corner and didn't seem unhappy to watch the people dance. She smoothed her skirts and leaned in closer to The Duchess as if to hear what she said.

Christel shook her head then looked up as if she knew someone watched.

He didn't want to wait a moment longer.

~ * ~

"Dance?" Ryder MacLaren set the glasses on the table then held out his hand, a smile on his face.

"You are next on my dance card if I had one." Christel McLellan searched Ryder's expression, wondering what he was thinking. Wondering if he cared for her even the tiniest bit. The first moment she saw him, he'd stolen her breath then as she grew to know him, he'd captured her heart. But she'd never known if he returned her feelings.

"I'm sure I'm the only one."

"Arrogant knave." She supposed he could afford to be arrogant. The truth was she didn't want the suitors who had appeared in the parlor or sent notes of interest to The Duchess. The last few months, Ryder had called on her several times and she was attracted to him; thought only of him when she closed her eyes at night or stared at the traffic passing by. Since Ravyn left, she'd had no one to talk to except Ryder.

"Really? Arrogant knave?" He quoted her.

It seemed he didn't understand her jest.

"No, you aren't." she told him, letting the palm of her hand rest in his hand. "I've given you every reason..." she paused, wishing she didn't feel the huge sigh forming. "I don't want to dance with anyone else."

"Even Rathen?"

"Especially not him. I heard about the horrible wager those men made. Thank Amorica's lucky stars Damian Andrews was only pretending to be like them. And Richy makes my skin crawl."

"Damian had to protect innocent people or the wager would have never been voiced. And I believe you girls made wagers too."

Ryder pulled her into his arms, swirling her around the dance floor.

"We did. Not well done but even without the bet, we would have dissuaded our suitors, Dicky and Richy."

Ryder let out a roar of laughter, pulling her closer. The colors in the room blurred, as did the people. Laughter and happy chatter rang out around them. A slight haze of smoke hovered near the ceiling.

He whirled her onto a balcony then stopped. "We need to talk."

A cool night breeze swept across her shoulders, the air felt good and smelled sweet. Dancing with Ryder's arms around her was heaven.

A bit winded from the dancing, she looked at him, her heart in her throat. Ryder had a reputation for chasing sunrises. He never stayed in one place, always searching for adventure. "I'm leaving."

"I guessed as much. That solemn expression you approached me with then the quick change, the smile on your face forming then evaporating almost in the same moment." Loneliness assailed her. In the few months she'd known Ryder, she'd fancied herself in love with him. "Do you know where you are going or when?"

"Leaving on the morning tide for the states."

"Visiting Damian and Aric?"

"Yes, they've asked for some help with their farms. I'm bringing three horses, three very special ones. Damian intends to breed them for racing."

"And there is nothing here to hold you?" She'd wished so many times he cared enough for her to stay, to ask her to wed. Now he was leaving.

He looked into the night, she supposed at the shimmering stars and the white moon. "I would ask you to wait for me, but that might be too big of an assumption."

She started to protest but he touched her lips with one fingertip. "Hush, more than anything I want you to wait. You could fall in love, and if you made a promise to me..."

I've already fallen in love.

"Then you would find yourself duty bound to return?"

She didn't want to hear about duty and honor. Instead, words of undying love would have been nice. Somehow she knew he would never tell her he loved her.

"Christel, I don't know how long I will stay, but I would like to make a commitment to you if you'll have me."

"Ryder, I would go with you." *If you asked me.*

He got down on one knee and slipped the ring box from his pocket. "Will you marry me?"

Her hands shook as she spoke. "Of course..."

He slipped the ring on her finger. "Are you sure?" He smiled up at her as he stood.

She nodded then he took her in his arms and kissed her. She closed her eyes and let his warmth envelope her soul. Yet she felt him stiffen.

"Ryder..."

A man Christel didn't recognize was tapping him on his shoulder. He held out an envelope. "Ryder, this is urgent. I wouldn't bother you, but..."

Ryder opened the envelope and studied the words on the parchment. He looked at Christel. "I'm sorry but this needs my attention."

"You have to go now?" She had thought to leave with him or kiss him again and perhaps have one more dance. This all seemed so strange, engaged one moment and alone the next.

"Then I won't see you again until you return." She had never felt so bereft. This couldn't possibly be happening.

He pulled her into his arms and kissed her again. "Christel, I am sorry. Will you wait for me?"

She nodded, trying to clear the tears from her throat but couldn't.

He touched her forehead, brushing a wisp of hair behind her ear. "Be careful of Richy Rathen. He is dangerous and he wants you. Wear the ring, its presence might deter him. Where is The Duchess?"

"I don't know. She was here a minute ago."

"Go home with her." Ryder held her hands in his. "Don't wait here one more minute than is necessary."

"Excuse me, Christel McClellan?

"Yes."

"The Duchess said she had a headache and had to go home. She couldn't find you but will send the carriage back for you. She assumes you will be with the MacLaren."

Ryder kissed the top of her hands. "Wait near the entrance and don't go outside until the coach gets here." He turned to the man who had delivered the message. "Will you stay by her side until the ride comes? I must leave."

"Of course."

"Really, I'm fine, Ryder, nothing will happen." Despite the brave words fear swirled inside.

"Promise you won't go outside by yourself."

"Promise, then this is goodbye." She stepped away from him, telling herself she would not cry and she prayed he would return to her.

He nodded and without another word left the room.

Christel found her cloak and slipped it on, waiting as promised at the door of the townhouse.

"Nice evening."

Richy Rathen stood beside her, his hand on the small of her back pushing her outside.

"Stop. What are you doing?"

"We're going for a walk."

"No, I'm not." But there was little she could do against his strength. With his hand over her mouth and his arm around her waist, he forced her down the steps and away from the townhouse.

Chapter Four

MacLaren Castle 1818

"You're trespassing." The arrow shot past the man's head. Christel withdrew another arrow and inhaling a long deep breath, pulled the bow string back then let the second arrow fly. Deep within she trembled, shook with the fury she felt at this moment.

"Bloody hell."

"Get off my land!" The firmness in her voice wavered with the last word. Christel's heart slid to her throat, lodging there. The lie did not sit well. This land wasn't hers to claim.

"It's my land and you can tell me why you're shooting at me."

His low, gruff voice drew Christel's attention, and she lifted her head, removing the focus of her arrow tip from the man's heart. She met his whiskey-hued eyes, and her stomach made a little catch. Surprised, she stared at his dark, furrowed brows, the well-chiseled lines of his rugged face. She remembered each contour, each line and dimple. His black hair was tied back, dampened as if he'd just taken a swim in the loch, a slightly off-center nose that spoke of an daring and bold past. A few days' worth of razor stubble covered his throat and jaw. A confrontation with this man would not end well.

Ryder?

"Put your bow down." The man strode forward with long easy steps that seemed to eat up the ground. Yet his expression was anything but angry. She could have sworn he was laughing.

Her heart lurched. He was still breathtakingly handsome, masculine in an emphatically sensual way. Christel slowly lowered the bow, watching with a wary eye. These past months her life had been in turmoil. In his buckskin pants and with a pistol slung at his waist, he reminded her of a time long ago. Despite all that had happened to her since the night he left her stranded at the ball, one sight of Ryder MacLaren had her senses spinning and her mind reeling.

The man moved with such an easy, fluid grace the vision near stole her breath and stopped her heart. Her hand rose to her chest as if she could hold back the multitude of emotions pummeling within. Emotions she couldn't define rushed through her threatening her newly conceived life.

"Why are you here?" Sure she didn't want to know the answer, yet relieved it wasn't the man she'd been hunting, Richy Rathen. So much had happened since Ryder had left her behind in London. He would never want to marry her when he discovered the truth. No man would want her.

"Christel, I'm so relieved I found you. I was afraid, so afraid for you. Your family is concerned as well. We heard rumors you ran from the convent and made your way to the MacLaren Castle. Why were you at the convent? Why didn't you stay in London? I've so many unanswered questions. We have to talk." He stood beside her now, tall and imposing yet seemingly gentle.

His gaze, focused on her, sent shivers sliding through her body. "I couldn't stay in London and you'd left. You were so far away you couldn't help." Hiding her shame from him would be so hard. Tears welled in her throat, but she didn't dare cry.

Ryder stepped forward arms extended. He looked tired. "I want to hold you, Christel, and chase all of the fears and demons away. I wish I could have stayed, but I came as soon as I heard from The Duchess that you had fled London and no one knew why or where you had gone." He paused, running his long fingers through his hair, "Where have you been?"

She closed her eyes, wishing for the courage to tell him all that had happened to her, but what would he think of her if she told him Richy had raped her? "I stayed at a convent as long as they allowed me then I traveled here, praying you wouldn't care."

"A convent? But you decided you couldn't stay? Did you forget about our engagement and that I would come for you? Didn't you trust me?"

She lifted her shoulders slightly. "The place didn't suit and..." Shamed, she looked into the woods to avoid his gaze. Recalling the horror she'd found with the nuns, wasn't something she wanted or needed at the moment. Besides, she didn't want his or anyone else's sympathy.

With the back of his hand, he touched her cheek. "A tear drop? You shouldn't cry. Why the MacLaren castle? Why not go back to London? Few live within this castle, or you could have returned to McLellan land."

"It was safe," *and I didn't want to explain myself, or what happened to anyone, even The Duchess.*

"Of course, I'm glad you feel safe here and I want to understand." He seemed to think about what she said, his brows drawing together in seemingly fierce concentration.

"I'm not really alone. I hear a woman crying every night when I go to bed." She had heard the low sobbing and tried to find the source but failed. "She doesn't frighten me and in a strange way she gives comfort."

"It's a ghost." He tossed her a cheeky grin. "Anyone around here can recount the story word for word."

Christel took a moment before she said, "I know, but I didn't think anyone would believe me, especially you."

"I grew up here, remember. There's nothing you can tell me about my land that I haven't heard before." He motioned as if he wanted to walk with her. "Let's go to the castle. I'm famished and tired. After I eat, I'd like a good hot soak in a tub. Then I'd like you to tell me what you're holding back."

"Of course, I'm sure Betsy will see to it." She strode faster, trying to distance herself from him then peered into the forest behind, hoping the MacLaren wasn't the only surprise she'd encounter today. Then she set off in the opposite direction.

"You're not coming?"

"No, someone has to provide the food. I was hunting and there is a herd of deer not far. I was closing in on them when you scared them off." She really hated lying to him, but she had a dual purpose.

"Then I will help. We will have enough meat sooner than later." He grinned at her. "How were you planning on getting the carcass back to the castle?"

"Angus helps. He has a travois of sorts. And I call him on this bugle when I need him." The lies kept mounting. At this rate she'd never remembered what she told Ryder.

"Angus? He's as old as these hills."

"I know." Christel pushed hair from her eyes, hoping to secure the wisps behind her ears yet knowing it would not stay. "But he's a good sort and he's all I have. He likes to help." She put her hands up as if to stop what she thought he might say. "I don't want sympathy. I'm just stating a fact. I've chosen to live here, and I will stay unless you kick me out. But I won't go without a fight."

Ryder let out a roar of laughter. "I'm sure in a battle of wills you would win. I don't want you to go anywhere. If you recall, I asked you to marry me. The offer still stands, Christel. You would make me the proudest man alive if you agreed to become my wife."

"Lady Christel, Lady..."

"Betsy? What are you doing?" Christel turned to face her friend and maid who was running through the woods, dress hiked to her knees as if all the demons in hell were after her.

"Blaine has fallen down the turret steps. I dinna ken if he's all right. He cannot move his legs and he's moanin' and groanin' an awful lot. Sounds as if he's dying."

"Where is the midwife? She usually tends to these things." Christel searched the woods and surrounding area as if she would magically appear.

"Gone, we cannot find her anywhere." Betsy bent over at the waist, heaving deep air.

"All right then." Christel slung her bow over her shoulder, thankful she did not have a skirt to contend with. She ran toward the castle, Ryder following. The ongoing hunt for Richy Rathen would have to wait.

Ryder stayed a few steps behind her. She heard his footsteps and for the first time is so many months, she felt a sense of security. Seconds seemed to pass like hours before they reached the portcullis of the MacLaren castle.

"Milady," the gatekeeper acknowledged them with a nod of his head. "Blaine is in the dining hall. MacLaren, good to have you home, sir. You going to stay this time?"

"How is he?" Christel asked, interrupting any possible answer.

"I believe his pride is wounded more than his body. He didn't want Betsy to make such a fuss. He told her several times not to leave the castle, but she insisted."

Betsy fancied herself in love with the young man. Christel thought a wedding might be in the near future, but one never knew. Young people always seemed to have a way of changing their minds. "Thanks, I'll see to him."

Once inside, Christel stopped to gain her breath. She grinned at Ryder who seemed to do the same. In the corner, she spotted the young man who was stretched out on a makeshift pallet, one arm over his eyes.

"How are you?" Christel knelt beside him. "You took a nasty fall, but I'm sure you'll be just fine in a day or two."

Blain looked away then back, "I'm alright, just a bit sore. I'm sure Betsy made this out to be more than it is."

"Let me be the judge, all right? Now, where were you hurt?"

Blaine pointed to his leg. "Just below my knee..."

Christel ran her hand down his lower leg.

"Oh..." Blaine jumped, moisture forming in his eyes, his lips pursed together and his browse furrowed. "Bloody hell, didn't think it would hurt that much."

"Think you have a broken leg." Ryder's calm voice penetrated the room. "I'll fix up a splint and we can find a pair of crutches. You'll have to stay off it for a while."

"Broken? But it really doesn't hurt that bad."

"Looks like it. But I think you'll heal in no time. Don't want to take any chances. See, it's a bit swollen and you've a lump growing right here." Ryder touched the spot then asked one of Blaine's companions, "Bring three strips of cloth, two sticks and if you can, locate the castle doctor. Bring me a pair of crutches."

The young man nodded then raced off to do Ryder's bidding.

The MacLaren had walked back into her life and just like that, he took over. Christel wasn't sure what to think, but at the moment gratitude filled her. "Thank you." She smiled at the man who seemed to laugh easily and make her forget the worst nightmare of her life. Yet she knew when darkness fell and she closed her eyes she would remember everything.

That had been a lifetime ago, and she knew she should put that horrible memory to rest, but she couldn't until Richy Rathen vanished from this earth. She was searching for him because she heard rumors he was nearby looking for her. If he touched her again, she would kill him.

Ryder was so devil may care and handsome, and she wondered if he would stay for a while or leave to find another sunrise. He'd returned to his home to check up on her and tell her he still wanted to marry her.

But did he really want that?

A few minutes later, "Here you go." Blaine's friend handed Ryder the requested items. Ryder set the broken bone then fastened the splints and handed Blaine the crutches, helping him up.

"Good as new. Was the doctor there?" Ryder asked.

"No, just his assistant. But he told me to have Blaine come by in an hour or so. The doctor will be back and will check on your handy work."

"Come on." Ryder put his arm around Christel's shoulder and led her toward the stairs. "What solar would you have me stay in?"

His booming laughter made her wonder why she felt so giddy and lighthearted, but she quickly stashed the thought to the back of her head. Yet she couldn't rid herself of the emotions spinning out of control, emotions Ryder set in motion.

"Why, the one with the ghost, of course." Christel smiled at Ryder, remembering the seemingly easy camaraderie she felt with him. So much darkness had filled her life since last she saw him and danced with him at the ball. In the middle of the night when she could not get Richy from her mind, she tried to hold onto those memories.

"Do you want me to go sleepless?"

"No, it was a joke. You can have the laird's solar."

"I would have thought that was your domain."

"I'm in the one adjacent. I didn't feel right about moving into your room. Seemed a bit presumptuous, and there was always the possibility you'd show up and demand I move."

"I would rather demand you marry me and share the room," he told her, his voice husky with emotion.

She wanted to discount so much, needed to forget London. The rake, Richy Rathen, was impossible, and when he'd cornered her the night Ryder had set sail to America, she'd been forced into a place she couldn't forget even though she needed to do that very thing for her sanity.

"A penny for your thoughts?" Ryder asked, a look of concern on his face that once again sent her senses reeling.

"Maybe sometime. I'm not ready to share." Maybe never. How could she tell him what that bastard did to her? And what she'd been forced to leave behind at the convent.

"I'll be here. Whenever or whatever you want to tell me, I'll listen." He put his hands on her shoulders then turned her and she stared into whiskey colored eyes filled with tenderness and concern. For a moment she thought she saw remorse then that emotion vanished. His ensuing grin lightened the black mood and washed away the bad thoughts of Richy.

"Really? For how long, a day, a month, a year." She didn't want to feel so close to this man, but in a few minutes he'd found a way back into her life and perhaps her heart. Now that he was here, she didn't want to think about losing him again. She needed him to stay. "I'm sorry. I had no right..."

"To ask me how long I mean to stay? You have every right since we are engaged. You've taken such grand care of the estate. I'm not here often, but the people I see, my clan, are happier now than I've seen them for a very long time. You have a magical touch that seems to warm the hearts of everyone you encounter."

"I have no hold on you. Expectations are not mine to have." The truth would always prevail. For the longest time she'd understood how alone she was. Returning to the McLellan castle, her home, was not a choice. Never did she want to live with Allura's and Hunter's sympathy. She knew her sister would bring suitable men to court her and she wanted none of that.

"Perhaps you deserve expectations of a place to call home." Ryder's voice was solemn and filled with kindness.

"I would love to call this home." She regarded him thoughtfully, searching his face for an answer. "Even if we no longer have a future together?"

"And..." he seemed to encourage her to tell him her thoughts.

"With your permission, I'd like to stay here even when you want to see another sunrise a world away. I don't want to live in London or the McLellan castle. I feel independent here and I love the people, your people."

"Who spoke of my adventurous ways? It certainly wasn't me, not for a long time."

She cleared her throat, not meaning to share the gossip at the castle and in London but knowing he deserved the truth. "Your clan. They talk of you with care and concern in their voices. They want you home because they all love you, but they tell me you have a lust for wandering. They called it chasing sunrises."

"A man can change." He shrugged broad shoulders. "Especially a man who has asked a woman to marry him, a man who has seen more of the world than he cares to speak of. Now the only sunrises I want to see are here with you."

"We are here. Where are your belongings?" She had not paid attention. He had nothing with him when she'd shot that first arrow at his feet.

"I've been at the castle and put my things in the solar. I went out to search for you. Some of my people told me you spend a great deal of time in the woods."

"Oh..."

"Sorry if I took advantage. I wanted to find you as soon as possible. My people advised me where you might have gone." He crossed his arms and leaned against the door jam, the expression on his face made her heart race and spin in a crazy disconcerting way.

"This is your castle. All of the assumptions were mine to make or break." She couldn't look at him. If she did, she might give herself away.

All those months of hiding her feelings would be for naught.

"Did you know it was me when you shot?" He pushed away from the wall then strode to the window overlooking the yard below.

Christel shook her head, smiling at his back. "No, but I knew you were not a deer." She wanted to follow but held back, her emotions too raw and she also knew he wasn't Richy.

"You missed me on purpose." He whistled through his teeth. "Wasn't that a pretty big chance? I could have moved a bit to the left and..."

"Meant only to scare. Before I shot to kill, I needed to know who it was." Christel pushed a piece of stray hair behind her ear, watching his every move. "I don't miss what I aim at."

Ryder turned and with a smile, "You succeeded."

"I'll leave you to unpack or rest or whatever you want to do." She backed from the room, her heart fluttering.

"When is dinner?" He stepped toward her.

"In an hour." She turned to run from him and her heart. When he touched her shoulder to stop her, she cried out.

"Do I frighten you? Christel, I don't want you to be afraid of me. Never that." His hand on her wrist, he pulled her toward him. With a finger he lifted her chin. She gazed into honest brown eyes, tender eyes.

"Ryder, please..." she didn't know what she wanted from him yet she remembered the simple intimacies they shared.

His lips lowered close to hers. "I want to finish what we began in London. Will you let me?"

His mint-scented breath was warm against her cheek. But she was terrified of what she might surrender and what he might never return. She backed away, one finger caressing the stubble on his jaw.

With his hand on the small of her back, he pressed her closer. The hard planes of his chest, the ridge of his cock against her belly all left her mind reeling.

"No," she told him. "I can't, not now." *Not ever. When he learns the truth, he won't want me.*

"I'm sorry. I didn't mean to take something you aren't willing to give." His brows furrowed together as if he tried to read her mind.

~ * ~

"My apologies. I don't know what possessed me." But he did know. She beckoned to him like a sirens' call. Her silken voice wrapped around him, sensually drawing him into her web. Gut instinct told him to go slow and not press her, finding out why she fled London imperative.

"No need for that. I must have..." she didn't believe that even if she tempted him in some way it would be her fault.

She swept long blond hair from her face; tendrils had escaped the bun she wore. Sky blue eyes stared back at him. "There is always a need for good manners. Christel, we will talk about what happened."

"I know nothing of bad manners. But I must go. The cook will need some direction for dinner and if I recall, you said you were starving. I'll send someone up with hot water." She turned, starting to leave but paused, looking over her shoulder at him.

She ignored his need for talk. Yes, he'd chased sunrises since he was a young man. The thrill of adventure had been his aphrodisiac. Discovering Christel in London and now arriving home, he realized how damn much he'd missed the land and his people.

His future waited here for him and he wanted her, no, needed her more with every breath. Returning from the states, he'd thought to find Christel in London. He'd hope to wed her and bring her to his home. She wasn't there and The Duchess had been afraid for Christel's life. Christel had left under unusual circumstances and in the dead of night.

Lord Rathen, Richy, had pursued Christel. The Duchess was not sure of the entire story. She knew Christel had left unexpectedly one day after she'd had a brief encounter with Richy at the party. She'd told him how she'd sent men out to scour the countryside, but they found no trace. Then she'd received a letter from Christel, telling her she was fine and she didn't need to worry. But the letter told The Duchess nothing about where Christel had gone. Even with all the favors she called in, no one could shed information on Christel's plight.

"Go on then. I'd like to get settled." His thoughts needed reconciling, and he knew his mind would continue thinking about what might have been if he'd remained in London instead of putting his friends in front of Christel's safety. He could have easily hired someone to deliver the horses.

Ryder watched Christel as she left the room then stepping outside the door, he stared at her until she was out of site. He closed his eyes, memorizing her slim features, straight long back and the slight sway of her hips as she strode past his people and into the kitchen. She belonged here even more than he did. This would always be her home if she wished it.

With a heavy sigh, he marched back into his solar. He wasn't sure where to start—with Christel or his unpacking. He didn't have much. He'd traveled fast and light. Christel had been away from London for over a year, and he was terrified something dreadful might have happened. The Duchess had pleaded with him to find her.

She's in trouble. I know she is. Find her, Ryder, please before it's too late.

The convent where she'd first gone had been rude and offensive to his inquiries. He imagined how they'd treated Christel, and he didn't like the direction his thoughts traveled.

Looking down at the courtyard, he was assailed with childhood memories. Had it really been ten years since he'd left this home? His father had passed on, and he hadn't been able to make it to the funeral. He'd always regret that. Now he intended to make up for lost time.

"Milord."

Ryder's friend from his childhood stood in the doorway, a grin on his roguish face. Together they'd found themselves in more scrapes than anyone before them.

"Owen, you surprised me. Come in. We have a lot to go over. You can tell me what has happened since I left so long ago."

Owen laughed then sat down in a chair near the solar window. "Life goes on, my friend. People come and go, babies are born and weddings are arranged. Is there anything in particular you would like to know?"

I'd like to know everything about Christel McLellan. "When did the lady McLellan arrive and under what circumstances?"

"So, that's the way of it." Owen rubbed his chin as if in thought. "About six months ago, give or take a day. She turned up here asking for a place to stay and telling us she was a friend of yours."

"I see and yes, I have a vested interest in her. I was charged with her safe keeping by her London chaperon. She is special to me in other ways. We are engaged to be married; at least we were when I left for Baltimore. Now I'm not so sure what our status is."

"Lady McLellan made herself right at home. But she is royalty and knows the ins and outs of taking care of the castle. If you must know the truth of it, she was a godsend. Started putting everything to rights. Took over the accounting of the livestock as well as the produce."

"I didn't know she had skills in mathematics. For that matter I didn't know she could read." Ryder wondered at that bit of knowledge. He had to admit he'd never given Christel's education much thought. He'd been infatuated with her from the start but in the scope of things, they'd spent little time together.

"She seemed sad..."

"How so?"

Owen shrugged then grimaced as if he didn't like the directions of the questions. "It's not my business, but the lady rarely smiled. But she's changed, happier now. It's strange though, she always seems to be looking over one shoulder as if she expects something bad is about to happen."

Ryder finished unpacking. What Owen told him weighed heavily on his heart. He suspected Christel's wariness might have something to do with Lord Rathen. The Duchess hadn't told him a lot, but he recalled the wager between Damian, Richy and Dicky then grimaced. Ryder needed to change the subject.

"You hungry?"

"Famished. I was deer hunting when I heard the news of your arrival."

"Really? That's odd. I found Christel in the woods. She told me she was hunting." Another secret he needed to get to the truth off.

"I've heard the lady can shoot the bow, but she never goes hunting. Many times she'll be out and about looking for something, and she always takes her weapon but..."

"Bloody hell, you mean she's..." *lying to me?*

Once again Ryder's thoughts jumped to Lord Rathen. He meant to get to the bottom of this and fix every bad thing that had ever happened to Christel. Why shouldn't she lie to him? He'd left her alone when she needed him.

The men walked down the stairs into the main room. Wonderful aromas wafted through the air, and Ryder's stomach growled. He didn't recall when he'd eaten last, but he knew it was sometime the day before.

As he moved through the large hall his clan, his friends waved and smiled at him. The greetings warmed his heart, knowing he had come home. For the first time in too many years, he didn't have the urge to see what was on the other side of the sunrise. Peace filled his soul and he returned the greetings with a smile and a wave of his hand. He was home and he meant to stay.

The young man who had broken his leg waved with one hand, the other was around his girl. Reminded of Owen's words, he wondered if there would be a wedding and babies soon for these two. He couldn't help but think about a life with children and a wife. Then his thoughts focused on Christel. He could still see her as his wife. She was beautiful and smart. She made him laugh and challenged him in so many different ways.

Ryder motioned to a serving girl. "Would you bring tea and some scones to the library, and if you can find the Lady Christel, would you ask her to meet me there?"

The girl curtsied. "Of course." Then she was off to do his bidding.

The library smelled musty. Ryder opened the curtains, letting the bright sunshine filter into the room. Then the windows were opened. He walked the perimeter of the room, picking up books to look at before setting them down. A small statue of a lion caught his eyes. Memories pounded through his head.

He recalled sitting on this old rug and playing with the lion, but there were four little statues. Where were the others? The lioness and her cubs were missing. But that wasn't all. Emptiness assailed him. It wasn't just things that had vanished from his life, family and friends were gone.

Ryder closed his eyes in thought. Did he regret the last ten years?

No, but he wanted the next ten to be different.

"Ryder?" Owen stood behind him. "Will you call me anytime? I've a home a little ways down the road, closer to town. If you need anything..."

Ryder nodded then extended his hand. Owen grasped it. "I'm pleased to see you again and I will stay in touch. I mean to make castle MacLaren my home now." He suddenly understood the complete truth of those words, but he also knew the only way it would happen would be if Christel became his wife.

"M'lord...?" Christel stepped into the library with a tray of scones and a teapot. "You were looking for me?"

"Good, you are here. You two have met? Owen is a friend, a good friend."

"Yes, we've met."

"I was just leaving..." Owen backed from the room, a wide grin on his face, his blue eyes shimmering with what seemed to be humor.

"I like Owen." Christel set the tray on a table then poured each a cup of tea. "He has been helpful."

"How helpful?" Ryder's tone caught him by surprise. He recognized the sensation of jealousy, something he'd never before encountered. But then he'd never cared for anyone—never loved a woman. "Sorry."

"What for?" Christel bit down on a scone then cocked her head as if waiting for an answer.

Ryder wasn't ready to blurt out his feelings. "I didn't mean to sound accusatory. He's a friend and of course he would be more than willing to help you. He has also helped me, and in doing so has managed to confuse things." Ryder wondered if it was too soon to confront her about the bogus hunting expeditions.

"Confuse you? What about?" Christel's brows furrowed as she appeared to think about his words.

"He told me a few minutes ago that you don't hunt but many times go to the forest with your weapons." *In for a penny in for a pound.*

Christel stiffened, her spine ramrod straight then her lips thinned. She set her teacup on the table and her scone on the plate. She paused for a lengthy time. Myriads of expressions appeared on her delicate face. Then pursing her lips for a moment, "He is right. I have other reasons for inspecting the woods."

"And they are?" Ryder drummed his fingers on the table then rose, walking around behind her. He rested his hands on the back of her chair then thought better of the gesture, not wanting to intimidate Christel. He had his suspicions but he hoped he was wrong.

Christel rose from her seat then turned to him, her hands shaking. "I'm sorry, but..."

"I only want to help. It's obvious you don't want to speak of this. Sit down and enjoy the afternoon tea. I won't pursue the topic. Keep in mind though, you can tell me anytime. I'm willing to listen." He wanted to solve the problem. If Lord Rathen was the man bothering her, he meant to put an end to her difficulties. He made a mental note to ask Owen to investigate.

"If the need arises, I will remember what you've said. Now, we should go over the books and the tallies. I found that when I arrived here, everything was in disarray. So, I decided to begin with a clean slate. You will find the ledgers are complete from the first of January, six months ago. I had no idea what to do with the ledgers for the years after your father's passing."

Ryder opened the book and looked over the work Christel had done. "It seems to be accurate. I'll examine the figures later just so I understand better what you have done. It will take me a few hours." How on earth was he going to chip away at the armor Christel surrounded herself with?

"I assure you the numbers are correct." As she spoke it seemed tension radiated through her.

"I don't doubt it and I didn't mean to offend. It's just that I need to understand all you've done here."

"I see..." Christel folded her hands in her lap, once again her back stiffening and her expression unreadable.

Ryder sighed wishing he could get across to Christel that he believed in her. He could say it so many times, but...

"No, you don't understand. I have every confidence in you. But look at it this way. If it were you returning home after ten years, wouldn't you want to look at every facet of your past life and understand what had happened since you left?"

"I suppose, forgive me." For a moment she smiled and Ryder knew he'd taken a step forward. Perhaps a piece of her shell had been nicked after all, but he had a long way to go.

Silence hung in the room and the meager sunshine from the earlier hour had vanished. From outside he heard the sound of fat raindrops hitting the earth. The scent of rain hovered in the air. At least he managed to remove the musty scent from the room. Now the fragrance of vanilla floated around him.

"So, there seems to be two sets of figures."

"There is, one is for the produce the farmers, your clan, bring to the castle to sell; the other set is from your merchant ships."

"What did you do with the goods the ships brought?"

"Some I sold to your clan, some to shops in town, and some are in the supply house in the castle."

He sat down then leaned back in his chair, aware of the fantastic job she'd done. "You have experience."

"Not much. Allura managed the McClellan castle. At times I followed her and tried to learn everything I could."

"Well, you've done an admirable job. Will you give me a tour of the castle?" He rose then held out his hand. She accepted, her hand in his so tiny and fragile. Yet she strode through the woods, bow held in delicate fingers, meaning to do what? It seemed to Ryder, Christel was a stronger woman than he'd previously thought.

"Where would you like to go first?" She smiled and he couldn't help but grin back, feeling lighthearted for the first time in too many years to count.

"Where does this castle ghost reside?"

"Wasn't she here when you lived at the MacLaren keep?" Christel asked. "You told me as much a couple of hours ago."

They walked through the library and up the stairs. "Yes and no, we weren't allowed to acknowledge her."

"That must be why she weeps. I'll show you were she resides now, at least most times."

"You jest. You hear her crying?" He squeezed her hand.

"She does cry. Sometimes I hear her at night. I'm not sure she has one room she stays in. I have heard her when I'm outside, looking over the castle grounds. And there are times when I feel she is beside me when I'm in the woods."

Ryder wasn't sure how to pursue this. "Is she scary?" Well that was stupid of him.

"Not at all. I feel sad for her and wish she would find a measure of peace."

"Here, this is where I first heard her." Christel stood at the top of the castle, where they looked out at the forest beyond. To the west the small town of Spotsberg could be seen, to the east the sea. North and south were small homes of the clan.

Wind whistled through the air and the rain changed to a slight mist. Christel rubbed her arms. Ryder wrapped her up in his embrace, cradling her next to his body. She shivered against him, but he wasn't sure the trembling was from the cold.

"We should go where it's warm." Her body next to his was an aphrodisiac to his soul. He wanted to keep her next to him and safe forever.

But Christel pushed away from him and pointing, "There, do you see her. She is sitting on the wall."

Ryder strained to see the apparition Christel pointed toward but he saw nothing. "No, but I think I hear her."

"Yes, she is crying, not weeping as usual. Do you know anything about her story?" Christel turned to him, hope shining in her soft blue eyes.

"I've heard her lover died. But that was a long time ago."

"How?"

Ryder pulled her back into his embrace, not ever wanting her to leave. He would hold fast to her for as long as she would allow him. "At war...I don't recall which one. The clans seem to have always been at war with someone, especially the English."

He felt the nod of her head against his chest. "Does anyone know the legend? I would seek them out."

Her breathing was slow and she seemed relaxed. But Ryder feared for her. If she started asking questions, would this ghost come to harm her? He didn't know anything about apparitions. But he also knew he would have to give her a chance to discover the truth. "Only if you let me go with you. I would be honored. There is a woman, older than time. She wanders the castle grounds. Most see her in the late evening and early morning."

"Old as time, no older?"

A shimmering silver light hung over the castle and floated above the turrets. Ryder pointed toward the light. "Is that her?"

"She's a bit reclusive." Christel turned in Ryder's arms. "Yes, that's her. Her light is very pretty, don't you think?"

"One might say that about her and yes she is very pretty." His hands rested at the small of Christel's back. He wanted to kiss her but didn't want to frighten her again. Maybe a lazy gentle kiss would be accepted. The thought made him grin and his heart pump harder.

He traced her neck with the tip of his finger, hoping she would find his attentions acceptable then bent close to her. "I want to kiss you. Will you let me?" She shivered in his arms but turned her face up to him.

"Yes." She breathed softly. Her words gentle yet hesitant.

Her reticence bothered him. What had happened in her past? Again his thoughts shot to Lord Rathen and her hasty departure from London. Every part of him tightened with disgust. He would discover the truth and make the despicable rake pay for any injustice committed against Christel.

Watching her eyes for signs of fear, Ryder lowered his mouth to hers. He touched her gently, molded his lips against hers, thrilled to hear the sigh of pleasure emanate from her. He ran one hand up her back, pulling her closer, reveling in the feel of her softness against his hard planes. Her breasts pushed against him. The need to feel every inch of her pulsed through him but he didn't dare.

He moved back and once again looking into her eyes. She lowered her lashes then returned his gaze.

"Don't think, little one, just feel and know that I would never hurt you. I want more but I won't rush you."

She touched his cheek with one slender fingertip. "Kiss me again."

He'd be crazy to say no. Once again, he lowered his mouth to hers, this time tracing the seam of her lips with his tongue. He closed his eyes, needing her, wanting her in the most primal ways. Mercuric energy ripped through him.

Hold back, I must hold back.

But she opened for him, touching his tongue with hers. He'd conquered one tiny step. With all the willpower he possessed, he ended the kiss.

"Is that all?" she asked, seemingly reluctant to move away from him.

"For now..."

"But."

"Hush, I will show you more to loving, but for now I'm tired and feel I must retire for the evening." God what a lie, after that kiss, it would take him hours to fall asleep.

"All right. I forgot you traveled today. I'm so sorry."

He laughed a deep roar. "Don't be sorry, don't ever apologize to me. Let me walk you to your room."

A loud wail pierced the night air, shards of silver knifed through the sky as energy seemed to push them together.

~ * ~

The corner of the tavern was dark, just the way he wanted it. Being seen and recognized was not his intent. He was here to gather information. At least the ale was good. The haggis had been awful, tasteless and not at all to his liking.

"There you are."

"Have you learned anything?" Lord Rathen took a long swallow of his drink then bored into Bromley's eyes. The man repulsed him. His hump shoulder and grating voice never ceased to aggravate, but he was good at what he did. Bromley seemed to be able to walk undetected anywhere.

"Yes." Bromley held out his hand in greeting, seeming to think he, Lord Rathen, would shake it. "What's it worth to you?" His gravelly voice sent a shiver down Richy's spine.

"You know I have no funds. But when I wed Christel, I will pay you. See that you frighten her into my loving arms."

"Bah! You don't know the first thing about love." Bromley pulled his hand back then spat on the floor. "This tavern is a hovel. Couldn't you find somewhere else to meet?"

"As I said, I have no funds. If you wish to be paid then..." He let the sentence finish itself.

"Ryder MacLaren has arrived at the castle. This will not be as easy as you once anticipated. She met him with an arrow close to his head. No doubt it was meant for you, M'lord."

"She loves me. She just doesn't know it yet." He would put the fear of God into her, wed her then find a bed partner who would meet his sexual needs. She was a frigid bitch. His pain shot down to his balls where she'd kneed him. He still remembered the deep searing agony that seemed to go on forever.

"Ah, me thinks you've been drinking too much of this ale. It's addled your brain. If she loves ya, why is she running from you and why is she hunting you with her bow and arrow?"

A serving wench brought ale for Bromley. Lord Rathen pulled her onto his lap, wrapping an arm around her waist. "As I said, she doesn't know it yet. Besides, I don't really care if she loves me. My aim is to get her to the altar before the MacLaren does. I need her money."

Bromley sipped long and deep on his ale, letting out a loud belch when he finished then wiped the foam from his mouth with the back of his arm. "Well, you got your work cut out for you. Saw them kissing tonight atop the castle walls. Then I beat it out of the courtyard before the gates closed. Here, I brought this for ya."

Bromley held out a folded piece of paper.

"What is this?"

"It's from your father."

Richy slowly unfolded the paper and read. When he looked up, rage boiled inside. "How dare he?" Spittle flew from his lips.

Bromley cocked an eyebrow. "Bad news?"

"He's disowned me. Says my inheritance is goin' to the baby."

Chapter Five

"I don't think your ghost wants us to leave." Ryder held a lock of her hair then brought it to his face. "Or maybe she likes to watch us kiss."

"It seems that way." Christel turned in Ryder's arms, watching the light display in the sky above the north turret. His warmth was something she never wanted to let go of. He had a way of making her feel safe and protected. The first time she saw him almost two years ago, he'd stolen her breath then he'd disappeared from her life only to reappear later and this time steal her heart.

Memories of Lord Rathen and his lips molded on hers assailed her. She closed her eyes and thought of Ryder, shaking thoughts of the other man out of her head. When she opened her eyes again, more sparks of silver light shot through the air. Energy pulsed around them and through her.

"Kiss me again, my petite one." Ryder whispered close to her ear, sending a myriad of pleasant shivers through her.

She turned in his arms, her face slanted toward his, his breath a soft sigh across her cheek. "Yes."

Once again, his lips molded across hers, their tongues mating. But this time his hands rested on her derrière, pressing her closer to him. She felt his rod against her stomach. Desperately, she tried not to remember another time and another place with a man she loathed.

But she failed and pulled away.

"Ryder, I can't, not right now. Give me time." Nothing about Ryder reminded her of Richy; his scent masculine, his chiseled features compelling her to watch his every move.

"Anything you want." He ran a hand through his hair, seeming confused and perhaps frustrated.

"It's not you." Christel ran her finger down his cheek. "Dear God, don't ever think this is about you."

"Who is it about and I—"

"No, I'm not ready to talk to anyone. Not yet... In time maybe I can come to terms with what happened."

Shaking, she turned and fled to her room. Yet she heard his booted steps following. He could have caught her but he did not. When she shut the door to her solar, she wanted to open it and call him inside. She needed to tell him everything, yet she didn't dare, terrified of what he might think if he knew the facts.

I have to tell him and see what will happen. He deserves the truth before I lose my heart to him. I already have lost my heart as well as my soul.

But when she opened the door, he was not waiting for her. His scent lingered.

Her heart in her throat, she raced from her room, knowing she had to speak to him now before she lost her courage, and it was strange how the ghost had inspired her and given her courage when she'd had none.

Nervous energy raged within, warring with the need to stay calm. One second she was ready to tell Ryder all that had happened that horrible night, the next she wanted nothing more than to hide in her room.

With her hand poised in the air to knock, she was startled by a ruff yet gentle voice from behind.

"Christel?"

"Oh!" Christel's hand slipped to her breast. "I thought you were inside."

"No, I wasn't ready to retire. I meant to walk and see if I could see the ghost again. I have thoughts that are confusing. I needed to clear my head." He stood in front of her, arms crossed over his chest, a look of grave concern on his face.

"I should go."

"Please stay."

"It's late and—"

"You didn't leave your solar to find me for nothing. You had a reason. And I think you have something you need to talk about. I'm ready to listen and I promise I'll have an open mind."

"Perceptive knave." Christel tried for a wee bit of Scottish humor, but it didn't come out quite right. Anxious to have this over yet afraid the truth would send him running, she debated with herself.

"Hardly, but you've grown pale. Your cheeks are white as if all the blood has drained from your face."

She put her hands on her cheeks. They felt like ice. "Really, my ramblings can wait until morning."

"If that's what you want, but I think you should come in and sit for a minute. I'm not at all sure you can make it to your room." He slipped past her and opened the door.

Christel followed and watched as he pulled the bell cord. A few minutes later a servant arrived.

"Would you bring tea and something to eat," Ryder said.

The servant bowed then left.

Christel sat in a straight back chair, feeling as if she were still a schoolgirl who had done something wrong.

Ryder didn't speak but sat in a chair opposite her until the tea and biscuits arrived. He poured her a cup of the hot brew, but he walked to the sideboard and found a bottle of scotch. When he returned, he sat back, watched and waited.

Swallowing hard and inhaling a long deep breath, Christel set her cup down and folded her hands in her lap. "It's a long story."

"I have all night."

"It might take that long for me to say the words." *That might condemn me to you forever.*

"I have all night and a great deal of patience." His voice calmed her, soothed her battered soul.

"What do you know of my last days in London?" She smoothed her dress then wrapped her fingers in the material, clenching them tightly.

"That you left unexpectedly without telling anyone where or why you were leaving."

"I couldn't stay." She felt what little blood that was left in her head drain away. Coldness swept within as she remembered the night, memories pounded a dreadful staccato in her mind. She didn't want to say the words, needed to run away as far as she could go.

"This has something to do with Richy Rathen." His voice was matter of fact, yet at the same time deadly. "I should have taken you with me."

"Yes, to both. I wanted you to ask me to go with you." She looked down, moisture forming in her eyes. Lord, but she didn't want to cry in front of Ryder. This was too difficult. She closed her eyes for a moment, hoping for courage.

"It's all right." He stood beside her then he knelt, drawing her hands into his. "If it hurts that much, I can wait."

"You are too patient." Looking up, she saw the concern and some other emotion written in his eyes.

"I've been lacking in my duties. The Duchess charged me with a task, which I abandoned. I was supposed to make sure nothing evil happened to you. And I left. Ran away from myself and feelings I didn't understand. I never realized I could care so much when I barely knew you. But I did from the first moment I saw you. I think I was in love. But I told myself I was crazy and that love didn't exist."

"I thought I wanted to live a life with God so I ignored all of the people around me. I was so sure I wanted to be a nun." *I lost my virginity to that evil man and now I have nothing to give the man I love.*

Ryder chuckled but it didn't sound joyful. "I'm so glad you did not get your wish. I'm not sure how I would have overcome that blow."

His laughter sounded bittersweet to her ears. "I'm nothing like them, at least at the convent where I lived for a few months. I could never preach one thing and act another way. They are all hypocrites."

"I'm not understanding what you're trying to tell me."

She sighed and clasped her hands tighter. "I know but... Looking back at my time in London with my cousins before they married and left to pursue lives with their new husbands, gives me some fond memories and some horrible ones."

"You should only have wonderful memories. I know about the wager, so that is nothing new."

"Ah, but Damian, the winner, bed his fair damsel, Amorica, before the wedding," Christel said.

"How would you know this?"

"Amorica told me after they were married. She explained everything—how she despised all smugglers save one, her husband."

"Richy and Dicky lost."

"Well, I'm sure Aric Lakeland did not woo Ravyn into bed easily. She was terrified of the marriage bed." Speaking of her cousins and friends lightened the mood and yet...

"What of you, Christel? Are you terrified of love making?"

She shook her head, her hair falling down and shielding her from his view. "No. I want you to make love to me." *But I'm terrified of rape.*

"Then tell me, Christel. What is it that is on your mind? Please. I promise not to judge, just to listen."

She looked up then licked her parched lips. "Promise me you won't do something foolish. Something you might come to regret."

"What..."

"Promise."

"I promise if the words will help you."

"The ball..." she paused, "...when you asked me to marry you then you were suddenly called to your ship." Her voice wavered. "Oh, lord this is hard." Determined though, she meant to get this over with.

Ryder tossed back another scotch then walked around her chair. "Christel, you can count on me. What I can promise is that I will never let you down again and I'll never leave you alone."

"I know but I've been judged and threatened. I've gone through so much to get here to MacLaren castle. I thought maybe this would be my home. But now you might not like what you hear and—"

"Toss you out? Christel, you know me better than that. We were at the dance. I left. I know The Duchess did not leave with you, but I assumed you would follow my instructions and wait until your carriage arrived before you walked from the parlor."

She rubbed her neck and shoulders, so tense from the fear and the need for this moment. "The Duchess arranged for the carriage to return and pick me up, but it was too late. Ryder, I did try to do what you said, but I wasn't given a choice."

The lines in Ryder's face tightened. "I'm at a loss for words. Too late? Too late for what?"

The breath Christel took gave her no bravery, but she intended to finish this tonight. "As I was leaving, Lord Rathen cornered me. I thought I could talk my way out of the situation I found myself in. But," she shrugged, moisture pooling in her eyes, "I found out differently." Remembering those horrific minutes made her shudder. She wiped the tears away with the back of her hand.

"I'll kill him." With his fist, he pounded the table. "I'll kill the odious lecher."

"No, you won't. You promised not to do anything foolish. And you want me to finish my story, don't you?"

"Of course." The once hardened lines softened. "Go on."

"I was terrified when he forced me into the darkness. When we were alone, he tried to be polite."

"Yeah, Richy can always appear the gentleman if he thinks it will get him what he wants."

"He was the perfect gentleman until I refused him. Under other circumstances, I might have accepted the ride he offered, but The Duchess had already told me she would send the carriage for me."

"You told him no."

"I didn't have the chance. He grabbed my arm." She closed her eyes, trying to stop the shaking of her body. This was not something she'd ever wanted to recall.

"You should have screamed. Everyone at the soiree would have ended up outside as witness to his perfidy."

"He anticipated just that. Before I could yell, his hand was over my mouth, silencing me." Against her mouth his hand had been sweaty and hot, so horribly revolting. She recalled that moment vividly.

"I should have been there for you." His lips thinned and the rage she saw in his face terrified her.

Christel jumped, surprised by his sudden vehemence. "You had no way of knowing. Just as I had no way to predict he would turn forceful," Christel said.

"Richy is seldom violent. He's a coward."

"I believe he thought I had a dowry he could get his hands on if he married me. But I don't have money. I'm the second sister. Allura has the castle and the wealth that goes along with the status. Actually, her husband Hunter Grey owns the land and the keep." [SEP]

"I'm sure Richy over extended himself in a game of chance that night and was more frantic than usual. He loved to bet on the horses. He spent the majority of the evening gambling. Who knows what he lost that evening." Ryder poured another cup of tea for her and set it on the table. "He bets on more than the horses."

"He said something about losing his ancestral home and he had to get it back before his father disowned him. I think he might have been drunk."

"So, he was desperate."

"I guess. He pulled me into the gardens. I fought him the best I could, but he ripped my dress, tore it to shreds then he..."

Ryder stood and gathered her into his arms. Her sobs made her body shake as she remembered that horrid night.

"Hush, you needn't tell me anymore. Rathyn's a dead man."

Christel soaked up the warmth of his embrace, needing the solace he gave her. But now that she'd started, she needed to finish. She pushed away then set one hand on his chest. "There is more."

"You don't have to say. I know the ending. I heard something of it when in London, but I didn't believe he'd go that far. A trip to Gretna Green or quickly arranged marriage without your consent."

"Luck, I guess, was with me. I got away, torn dress and all then found the carriage The Duchess sent my way. When I was home, no one was up so I ran to my room. A servant brought me hot water for a bath. She was so sweet. She told me what to expect. She told me I could be pregnant, but I didn't want to believe that could happen."

"Luck?" Ryder sounded incredulous.

"The next morning I ran to the convent near here. I stayed there until they kicked me out. I was so afraid. I knew your home was nearby and I hoped your people would accept me. I couldn't go home." Tears flowed down her cheeks. She tried to wipe them away with the back of her hand but to no avail.

"My dear petite, I'm so glad you chose to come here. I followed your trail to the convent, but the nuns there would not speak of you. I went to the McLellan estate but, Allura had not heard from you. I was beside myself. Knowing I needed rest and information, I headed home."

"I didn't believe I could really get pregnant."

"There is a baby?"

"Was."

~ * ~

"Stillborn." Tears streamed down Christel's cheeks.

The fury Ryder felt swept within. He'd promised Christel not to do anything foolish and he wouldn't be irrational. But Lord Rathen would be punished for his misdeeds. Somehow, he would make sure Richy never had another dime to his name. An idea formed in his head then reality crashed down around him.

"Are you all right? You shouldn't do anything. A bed...a bed, I need to get you to a bed." He turned in circles, frantic with fear and need. He wanted to pick her up and hold her in his arms, needed to keep her safe. "Bloody hell, I don't know what to do."

Christel rose and placed a small delicate hand on his arm then laughed. "You don't need to do anything. I'm fine. It was six months ago, the birth. I came here right after."

"Sit." Still frantic, he picked her up and put her on his bed. She was so tiny and delicate. The panic he felt flowed through and adrenalin sped inside. He clenched his teeth, wishing he could find some way to turn back time.

"Ryder, stop." She pushed back hair that had fallen in her face and tried to get up, but Ryder sat down next to her, stopping her with a look.

"Humor me, I need to hear the rest of your story. Just let me be crazy for a few minutes. That's all I ask. I need time to figure all this out and make plans." Plans that would keep Richy celibate and working the rest of his life.

"Alright." Her voice was hesitant then she slanted him a rather sheepish look as if she truly thought him insane.

"Don't laugh at me." Embarrassment was a trait he seldom felt. "I know I must have over reacted. If it's been six months since the birth, you are healthy." His words sounded more like a question than a statement.

"Yes." For the first time since she'd entered his solar, she smiled through moisture filled eyes. "Ryder, I am fine. The pregnancy was normal. The birth seemed normal too. After I delivered the baby, that's when the nuns told me I could no longer stay. They told me I had a girl, but I saw the baby. The child was a boy." She paused, "I didn't even get to hold him, not for one second."

"Hypocrites." His mind churned, trying to make sense of her story.

"Would you have wanted me to stay, to become a nun?" She cocked her head to one side, apparently waiting for an answer.

"Of course not." This was something that needed his full attention now.

"Do you think less of me? Are you going to kick me out?" She clasped her hands tightly in front of her waiting.

"Hells bells, what kind of question is that?"

"The kind a girl has to ask." Christel's voice was soft and barely audible. "I've endured much this last year and a half. I just need to know how you feel. I want to know if you blame me for what Richy did. Some men would."

"Christel, if I could wrap you up in my arms and somehow erase all the bad things that have happened to you, I would. But we both know I can't. Judging you for an evil another committed at your expense is not who I am."

"Thank you." Tears flowed again.

"You are strong, braver than most. I don't know if I could have found a way to survive, and I'm a lot bigger than you." He touched her shoulder to comfort. "What can I do? I want to make this all go away."

"Honor your promise." Christel took his hand in hers, looking at him with steady eyes. "Please, don't do anything stupid, anything that would get you in trouble with the law that would put you in jail."

"I will find Richy and I will do nothing that would cause the police or the Bow Street Runners to come after me. I don't want to spend my life in jail, nor do I want to hang for the murder of Richy, vile scum that he is. However, I promise you, I will find a way to keep Lord Rathen's pocketbook empty. He will live the rest of his life disowned by his family and in disgrace."

Christel dropped his hand and leaned back, her expression one he couldn't read. "You can do that? How?"

"I don't know yet. First, I have to find him." He paused for a few seconds. "You thought I was him when you shot the arrow at me."

She nodded. "Yes and no. I knew it wasn't Richy, but I didn't recognize you right away."

"So you think he might have followed you. Why?" He rose and paced the inside of his solar.

"After I kneed him as hard as I could, I ran and he yelled at me. He said he'd find me and there was nowhere I could hide."

"You hit him in his whirlygigs?" Ryder let a deep belly laugh roll then checked himself when he saw her cheeks turn pink. He knelt beside the bed and brought her hands to his lips. "I'm sorry, I shouldn't use such language in front of a lady and what happened is nothing to laugh about."

She grinned again. "He was naked, his pants still down. If I could forget the hurt and the sight of him, I would laugh too."

"Good girl, you should try to forget the agony and remember what you did to him." He would always remember the pain and suffering Richy caused Christel.

Ryder left her side to rummage in a desk for paper and pen. Sitting down, he made notes and wrote out directions. When he looked up from his work, Christel slept. He would have loved to cover her and let her sleep in his bed. It was where he wanted her for the rest of his life. But she'd been through enough scandal. He didn't need to add his name to the list of men who caused Christel distress of any kind. She didn't need the label that would come from spending the night in his room.

After opening the door to his solar, he lifted her in his arms then carried her to her room and managed to open the door. Setting her on the bed, he covered her with a warm quilt then kissed her on the forehead.

"Sweet dreams, my petite one."

A few minutes later he was striding through the castle, barking orders at his servants who were already awake and waking others.

"Stewart, just the man I was looking for. Glad you weren't asleep. I need you to make a sketch. Do you think you can do it?"

"Of course. I just arrived. I was drawing near the loch, a great place to paint a sunrise." Stewart pulled paper from a satchel he carried over his shoulder and drew from the description Ryder gave him.

With that accomplished, he left for the stables, not realizing the hour until he saw the sun peaking over the trees.

No wonder Christel had fallen asleep. No wonder Stewart had been out painting sunrises.

He'd kept her up most of the night. The only regret he had though was that he'd exhausted her. But now he had a mission of revenge, one he would accomplish as soon as possible.

"I need a horse." His voice echoed around the stable.

A young man raced from a back room, pulling on his pants and doing a bit of jig in the effort. "M'lord."

"I need my stallion, Finian." In his haste he'd forgotten to put on his riding boots. What he wore would have to do. He'd worn less on his feet when he'd been in the states with Aric and Damian.

"Since last night..." the boy sounded breathless, "...he hasn't been fed or watered this morning."

"I'll wait. Give him a bag of feed. He has water in his stable?"

"Of course." The boy rushed to do Ryder's bidding, much faster now that his pants were fastened.

Ryder paced, thinking of all he must do before returning, belatedly realizing he should have left Christel a message. She would understand his absence, and he didn't intend to be away for too long.

Moments later, "Here he is, M'lord." The saddle was on the horse, which pranced, looking ready for his next adventure.

"Thanks." Ryder tossed the boy a coin. He caught it with astonishment clearly written in the lines of his face. Yes, once more realizing the home had been without a laird for too long.

Ryder led Fin from the stables then mounted. The horse started at an easy pace through the castle keep. Once beyond the gates, Ryder let the horse gallop, reveling in his smooth gait. Early morning sun lit the road, and the wind rolled across his face.

His thoughts went to Christel and how beautiful she had looked when he set her on the bed, her long blond hair in disarray, sooty black lashes on alabaster flesh. Where Christel was concerned, none of his feelings were platonic.

At this point in time, his focus needed to be on Richy Rathen and Christel's baby. The nuns had not let her see the stillborn baby and he had a hunch, a gut instinct, they had lied to her. Proving this fact might be impossible but he meant to try.

Pulling back on the reins, he let Fin walk. He was near Owen's home and while he'd rushed from the castle at an early hour, he needed to respect the time of day. He guessed it would be nearing six am.

Owen was outside chopping wood. "My friend? What can I do for you?"

Ryder dismounted then let Finian's reins fall to the ground. "A favor and I will pay handsomely."

"No need for payment." Owen wiped sweat from his forehead with the back of his sleeve, a wide grin on his face.

"I will pay you or I will seek out some other who I might not trust as much," Ryder told his childhood friend.

"Well, that's a deal I can't refuse. Let's go inside where we can talk over a cup of hot tea."

Ryder had come to prefer coffee since his time in the states, but he doubted if Owen had any. He made a note to himself to import coffee.

Ryder accepted Owen's hospitality, sitting in his kitchen with the hot tea. "I need you to find out if a man by the name of Richy Rathen has been seen in these parts. He pulled the sketch from his pocket.

"Stewart?" Owen looked up from the picture, a grin on his face. "The likeness is good, I assume."

Ryder nodded. "A talented man, that one. This sketch looks exactly like Richy including the baggy eyes and belly."

"How do want me to proceed?"

"Richy loves to bet the horses, but there are no races in these parts. He also loves whoring and drinking. Can you send some men to the taverns between here and Edinburgh? Show everyone the picture. Stewart made several copies." Ryder rummaged through his satchel and handed all but one to Owen. The men shook hands and Ryder mounted Finian and headed back to the castle. His mission was not finished.

The sun, now high in the sky, shone down on him. Light played with the leaves on the trees, casting shadows on the road. Ryder's heart was a little bit lighter. He wanted to see Christel and tell her about all he'd done. But first he had some letters to send.

Time had created a vacuum in his life. He wasn't sure who could be trusted and who could not. Just because he was the laird did not mean he had the loyalty of all of his clan. Owen and Stewart had helped him.

Two letters were in his satchel, one to The Duchess and one to Hunter Grey, Christel's brother-in-law. He hoped Hunter would send Blade, but whoever Hunter sent to help, he would make sure every convent between his castle and London was searched, including the one where Christel had stayed.

When he entered the keep, he expected to see Christel but she was nowhere to be found. He knocked on her door and there was no answer. He wondered at that but perhaps she was still asleep. He resigned himself to seeing her this evening. But she did not show up. All his inquiries went unanswered until one of her serving girls found him with a note.

Ryder,

Please do not worry over me. I am a bit under the weather. I will see you soon.

Christel

~ * ~

Sarah, you're a bonnie lass." Richy's hand slipped beneath her skirt. He ran his fingers along the inside of her thigh and prayed she could give him what he needed.

When he found her swollen folds and felt her cream, he sighed and as he rubbed the tiny bud, he reveled in her moan of pleasure.

Yes, this would work tonight. His cock would grow hard and he'd be inside her. Then he could stop thinking about Christel for a few minutes. If he'd won that damn wager, his life would be far different.

His other hand played with her breast, teasing her nipple. Then he kissed her neck and bit then licked.

"Richy," she sighed.

"Do you have a room?"

She nodded, "Upstairs, first door on the right."

He stood, carrying her as he took the steps staggering a bit under her weight. Bloody hell, but he hadn't risen to the occasion since Christel kneed him in the balls. He wanted his hard rod inside Sarah.

She bent down to open the door and as he kicked it closed, he was ripping her clothes.

"Richy," she screamed.

But his mouth found her and silenced any more words. Her breasts bobbed free. Seconds later she lay naked on the bed, his clothes joining hers.

"Touch me." He moved her hand to his limp cock. "If you don't work your magic, I won't pay you. He bit on a nipple and she yelled in pain.

"Lick me. Put that tongue of yours to good use." Bloody hell, but he couldn't get it up.

She bent at the waist, licked and sucked but to no avail.

Richy tossed her from the bed. "Incompetent whore." Yet he knew he was incompetent or impotent. Until now he hadn't thought of himself in that manner. Perhaps if he forced her, he would get the desired results from his limp cock.

"I'm going to fuck you." He strode to Sarah and grabbed her by the arms. Lifting her, he threw her back on the bed and spread her legs.

Tears streamed down her face. "Please don't hurt me."

"That's it, beg for your life." Lord Rathen rolled off Sarah, frustration eating at him.

"Don't hurt me." Once again, she begged but with Richy on the floor, she took the opportunity to grab her clothes and flee.

"No..."

Chapter Six

The loud incessant knocking was giving her a headache. Christel closed her eyes and put her hands on her ears to block the noise.

"Christel, open the door. It's time to rise and shine. It's a beautiful day, the sky is clear and it's calling your name."

No, she didn't want to see anyone today or tomorrow or even the next. She pulled the covers over her head.

"Christel, like it or not, I'm not going away."

Aidan?

A fog filled brain cleared. "Aidan? Is that you?" Christel opened her eyes. The banging had stopped and for a moment she thought she must have imagined her little sister's voice on the other side of the door. She hadn't seen Aidan since she'd left for London.

"Are you going to open the door or not?"

She imagined Aidan, hands on hips, tapping the floor with her foot. "Yes, just a minute." She pulled her robe on and raced to the door.

"Christel." Aidan fell through the now open door, arms flung wide then embraced her sister.

"What are you doing here?" Overwhelmed at the sight of her and depressed from the realization Ryder left her, she waited for an answer.

"Ryder sent a request for help to Father. Blade was visiting Hunter and decided he was the one for the job."

"And you tagged along. Are you still smitten with Blade?" Christel looked at her little sister. Her fiery red hair had not changed, nor the clear sky blue of her eyes, but she'd grown up, her figure beginning to mature into beautiful curves.

"I love him and always will but, no. I have given him more than ample breathing space. I don't want to talk about me. I want to know why you've scared Ryder half to death by staying in your room for over a week. He's beside himself with worry and thinks he did something wrong."

"Come and sit with me." Christel pointed to one of the chairs in the solar. "I can explain everything."

"First, I'm going to cheer up this dreary room." Aidan flung the curtains open. Sun poured into the area. "There now, isn't that better?" She turned, hands on hips and an impish smile on her lightly freckled face.

Christel looked up from her chair. "I'm not sure. The blackness fit my mood much better." Yet she understood she couldn't stay in the darkness of her solar forever. She needed to confront life again no matter what waited for her.

Yet when Aidan opened the window, the scent of roses filled the air and she had to admit her mood had lightened.

"You've been crying..."

"You noticed red swollen eyes, how astute." Still, Christel didn't want the sunshine and she didn't want to be cheered up. But she knew from first hand experience there was no stopping Aidan. If Aidan intended to make her feel better, that's what would happen.

Aidan sat for a second then rose and wandered around the room. "Tell me, what has you shut away from everyone?"

"Always to the point." Christel wasn't sure if she wanted to tell anyone else about the child she'd never been able to hold—her stillborn tiny baby boy. Ryder had vanished after she'd told him. Aidan might do the same. She couldn't handle another rejection.

"Well, talking things out has a way of clarifying the condition, makes it seem less, not quite as horrible." Aidan flipped her hair from her face with a wave of her hand then poured tea for both of them. "Here you go." She held out the cup.

"Wise words but very wrong." Christel knew she had made the situation worse with Ryder, not better.

"You don't know that," Aidan said, still grinning and so happy Christel wanted to cringe.

"I do, but I will tell you all about what sent Ryder scurrying into the hills." Thoughts of Ryder leaving sent moisture pooling in the back of her throat again, but she stiffened, straightening her back as she recalled the words.

"He didn't run from you. He set out to help you," Aidan confronted her, frown lines on her forehead.

"I won't argue." Christel told her story to Aidan. It did seem easier this time and Aidan listened with tear-filled eyes.

Aidan took Christel's hands in hers and spoke slowly. "Ryder loves you. He sped away to look for this Rathen fellow. He went to see Owen and several other people to ask for help. He even had one of his friends draw a sketch of Rathen so he could show it to people."

"He promised he wouldn't do anything that might put his life in danger." Christel's heart raced with fear for Ryder.

"He won't, but he is a man who is determined to right any wrongs done to the woman he cherishes."

"I don't understand why you persist in this notion that Ryder loves me." Christel wiped the moisture from her cheeks. "He's never said so."

"One only has to watch him looking to your solar. His eyes are sad and he has tried to talk to you, but you have rejected him each and every time he has tried to approach you. Now I understand love and I understand why you are afraid, but his opinion would never change because some insipid fop abused you."

"Perhaps you are right." She didn't want to put her hopes into believing something she was sure was not true, but Aidan had a convincing way about her.

"Of course I am right. Now let's put a smile on your beautiful face and wash away the red, tear swollen eyes." Aidan walked to the bell cord to summon a servant. "In a few minutes you'll feel more like yourself."

"M'lady," the servant entered.

"A bath please."

A few hours later, Christel stood in front of a mirror, dressed in a lavender day gown, her hair expertly coifed by her sister.

"You are so beautiful." Aidan danced around her, giving her hair finishing touches and singing a bawdy song about sex and love.

"Aidan, really..."

"Yes, really, come on, let's go see if we can find Ryder and set his mind at ease." Aidan wound her arm in one of Christel's. "It's time, you know, past time."

Christel inhaled a long deep breath and with unsteady legs, descended the long stairway to the first floor. Ryder sat in the library reading.

For the longest time, Christel stood in the doorway, wondering how to proceed.

Aidan gave her a tiny push. "Go on, he's not going to bite."

Ryder must have heard them. He rose and set the book on his desk, a smile forming on his handsome face his eyes alight with what seemed like pleasure. "Christel? I'm glad to see you."

The moment froze in time, and as she walked toward him, everything moved in slow motion. "Ryder."

"I'm glad to see you're feeling better. Were you sick?"

"In a way. I..."

"Come, sit down." Ryder pulled out a chair for her. "Can you tell me what I did wrong?"

Does love sickness count? "I believed that after I told you what happened, you thought less of me and left." Honesty? Is it always the best course of action?

At his sides his fists clenched then loosened. "I had errands. But when I returned that evening, you were nowhere to be found."

"You put me in my room when I was sleeping. I thought you didn't want to be with me." Her stomach rolled and the lightheadedness that consumed her made her reach for the arm of a chair to steady herself. The floor beneath seemed to undulate in waves. Quickly, she sat down.

"There was too much scandal associated with you. I didn't want the clan to think I was using you by bedding you before we were wed. Your reputation is important to me. If you were found in my bed..."

"Thank you. Aidan said you sent a letter to my father for help. What do you need assistance with?" She was afraid to ask, terrified he'd still do something they both might come to regret.

"Finding Richy, I've heard he is in the area. I want to make sure you are protected." Ryder sat on the corner of the large desk. His gaze riveted on her.

Her emotions frayed, her heart fluttering in her chest, she smoothed the folds of her dress. "You promised you wouldn't do anything stupid."

"Leaving Richy Rathen to find you would be stupid. Christel, he wants you, perhaps needs you would be a better word and will stop at nothing to get you. He doesn't seem to understand you have no great inheritance to bring his way."

"I would never willingly go with him." She straightened, shaking her head at the thought of her voluntarily leaving with Richy.

"I know. Come let's talk about something else—anything else, something that will put a smile on your face as well as your heart. The sun is shining and the weather is warm. Would you like to walk?" He rose and held out his hand. "A soft breeze rustles the leaves and it's not too hot. Sunshine might help you feel better."

"Of course, I'd like to feel the sun on my face. After a week of sulking, I should make amends to the clan and to you. I was stupid." Guilt swamped her, filling her heart and soul. If she'd taken a moment to talk to him, all of this could have been avoided. She would not have lost a week with him.

"You can do that later."

The feel of her hand in his large one sent her mind spinning and her heart racing. "Where are you taking me?" She felt the anticipation all the way to her toes.

"To the gazebo in the rose garden. Where I can kiss you if you'll allow it? Have you seen the gazebo?"

"No, but it must be gorgeous. I'm sure the roses are in bloom by now." His thumb traced a path on the top of her hand. The sensation made her a little bit crazy, reminding her of the night in his solar when he'd kissed her. Yes, she'd love another kiss.

Outside, the air smelled clean and fresh and a soft breeze blew from the ocean. Birds chirped in trees and tiny frogs with loud voices croaked. When they were away from the castle and seeing eyes, Ryder let go of her hand and wrapped his arm around her shoulder, drawing her to him.

She leaned into him as he pulled her closer, so close she heard his heartbeat and felt every breath. For a moment, she shut her eyes and let his warmth heal wounds created by Lord Rathen. Where she was terrified of Richy, she knew Ryder would never harm her. He would always look out for what was best for her.

"Look," Ryder pointed toward the sky, "it's a hawk. What do you suppose it's hunting?"

Christel watched as the hawk caught the air currents above. "So graceful and free. Hope it's not the little bunnies we saw a little ways back." Soaring above the earth on the wind, the hawk looked down upon them. She wondered what it would feel like to be so free and without a care in the world.

He bent and kissed her on the forehead. "Christel, I never meant to leave you that night a week ago. But I had a mission and the sooner I accomplish it, the safer I'll feel. I fear for your life. See, here we are."

They stopped. Covered in trailing roses, the inside of the gazebo was hidden from prying eyes. All around the little house were different colored rose bushes. Inside, it would be private and no one would be able to see them.

"It's beautiful." Leaving London, everything had seemed sordid and dirty. Now at Ryder's home she found herself surrounded by peace and beauty.

"I have a gardener whose sole duty is to tend to these beds. He was hired by my father ages ago." Ryder pointed toward a red rose before plucking it from its stem and handing it to her.

"Can we go inside the gazebo? The air smells so sweet."

"Like roses," Ryder laughed then hugged her.

Inside, the chairs were made from whicker and had been painted white. On the couch, colorful pillows adorned the corners.

"What happens to these if it rains?" She didn't want anything to change or become damaged.

"The gardener races out here and retrieves the pillows." Ryder sat down on the couch then patted the place next to him. "You can sit too, right here beside me."

She smiled, wondering what Ryder had planned. A few minutes

later, a servant arrived with lemonade, a basket of strawberries and steaming hot bread. Another servant walked in behind with a platter of cheeses and meats.

"When did you plan all this?"

"When Aidan arrived in a flurry of petticoats and assurances, she would have you feeling better before I could count to ten."

Joy bubbled up inside Christel and made its appearance in laughter. "She does have a way about her."

"It's good to see you smile. I want that smile to stay on your face forever." He lifted her chin and she looked into dark brown eyes, caring eyes.

"You really mean that, don't you?" She moistened her lips, anticipating a kiss.

"Yes, and I want to erase the memory of Richy's touch from your mind." He bent and gently brushed his lips against hers. He ran his tongue along the seam of her lips then moved away. "Do my attentions frighten you, my petite one?"

"No, they make butterflies dance in my stomach. I like to be close to you." She reached up and smoothed her hand along the stubble on his face, adoring the way it felt to her touch and how his unshaven whiskers scratched her face when he kissed her.

"I brought you out here so I can try to make new pleasurable memories in a beautiful rose filled garden. Will you let me?" He brushed a kiss across the back of her hand, before backing away.

Christel paused, wondering what his intimate touch would bring—pleasure or pain. Somehow, she knew he would never hurt her and he would always bring her pleasure. "If I want, I can tell you to stop?"

Ryder smiled, his eyes seemed to dance and glimmer then he nodded and kissed the tip of her nose. "Of course, my petite one."

His lips found hers again and this time he didn't draw away from her. She felt his hand at the nape of her neck, urging her face upward and deepening the kiss. Then she wrapped her arms over his shoulders and opened her lips. His tongue touched hers, danced with hers before exploring more intimately.

With his hands, he framed her face, holding her still. She moaned softly and wondered at the sound of her voice as it whispered into his mouth. Their tongues danced and played together. Her body softened, needing something he wasn't giving her, sensations she didn't understand whirled inside. But she didn't know what they were or how to return the sensations. She'd never felt anything like this, this fantastic relentless pleasure.

He pulled back and seemed to look at her as if he wanted to read her mind. "Did you like the kiss?"

"Yes." Of course she did, she loved every moment with him.

His thumbs traced circles on her neck. Then he bent and kissed her again, sucking her tongue inside his mouth. Ryder pulled away and trailed light nipping kisses down her neck and across her collarbone. With each kiss, his teeth settled on her dress and pulled it a fraction of the way until her shoulder was bared to him. Again, he kissed and tugged then kissed again, turning his attention to her other shoulder.

"You are so sweet," he said against her cheek. "So absolutely perfect. Do you like this? May I kiss you again? I don't want to ever stop."

"Ryder, please." Was all she said, and her voice broke on the words.

"Oh, yes my little one, enjoy and relax." He kissed her once more and as he did so, he used his palms to push the fragile sleeves that were scarcely more than straps from her shoulders and down her arms.

~ * ~

Ryder could restrain himself no longer. He lifted his face from hers and looked down in time to see her breasts slip from her bodice. For a moment he closed his eyes. At the sight in front of him, he could barely breathe. She was so perfect and she was made for him and always would be.

She wrapped her arms around his neck, seemingly oblivious to her state of undress. Running her fingers through his hair, he groaned and knew he had to stop her explorations before he took more than she was ready to give.

"Touch me later." Ryder took her hands in his then held her arms to her sides while he feasted his eyes upon her. "You are so beautiful. Do you like this? What I'm doing?"

"I want to see you," she whispered. "It seems only fair after all."

"Later, you can see all of me."

Chuckling softly, he cradled her in one arm, urged her back into an arch that offered her breasts as a gift to be taken. He looked into her eyes, searching for any sign of fear before he bent to take a nipple between his lips. Her tiny moan of pleasure caused him to smile and he returned to her mouth for an instant, silencing her. Soon he touched the tip of his tongue to the nipple again, flicked it back and forth until she brought her hands up to wind her fingers into his hair.

Needing to take his time and introduce her to the joy of making love was something he had to accomplish. Nothing would please Ryder more than to expunge the memory of Lord Richy Rathen from her mind.

She surprised him, catapulting him from his thoughts of Rathen. With strength she couldn't have known she possessed, Christel forced his mouth hard against her breast and he obliged by sucking her nipple deep inside his mouth and biting gently.

"Ryder..."

He looked up, "Yes?"

"I don't understand the feelings. They are like nothing I've known before, and I want them to go on forever."

"Then you don't want me to stop?" God but he didn't want her to say yes.

"No, please, touch me, kiss me again, touch me. Help me forget everything that came before you."

"I promise, you will come to understand all of your feelings and more." Smiling inside, he moved to the other breast, laving and sucking while he listened to her respond so beautifully to the attention he gave her and used his fingers on the nipple he had abandoned. Her flesh was silken and seemed on fire, beckoning for more.

"Ryder, dear God, I feel so hot inside and, and..."

He watched her swallow then kissed her neck, nipping the length. "And?" What he wouldn't give to know the answer. Could she tell him? He needed her to understand she could tell him everything.

"The sensation, something I can't..." In his arms she tensed, her eyes open wide where they'd been closed before. "I don't know how to explain what I'm feeling."

He feared she would remember a past he needed to obliterate. Ryder lifted his mouth but could not bring himself to think about what happened to her in London when all he craved was to give all his thoughts to Christel.

When she didn't say anything, "The sensations? Are they good ones?"

"I think so, yes." She ran her hands up his chest then down, resting a moment at the waistband of his trousers. "I want to feel you, all of you. See you."

He laughed. "You don't know, my little one, that you can touch me anytime you want, anywhere you want." He moved back a fraction then undoing the laces on his shirt, he slipped it off.

Her hands flattened against his chest. When she touched his nipple, it was all he could do not to whip off her skirts and take her right then. He forced himself to hold back, willing himself to have patience. In time she would come to him, eager and knowing there would be no pain only pleasure.

"I believe I like the way you feel, nothing like me."

Ryder smiled again and returned his attention to her nipple. While she tugged and pinched his nipple, exploring his body, he slipped a hand beneath her skirt and ran his palm up her leg, over a silk stocking, until he reached incredibly soft skin.

She stilled. "Ryder? What are you doing?"

He knew he had to take incredible care, ease her into the joys of creating and giving pleasure. "Just something to give you pleasure, my petite one." Then he tucked his hand around the brush of hair at the apex of her thighs. His finger delved through slick wetness, her cream flowing for him. He knew her body was ready and that gave him great pleasure.

"Ryder, do you think you should do that? I mean," she licked her lips.

"If you like it, yes." He touched the tiny nub between her swollen folds, rubbing gently, thrilled at the way she moved with him. Then he parted her further, slipping a finger inside, letting her body ride him.

"I don't want you to stop," her breath swept lightly against his face. "Please don't stop."

"Then I won't." Her words were an aphrodisiac to his heart. Giving her pleasure and erasing the pain was his mission. He raised his head and listened but heard no approaching footsteps. Watching her breasts as they moved and swayed with the rhythm he set. Ryder gave full attention to the tiny bud until Christel's hips rose meeting him, begging for more.

His lips parted, drew back with delight at seeing what he gave her. He needed her aroused body to reach its release. But he wanted to see her too, revel in all her beauty. He pushed up her skirt until it bunched around her hips. Her thighs jerked and her cream slicked his fingers. She appeared lost, carried away on the sea of wanting he had created. The tops of the embroidered silk stockings had worked down to rest at her knees.

Ryder bent over her, laving her nipples with teeth and tongue, tracing the fullness of her breasts, before driving her, with a last strong stroke, to her release. He was enchanted by the bucking and intense spasms of her body.

"I never knew." She whispered as she sagged in his arms. "I don't think I'll ever be able to move again."

Ryder gathered her close, held her while her eyes remained closed. He thought of watching her as she slept, lying close to her throughout the night. He knew then he needed to wed her as soon as he convinced her to say yes, afraid her fears would make that difficult. But he was sure this new revelation of sexual pleasure might help persuade her.

His breathing calmed but his cock had not. He needed to divert his mind from his discomfort. From here on out he must move with care. Thoughts of Richy and his whereabouts flashed through his head. He should hear from the scouts Owen had sent out a week ago.

Regretting his actions as soon as he put them in motion, he pulled Christel's bodice up then her skirt down. Bloody hell, but he wanted to keep her naked for a few minutes more but didn't want to take the chance of anyone coming upon them. This afternoon he knew luck had been on his side.

"Come, sweetheart." He bent and whispered close to her ear. "You know how impulsive your little sister is. She could come looking for you."

Her eyes opened while she focused on him, her voice wavering. "You're right, of course. Aidan will want to know where I've been."

"We must be wary. Richy will be looking for you too, and he won't ask you to wed him, he'll force you. We should talk of marriage— say our vows as soon as possible." He realized that was a bit abrupt and it didn't sound the way he intended but there was nothing to do about it now.

"After what happened with Rathen, you shouldn't have to marry me." She sat up, smoothing her skirts then turned her back to him with a slight lift to her delicate shoulders. "I have nothing to give you."

"I'm sorry but I would have the reading of the banns by sunset. We must wait a week to make sure everything is done right."

She turned back to him, pushing her hair from her face. "I'm not going to marry you when I know you don't want to be tied down to one place, if you still wish to chase sunsets."

Ryder took her hands in his. "I'm not chasing any more sunrises. I didn't know what I wanted and so I searched the world. Now I understand everything I hold dear is in front of me."

"You're not saying this because you feel duty bound to protect me?" Moisture pooled in Christel's eyes, and he felt the cad for putting them there.

He touched a drop of liquid as guilt swamped him. He intended to find a way to convince her his intentions were pure. "I never want to make you cry, and I never want to leave the MacLaren land unless you are by my side. It's a family I crave as well as you as my wife."

"You make me happy. It's just that I'm not sure I believe you. So many times you've said the opposite."

"Do you trust me?" *Will she give me her heart and soul?*

"Yes, I always have and I believe I always will."

"Then you know I speak the truth. I want to marry you and I want to keep you safe. They are not separate concepts. A man can change when what he wants is within his reach, perhaps even sitting right in front of him. You are what I want and crave more than seeing another sunrise unless we see it from our land, perhaps at the top of the castle."

"But they are separate ideas." Her chin rose a notch. "The situation has changed. I'll think about your proposal."

He stood, hand extended, terrified Christel would say no. If she changed her mind and didn't except the second proposal, he wasn't sure how to keep her safe from Richy Rathen. First, he needed to find out the truth about her baby. If the baby lived, she would need protection from Richy's father too. His father, the earl, was the only person close enough to Richy and with enough resources and wealth to steal her baby.

His gut rolled. He'd never felt terror like this. Always, when danger threatened, there had been a rush of excitement pulse through him, and what fear there had been vanished in the exhilaration peril created.

"Christel, where are you? I've been looking everywhere..." Aidan's voice permeated his thoughts.

"I'm here, with Ryder." Christel stood and what seemed to be relief swept across her face.

"Oh." Aidan stopped. "I didn't mean to intrude."

"You didn't. We were finished." Christel adjusted the bodice of her gown.

"I'll walk the two of you back to the castle. Aidan, you shouldn't be out here alone." Ryder was amazed at the changes in Aidan. Several years had passed since he'd last seen her. Blade would have a devil of a time resisting her now, if he even wanted to keep her at arm's distance.

"You all right?" Aidan's gaze was focused on Christel. "Something is wrong. You look different."

"I'm fine and out of the horrible depression you found me in." Christel smiled, relieved her sister was here.

"That's good." Aidan skipped along the path away from the castle then bent over to pick up a wildflower. "One should never feel sad. It's a waste of time." She turned around and gave them both a huge grin.

Blade crashed through bushes, wiping cobwebs from his face and swearing. "I should put you in your solar, lock it and lose the key, Aidan."

"You could try, but I'm sure I'd find a way out." She winked at him then skipped down the trail again, looking back long enough to call out to Blade over her shoulder. "You should channel your energy in some of other way, something more constructive."

Aidan and Christel clasped arms at the elbow, leaving the men to follow behind.

"Come on, Blade, we need to keep up. Why did you let her traipse out here?" Ryder had been interrupted too soon. He wanted more time with Christel to explain all he was trying to do. He wasn't sure about the baby though and he didn't want to get her hopes up. He needed proof and intended to find out if the nuns had really lied to her.

Blade ran his hands through his hair, exasperation showing clearly in the lines on his forehead. "If you haven't noticed, the little one has a mind of her own. And to my horror she's fearless."

"I've observed." Ryder tilted his head back and let out a roar of laughter then on a more somber note, "Christel has had too much fear. I wish I could change that for her, but all I can do is make each day forward better."

Blade whistled through his teeth. "I've never met Richy Rathen, but I've heard stories. The gaming halls in London know him and have fleeced him of much of his family's fortune."

"I'm on my way to..." Ryder paused mid-thought. "Bloody hell, where are those two going?"

"Damned if I know." Looking perplexed and resigned at the same time, Blade ran his hands through his hair.

Blade and Ryder set off in a trot in an attempt to shorten the distance between them and the ladies. How the girls got so far ahead, Ryder wasn't sure, but now they had to catch them before something untoward happened. Only a few minutes passed and the men were within a few feet.

Aidan skipped backward, grinning and shaking one finger at them. "What took you so long? I thought for sure you would have tied a rope to our waists so you could keep us close. You're slipping, Blade."

"Where are you going?" Ryder felt sure he knew the answer and dreaded the girls' reply. He always liked a good swim and he'd give anything to have Christel out here alone, but he didn't want company. Besides, skinny-dipping wasn't in his plans at the moment.

"I had a hankering to dip my bare feet in the creek and share some girl talk with my sister." Aidan turned and tilted her head, staring at them as if she expected an objection.

"What do want, Christel? You've been quiet." Ryder needed her to show him her beautiful smile just as Aidan was slanting Blade hers.

"Thinking about your question and trying to decide."

"Have an answer?" He was not a patient man and he hated waiting, but in this case he had no choice.

"Not yet, but I'm closer."

"Here it is. This is the spot I remember." Aidan danced toward a tiny pool made by the creek as it meandered to the ocean. "Come on, Christel, leave the men to guard duty."

Ryder rubbed his hands over his face, thankful Christel was nothing like Aidan. But then if she were half that impulsive...

He suddenly realized the two sisters were very much alike. It's just that he was in love with Christel. On an impulse, Christel fled London. He was sure she could have solicited aid from The Duchess, but she'd decided to take on the world all by herself.

You're a fool, Ryder MacLaren. You've never been raped or pregnant. How on earth could you ever judge or figure out why?

Ryder leaned against a tree, arms crossed over his chest and the back of one booted foot placed firmly on the trunk, admiring the love of his life. He remembered one afternoon by the pond before he left her alone. They had almost made love, but The Duchess had interrupted them. She'd scolded him, shaking a finger at him then promptly grabbed Christel by the wrist and ushered her home. Watching them leave, he knew in that moment there would never be anyone else for him.

So why have I waited so long to act on my feelings and cement our relationship? Because I'm a coward.

Christel was bent over and he was blessed with the gorgeous view of her backside. Her softness, her breast made for his hands, he sighed. Good God but he wanted, needed, that woman to be his.

"I asked her to marry me." Ryder didn't know why he told Blade. Maybe he needed moral support, maybe he was a bigger idiot than he could imagine.

"You did what?" Blade choked, sounding surprised.

"I want her to be my wife."

"Did she agree?"

"Nope, said she'd think about it."

~ * ~

The Duchess held the letter in one hand as she paced. She had feared the worst but never this. Thank the gods above Christel was still in one piece and that cad Richy hadn't found her. Thank her lucky stars she'd found her way to Ryder's home.

"Scarlet." Where was she when she needed her?

"Yes, M'lady."

"We're going to take a ride. I hear the Earl of Rathen resides at his country home. I need to chat with him. Call the groomsman and have the carriage prepared. The sooner I arrive the sooner I can act, if my fears are correct."

"It will be done post haste." Scarlet curtsied and left the room.

The Duchess sat down and reread the letter. How many times had she stared at the words written on that piece of paper? Ten. Twenty. She crumpled the paper into a tiny ball and started to throw it in the trash then thought better of it. Smoothing the wrinkled lines of the paper, she drew in a deep breath.

I will get to the bottom of this then I will go to Scotland and make sure nothing else bad happens to Christel. I've failed miserably as a chaperon, but I will set things right if it is the last thing this old lady does.

"The carriage is ready." Scarlet appeared in the room. "Would you like me to accompany you?"

"Yes, my dear, please. You can help me find out the truth."

"The truth about what?" Scarlet helped The Duchess stand and escorted her to the carriage outside her residence.

"I'm on a mission. You remember Christel. She's had a bad encounter with the earl's son, Richy, and I mean to discover what happened. Ryder was vague and yet in a strange way to the point. But then I'm not sure how much Ryder knows or is guessing."

"I see." Scarlet leaned over and patted The Duchess' hand. "I'm sure the earl will tell you the truth."

"I'm not so sure about that. In his younger days, he was not that much better than his son. As the old saying goes, the apple doesn't fall far from the tree, if you get my thoughts. At least he wasn't a wastrel."

"I'm beginning to understand."

The Duchess felt older than her years and twice as helpless. When she looked in the mirror, she saw wrinkles and snow-white hair, hair that in her younger days was as black as a raven's wing. She didn't want to go to her grave with regrets.

"I think Richy raped Christel. Now don't go spreading that around. We both know about reputations and the like. She could be tarnished in a blink of an eye."

"You know I empathize and I'll never forget you took me in when the same happened to me. I was so relieved when there was no baby."

"Well, we cannot say the same for Christel, poor child."

Scarlet drew in a sharp breath. "She was pregnant from the rape? You think the earl knows something?"

"I believe he stole the baby before Christel could hold her child."

Chapter Seven

Christel sat on the edge of a rock, flicking water into the air with her bare feet. Droplets fell around her and the lightheartedness between the sisters was so welcome. Next to her Aidan giggled while she leaned back and pointed her face to the sky.

Sunshine felt warm and a soft breeze filtering through the trees whispered against her face.

"How do you always stay so happy, Aidan?" Christel watched a squirrel race down a nearby tree and scamper into the bushes beyond.

"I have never been outside in the real world. Allura and Hunter protect and shelter me more than a doting father would. When they aren't watching, Blade doesn't even let me breathe. Do you think those two stodgy guys will come play in the water with us?"

Christel turned to look at the men and laughed. Aidan had a way of doing that to her, chasing her cares away. "Probably not, Ryder is too concerned about my safety. If we were alone, he might play in the water."

"They are too unadventurous, too stern. We need to wear them down a bit, you know. They think they hold the weight of the world in their hands." Aidan bent over and cupped water in her hands then tossed it into the air, batting the droplets.

"Ryder is the most risk-taking man I know. He's traveled around the world and seen so many different things. Once he told me about the Acropolis and Delphi. I believe traveling with him would be adventure I'd like to have."

"He's been to Greece? I suppose I didn't use the right word. I just don't think they like to play. I've never seen Blade outside his serious, stern face except when he's flirting with a woman he wants to bed."

Christel grew thoughtful. She didn't know if she should tell Aidan or for that fact anyone, but she needed to share. "Ryder asked me to marry him. Twice, once in London and today."

Aidan clapped her hands together. "What did you say? Tell me all about it. How did he ask you? Oh, I'm so excited. We're going to have to write Allura and The Duchess and I can start planning the wedding. My goodness, when will he have the reading of the banns—"

"Aidan." Christel put her hands on Aidan's to stop the flaying arms and the nonstop run on of words. "How on earth do you breathe?"

"I don't know. I want to know everything and you will have the most glorious day. I've got to—"

"I told him yes in London but Aidan, this time I haven't decided if I will accept the proposal." Except she did know she'd say yes.

I want nothing more than to live my life with Ryder and wake up next to him every morning.

Behind them Ryder cleared his throat but said nothing.

The girls whirled to face the men. Ryder's jaw ticked and Blade's shoulders had stiffened. They both appeared as if they wanted to say something, yet not a word was uttered.

"When I decide, you'll be the second to know." Still looking at Ryder, she noticed a slight smile form on his lips.

"Second?" Aidan questioned.

Ryder's smile had not faded. "Don't you think I should know first?"

"Well, of course. Guess I wasn't thinking," Aidan was quick to say.

"Guess you weren't," Ryder acknowledged.

Christel stood and shook out her dress then slipped on her shoes without the stockings, which she carried. Aidan did the same.

Christel dropped back and accepted Ryder's arm. She liked the feel of his strength next to her. It gave her confidence and security.

"Ryder!" Ahead of them Owen strode down the path from the castle. "There is news."

Ryder waved at the man. "We'll talk in private."

"Very well," Owen said.

"Ryder, is it about Richy? Don't you think I should hear this too?" Christel did not want to be left out of any discussion about Rathen. Yet she feared the outcome and what Owen had to say.

"We came all this way to help." Blade put his hand on Ryder's shoulder. "You don't have to do everything by yourself."

"I acknowledge all of your concerns. But this might not be pleasant. Let's wait until we can have the privacy of my office."

Her mood darkened as they walked through the portcullis and on to Ryder's workplace. The sun hung low in the sky, evening coming soon. Aidan had brought her emotions back to normal, but the possibility of seeing Richy Rathen again terrified her. At this moment her patience had vanished.

"It's going to be fine." Aidan walked beside Christel and tried to reassure. "Really, Ryder and Blade won't let that horrible man near you. Nothing is going to happen."

"I know, but there are no guarantees in life. He shouldn't have discovered me alone that night in London either, but he did." At least I have found a man who cares enough to protect me and not hurt me. I am indeed foolish to make him wait for an answer to his proposal. I should tell him yes, tonight."

She heard Ryder growl low and watched as he raked his hands through his hair. "I promise you, Rathen will rue the day he touched you."

Moisture filled Christel's eyes when she heard Ryder's vow. Her heart was so full of love for this man, she didn't know how to show him and she was too terrified of his reaction if she told him.

Inside Ryder's office, he called for a servant who brought a platter of cheese and meat, another brought tea for the women. Ryder poured Owen and Blade a glass of scotch.

Silent tension hung in the room until Ryder cleared his throat. "What can you tell us?" He directed his question at Owen.

Nerves frayed, Christel sat with stiff arms, fingers folded around the edge of her chair. She drew in a deep breath to steady herself. Maybe Ryder had been right about speaking with Owen privately. But she needed to know.

"First, about Richy. He's been seen frequenting several taverns.

He still doesn't know that Christel is here. He thinks she's with Allura and Hunter. Believes they are keeping her hidden away somewhere in the castle."

"That's good. We have time then to find him and send him on his way." Ryder downed his drink in one swallow.

"You're not going to kill him." Christel wanted him to suffer but she didn't want anyone dead because of her.

"The task might prove difficult. He has a few friends with him, and I'm sure while they don't have a lot of loyalty to the scoundrel, they enjoy Richy's money. Bromley, his main man, is an evil, ruthless person."

"He has money to pay them?" Ryder set his empty glass on the table. "I can hardly believe it."

"From what I understand, his father gives him a stipend to stay away from London. And that brings me to the second and probably most important piece of news." Owen sipped his scotch before turning his attention to Christel.

"Not sure how to go about telling you this or how you will take it but if what I've learned is true, we will get your baby back to you."

"My baby? My child was stillborn." Christel's heart thundered beneath her ribs, her breath shaky. "I can't believe you would be so cruel as to tell me my baby is alive and break my heart once more."

"I have good reason to believe the child you bore at the convent is alive." Ryder sat beside Christel then took her hand in his. "When you told me your story a week ago, there were certain things you said that did not make sense."

"I never understood how I could hear a baby crying yet mine was dead."

Ryder's gentle words and touch gave Christel hope where there had been none.

"That's what bothered me, too, so I had Owen send someone to the convent to ask a few pointed questions."

"The answers?"

"If your baby was stillborn last May, then a second baby was born on the same day in that same convent. That is too big of a coincidence to believe."

Christel inhaled a swift deep breath, her fingers wound tightly into Ryder's. She prayed her child lived. "There was no other baby born that I know of. The sisters did not like pregnant women in their domain. I was the only one, and they made it clear I could not stay after my child was born. I never understood why they let me live there."

"Oh my God." Aidan had been silent until now. "The nerve of those seemingly pious nuns. I'll bet someone paid them."

Ryder brought Christel's hand up and kissed the back. "We will do everything humanly possible to find your child. I promise. The Duchess might be working on that even as we speak."

Owen cleared his throat. "I've more news."

"There is more?" Christel thought her nerves and her emotions had been wrenched apart. What more could Owen know?

"Yes, it seems your child was a boy and not a girl. He was much more valuable to a wealthy earl from London."

"They sold my baby?" Christel could not believe what Owen told her. The earl bought him?

"Bloody hell." Ryder touched Christel's cheek with the back of his hand. "I believe I know who and why. Good God, but I should have been there for you. I'll never forgive myself."

"I'm sure you've guessed it. Lord Rathen paid handsomely to have his grandson taken from you," Owen said.

"He disinherited his son so he grabbed the babe in hopes he could do better a second time." Ryder whistled through his teeth. "How had he learned about the son?"

"We don't have proof it was him, but I suggest you write The Duchess. Perhaps she knows a good person to hire. One who can discreetly discover the truth. The earl always kept tabs on Richy. I'm sure he must have known you were raped by his son." Owen directed his conversation to Christel and Ryder.

"I will do that." He turned to Christel. "Do you wish to go to London? We could take care of that matter together."

"What about Richy? It could be a trap." Christel wanted nothing more than to rush to London and find her child.

"I will find Richy Rathen. I'm sure there is a cell in your

antiquated dungeon just waiting for someone like him." Owen set his glass on the sideboard.

"My first priority is Christel's safety." Ryder strode to Owen then shook his hand. "Take care. Richy can be dangerous. He's doesn't fight fair."

"I want my son back." Christel knew what she must do, but it sounded as if Ryder meant for her to stay here.

"I understand, but we can't march into the earl's home and demand the grandson he now raises is your child."

"Why not? If you won't take me, I'll hire a carriage and go by myself."

"I'm afraid you would do just that. Alright then, we will go to London together if you promise to listen to my counsel and not go running into a dangerous situation."

"I vow on my baby's life I will heed your advice."

"Good then, is it settled? Are we going to London?" Aidan asked, clapping her hands together.

"You're not going," Blade said, his voice gruff and seemingly determined to dictate Aidan's life.

"You can't tell me where I can go." Aidan stood, her hands fisted at her sides. "If Christel and Ryder find her son, she will need help with the baby."

"She has The Duchess and The Duchess has funds to hire a nanny if necessary." Blade stepped toward Aidan, looking as if he wanted to shake her until she did what he advised.

"I promised Allura I would make sure you didn't do anything stupid," Blade said. "And I aim to keep that vow. You're not going to London."

"Going to London isn't stupid. Besides, I've never been there," Aidan finished, cocking her head a bit, seeming to know Blade would lose this battle.

"Very well," he said, backing down. "We're going to London then."

"You don't have to go, Blade. I'm capable of riding in a carriage without your supervision. I don't need you."

Blade ran his hands through his hair and inhaled a long breath. "I'm going and that's final. Pack your bags."

Despite the gravity of the events spiraling out of control, Christel felt a moment's lightheartedness at her little sister's relationship with Blade. She was sure Aidan had the noose wrapped around Blade's neck and was slowly pulling him in. Blade wouldn't know what happened to him when Aidan finished. For that matter, he didn't know what was happening to him now.

Then her thoughts turned inward. Her baby was alive, might be alive, and she was pretty sure this child Owen spoke of was hers.

"Christel, I think we should stay here." Ryder seemed to have a sudden change of heart.

"Why, I want to see my baby."

"We should let our friends make the confrontation. The earl does have a connection with the child, and he won't give your son up easily. I'm not sure of the legalities, but I know he will do everything in his power to keep the baby."

Christel's heart dropped to the pit of her stomach. Deep inside she understood what Ryder said, and she agreed with him. They had much to do to prepare this home and make a case the earl would not be able to win.

"All right then. We will let Aidan and Blade go in our place. You have written The Duchess, and I believe her name is in better standing than that of the earl or Richy."

"I know how hard this is for you." Ryder pulled Christel into a quick embrace then kissed her on the forehead.

She wanted to lean on him and absorb his strength into her. Teardrops formed again, and she felt as if she'd spent the last week crying. These should be tears of joy. In part they were. Elated to learn her child had survived, yet in the deepest despair knowing she would have to wait to hold him.

"Ryder, I know this is not the best circumstance to accept your earlier proposal, but I believe if we are married and presenting a united front, we'd have a better chance of winning the court's favor."

Ryder stiffened when she agreed to wed on the terms she'd just spoken. "I will attend to the reading of the banns."

She put her hand on his chest. "Ryder, I'm sorry. I know this is for the best. After we are wed, if you want to chase a sunrise or two, I will understand and give you my blessing. If you want my company, I'll be honored to go with you."

"Nothing will change. I've seen everything in this world worth seeing. I want only to settle down with my wife and her child. Perhaps make one or two of our own. Don't worry about my leaving. It won't happen." He spoke as if he still had regrets about her or possibly the marriage.

"I don't understand. I thought you'd be happy," Christel said.

"I am." His voice was curt.

Christel pulled away, studying his face yet not seeing joy. "I would have never guessed you were pleased with my acceptance of your proposal. Should we set a date?"

"Oh, you can't wed if I'm not here to help you plan." Aidan looked horror struck. "Blade can go to London by himself."

"But you've always wanted to see London," Blade unexpectedly protested. "Besides, I don't want to leave you here alone."

"There will be another time. It doesn't have to be today or tomorrow or even this year. This wedding is far more important to me." Aidan danced around Ryder's office.

"Send Owen." Blade watched Aidan, a sour look on his face.

"You just don't trust me by myself." Aidan planted her feet firmly then poked Blade in the chest a couple of times. "I'm right and you know it."

"I'm not leaving you alone." To Christel, Blade sounded adamant.

"Then it's settled." Christel didn't think Blade would change his mind. "We're all staying. Ryder will send Owen, and Aidan will help me plan the wedding."

Aidan clapped her hands together. "Let's start." She linked her arm in Christel's.

"Right now?" Christel asked, feeling skeptical. Truly, she didn't think there was a lot to do in planning a wedding.

"No time like the present." Aidan tugged her from the room. When they slipped through the doorway, Ryder waved at her.

She wasn't sure how Ryder felt about any of this. She needed time to sit and talk with him. Aidan had other plans though. As they walked through the hallways to Christel's solar, Christel's emotions soared, her thoughts jumbled.

"If you wish to go to London, we can postpone the wedding. I don't think Ryder was too enthusiastic about staying here."

"Well, what do you think? A man asks a lady to spend the rest of her life with him and she tells him he can leave any time he feels like wandering."

"That wasn't well done of me."

"Nope."

"My life is an upheaval, and I don't know whether I'm coming or going. I'll apologize," Christel said, regretting so much yet cherishing the thought of marrying Ryder.

"The wedding, now where do you want to have it?"

"A church."

"Which one? Do you know what..."

"He's protestant."

"And we're catholic."

Christel thought of the nuns who had cast her out after selling her son. "Not anymore."

~ * ~

Ryder poured himself another drink then relaxed behind his desk. Looking over the rim of his glass, he studied Blade. The man was smitten with Aidan. Too bad he didn't acknowledge his feelings.

He didn't understand why Christel was in such a hurry to get rid of him. He would change that. Needing her love seemed imperative, but he wasn't any closer now than he was when he was in London.

"You look pensive." Blade leaned against the wall before walking to a chair across from Ryder's desk.

"You don't?"

"She's a little devil with the most beautiful face and soul of anyone I've ever met." Blade sipped his drink then set the glass on

Ryder's desk. "I've been enamored with her since the moment I first saw her. She was thirteen then perhaps younger than that."

"She doesn't love me." God, but he wished he hadn't realized that. Christel agreed to marry him because it was the best way to get her baby back. But all he wanted or needed was her love. Guilt swept within every time he thought about the ordeal she had gone through. Raped. He'd never thought Richy would stoop so low.

"You're wrong. Anyone can tell how much she loves you," Blade said.

"How would you know?" Ryder shot back, rubbing his temples in an attempt to rid himself of his sudden headache and knowing nothing would ease the nausea rolling in his gut.

"I saw the way she looked at you."

"Then why did she have to think about marriage then decide it was a good idea as long as I understood I could keep my freedom to come and go as I please?" Ryder knew he needed time to talk with Christel. He'd hoped Blade and Aidan would follow up on their offer to travel, but he knew Aidan wouldn't forgo the wedding plans.

"I don't know," Blade said. "Some men would jump at the chance to have that type of relationship with their spouse."

"Not me."

"No, I wouldn't either." Blade held up his hands and laughed. "I know what you're thinking but when I find the right woman, well, I won't want to stray very far from her side."

"Haven't you found the right one already?" Ryder had watched him and the way he stared at Aidan, followed her everywhere.

Blade drummed his fingers on the desk then sipped from his drink. "I don't know. Maybe."

Ryder would like to know what was whirling around inside Blade's head. What a convoluted mess. He didn't know whether he was gaining ground with Christel or losing. But he wasn't about to give up on her. And he meant to erase every wrong that had been done to her.

"Sir?" One of his servants stood at the doorway.

"Yes."

"You have a letter." The man walked in and handed the paper to

Ryder as he stood to accept it.

It was from The Duchess. Terrified to open it, he stared at it.

"You going to see what's inside?" Blade asked. "Or are you just going to stare at it all night."

"Oh, yes." Ryder breathed deeply then picked up the letter opener sitting on his desk.

My dearest Ryder,

I have considered the information you sent me, and after careful thought, I've decided to pay the earl a visit. I will let you know if anything positive comes from this, but I have the feeling he will have his grandson closeted at his country home near Sussex.

I've retained the best solicitor in London to work in our behest, but this will not be easy. It might prove useful to plan a kidnapping. I say this in partial jest simply because it has been said possession is nine tenths of the law.

I will keep you posted.
The Duchess

Ryder's heart leapt to his throat when he read the word *kidnapping*. He had thought that too but had dismissed the idea as foolhardy. To have someone as respected as The Duchess suggest the crime told him how dire the situation really was.

"What's the letter say?"

Ryder strode to the fireplace and tossed the paper into the flames. Watching the words vanish made him feel much more comfortable about the future.

"How loyal are you?" Ryder realized the fewer people who knew what he planned the better.

"I would give my life for the McLellan clan and now yours since you are about to be united to Hunter and Allura by marriage."

"What I'm going to tell you remains a secret."

"As you wish."

"The Duchess believes the only way we will be able to lay claim to Christel's son is if we kidnap him." Plans began to take shape in

Ryder's head. The earl had stolen the baby from Christel's arms, and now he would steal the child back.

"Easier said than done, but I'll give you whatever help you need. Do you want to raise a bastard?"

Blade's question stopped his heart. "No, who would? But I love Christel and she deserves better from me. It's not the child's fault nor is it Christel's. The child will need a father and I prefer that father not have Rathen as a last name."

"Then, as I said before, I will be at your beck and call."

"Thank you." Ryder's fears were lightened with the promise Blade gave him.

"Do you plan to tell Christel?"

Blade's question jolted Ryder. When he told her, it would be real. How much could he say? She'd want to be with him, yet he didn't want her in danger. "Perhaps it would be best to leave both Christel and Aidan without the knowledge of our misdeeds."

"They can plan the wedding."

"Yes, and what plausible excuse pertaining to our absence could I give Christel that she would believe?" Ryder felt frustration roll within, his fists tightening. She would guess his intent and call him out.

"Then you tell her, she tells Aidan and we have two hot headed and impulsive women to watch out for." Blade ruffed his hair a frown creasing his face.

"And a young mother who has never seen her son," Ryder added, feeling the frustration eating at him. This would not be an easy trip for any of them, and lives would be at stake.

"Is it a crime if you steal your own baby?" Blade asked.

Ryder let out a snort. "Bloody hell, I wouldn't think so. It's the earl and the nuns who committed a crime."

"One I'm sure the nuns will go unpunished for at least until their day of reckoning."

"I have to talk to Christel, and perhaps I can convince her staying at the castle would be the safest for her. There can be no secrets between us. I won't ride off to London without giving her a choice." Ryder rose and without another word, left his office, heading for Christel's solar.

When he reached the door, he heard happy chatter from inside. He didn't want to intrude and change the mood, but he had two items he needed to talk to Christel about. He prayed their exchange earlier was just a misunderstanding, but he couldn't be sure until they sorted this out.

He knocked and was greeted with silence then giggles. He couldn't help but smile.

"Come in."

He recognized Christel's voice. "Thought you'd never ask." He stepped into the room.

"So...what brings you here?" Christel rose and strolled toward him.

He wanted to pull her into a tight embrace. Instead, he looked pointedly at Aidan and with a slight nod of his head, encouraged her to leave.

Aidan grinned then hugged her sister. "Think I'll go see what cook is brewing in the kitchen."

"Perhaps you should check on Blade," Ryder said. "He seemed lonely to me."

"Perhaps not. He's never lonely. There is almost always a lass or two hanging on his arm, waiting for his words of wisdom and perhaps something more." Aidan left the solar in a whirl of petticoats, laughter from the hallway floating to the room.

"We need to talk." Ryder sat down near a window then patted a seat next to his for Christel to sit.

"That dire?"

Where to start? "First, I'm hoping what you said in my office was a simple misunderstanding. I want to marry you and settle down. I've no thoughts of wandering the world. I've done that."

"I didn't mean...I just don't want you to think you have to do this because of Richy. I want you to be happy."

"I'm happy with you, here at the MacLaren castle. You need to understand I'm won't ever lie to you." Bloody hell, but all he craved was to live on this land, his land with the woman he loved.

"Do you mean that? Really, truly mean it?"

Ryder reached for her hands. "I thought you knew that I'm a man who charts his course. If I didn't want you for my wife, I wouldn't have asked." He rubbed gentle circles on the back of her hand. He wanted to pull her into his arms. Hell, he wanted all of her, now, before the wedding.

"What you're telling me is the truth? I was frightened, no, terrified. I'm not sure if I can be a good wife to you. I didn't think anyone would want me after..."

"Hush, I don't want to hear any more talk of Richy Rathen and his misdeeds. He will soon be no problem for us. Last I heard he dropped a cool thousand on a horse. Lost everything he owned that day. I don't think his father plans on giving him any more money."

"You didn't set him up?"

"I don't have to do anything nefarious. Richy is his own worst enemy. I am still concerned, however, that he might have plans where you are concerned. He believes you have the funds for him to maintain his current lifestyle."

"I'm terrified he'll show up at the castle."

"He can't get in. His portrait has been shown to all of the guards. The only way he'll come into the MacLaren castle is in chains."

She closed her eyes and inhaled a long deep breath. "Thank you, now what else do you wish to talk about."

"I received a letter from The Duchess."

"Can I read it?"

"No, I burned it. But The Duchess believes we might have to take matters into our own hands. She thinks we should kidnap your baby." The notion sounded more incredulous every time he spoke the words.

Her eyes grew wide, and it seemed to Ryder that Christel stopped breathing. "All right. You would do that for me and a child who is not your son?"

I would do anything for you. "Yes." Ryder wasn't sure where to go with this. "Blade and I plan on traveling alone. We should be back in three weeks and in time for the wedding."

"I want to go with you. The sooner I can hold my child, the better I will feel," Christel said.

"Somehow I knew you would say that. But I don't want you implicated in anyway. And if you went, Aidan would follow and we both understand the possible repercussions of that."

"Blade swore he wouldn't leave her alone. If he goes with you..."

"He has no choice. I can't tell anyone and I have his pledge of loyalty." This conversation wasn't panning out the way he wanted. He didn't have a doubt in his mind the girls would follow them. Perhaps they would surprise him and stay put.

"I see."

"I hope so." Concerned for Christel, Ryder pulled her into his arms. "Trust me, this is the best solution."

He kissed her, a daytime kiss intended to reassure. But the kiss turned when Christel traced the seam of his lips with her tongue. He opened for her, thinking he'd taught her well. It didn't take much, just a hint of sex and he was fully aroused and craving more than he wanted to take right now.

She wrapped her arms around him, winding her fingers through his hair. He pulled back to look into her eyes. What he saw made him catch his breath. She closed the lids of her eyes then opened them seductively. He kissed the tip of her nose then her cheeks, and knew he wanted more.

"I want you," Christel whispered close to his ear.

That was all the encouragement he needed. He trailed kisses down her neck and across her collarbone, lingering near the swell of her breasts. "Are you sure?"

"It's not like I'm a virgin."

"You are to me. We should wait until the wedding night." Those were among the hardest words he'd ever said to her.

"No, when we say our vows, I want to think about your touch and yours alone. I want to know that you will bring me only pleasure."

Her smile melted his heart, the expression expectant yet wary. He slipped the tiny sleeves of her gown down her shoulders and watched as he revealed her breasts, the nipples hard and begging for his attention.

She undid the laces of his shirt. "I want to see you, touch you, all of you."

He slipped it over his head. She ran her hands across his chest, her fingers so tiny and delicate, her caress erotic.

Sweeping her into his arms, he strode to the door and bolted it shut then continued to the bed where he set her down. He followed her, pulling her into his arms. He felt blessed a thousand times.

Within seconds she was naked beside him. His hands trailed over her flesh as he pulled her closer, his blood rushing. Her fingers dug into his back as she moved her head back to look at him.

"Your clothes?"

He laughed, surprised she wanted him naked. "Of course."

Unfastening his pants, he took them off then settled next to her, and for the first time in his adult life with a woman, he was unsure what to do.

"Touch me." Christel's hands roamed across his back then wound through his hair. He bent to take a nipple into his mouth, laved and caressed it while one hand caressed her other breast. She moved against him. The tiny moan she gave made him pulse with need. Kissing her body, he moved downward to her belly, one hand at the apex of her thighs. He found the tiny nub that would give so much pleasure and teased.

Then he rose and kissed her. His tongue delving inside set a primal mercuric rhythm that she followed. Her body moved against him, and he wanted to be inside, feel her heat and sex. Good God, but he'd never felt this urgency. He didn't know if he could wait. But in a few seconds her body bucked and trembled.

"Ryder..." Christel cried out.

Knowing it was time, impatient, he plunged inside. Her warmth spread through him like an inferno. He couldn't hold back. They were as one with each other. His body raged for her and he shook with need. Deeper inside, he felt her walls squeeze around him until they climaxed.

Her silken flesh, sheened and moist, trembled. Her hair in disarray around them, he wove his fingers through it. "Christel?"

"Umm..."

"Are you all right? I didn't hurt you, did I?" Afraid because of her silence, he wasn't sure how to proceed from here.

"No. I didn't think sex could be this good." She put her head on his chest. "I can hear your heartbeat."

"And it is racing."

"Yes, did I hurt you?" Christel's question was innocent.

"You pleasured me beyond anything I've felt before."

She pushed up, her breasts swaying provocatively. He touched the nipple, knowing he would never get enough of this woman. Then she kissed his lips but pulled back before he could deepen it.

"I felt pleasure too."

"Good, I want you to always be able to say that."

"Do you think we made a baby?"

~ * ~

Whistling, Blade strode to the door of his solar. The only thing that would make this night better would be a willing woman in his bed. His thoughts drifted to Aidan and her beautiful red hair along with her shimmering blue eyes always filled with mischief and the desire she never hid from him. Because of Aidan, he'd been celibate for the last year even when he knew she wasn't going to be ready for him for another couple of years.

Ah, but in a few years, god willing, she would be his wife and in his bed. Patience and control haunted him when she flaunted herself in front of him. The little she-devil knew exactly what she was doing. He vowed to himself he wouldn't touch her until she was a woman grown. By his calculations, she was just seventeen. Some might call her old enough, but he didn't. He craved her, had for a very long time but he would wait. He kept telling himself he had her best interest at heart, but what about him? Even now his heart pulsed as intensely as his arousal.

Aidan never lost a chance to flirt, and he had to admit he enjoyed her antics, looked forward to them. He smiled, thinking of how she might look naked, having envisioned her that way just this afternoon when she was splashing water and he was treated to the sight of the length of her leg. For a moment, his gut tightened and he could have lost control. She tempted him day in and day out and bloody hell, but she must know it.

He grinned. The simple truth was that he wouldn't have it any other way. When he finally made her his, the act would have more meaning and the joining sweeter than anything he could imagine. When all this came about, he intended to savor every second.

Blade pushed open the door and came to a sudden and very abrupt halt. "Bloody hell." The object of his imagination was lying on his bed, naked. While he gaped at her, she rose, an angelic smile on her face. For whatever reason, she pulled her hair behind her back. He saw all of her, every beautiful and erotic curve.

Coughing then searching for the right words, "Aidan, what are you doing? What are you doing here in my solar, in my bed?" When she moved, her long red hair swirled around her, covering then uncovering her breasts, tantalizing in every way. Breast that were barely there, confirming his thoughts abut her maturity. Once again, she pushed her hair behind her back. Then she paused, a wavering smile on her beautiful face.

She didn't answer him but stood in front of him, seeming to wait. He didn't need her answer to understand her intent. She stepped forward, her face pale and he half expected her to faint.

Truly, he didn't know what to do or say that wouldn't belittle her. Yet his entire body shook with the blood pulsing through him, and his need to possess her increasing tenfold with each second. Closing his eyes for a moment, he prayed for strength, for the will to make sure she made it to her solar unscathed by him. Bloody hell, but he wanted her, craved her more than life itself and here she was, the young lady he hoped to someday call his wife, blatantly and willingly giving herself to him. Why the hell should he refuse?

"Aidan, where are your clothes. You need to put them on before I do something we'll both regret." His fists clenched and unclenched at his sides. "Aidan..."

Walking toward him and shaking her head, "I won't regret anything we do. I want you, Blade, have always craved you. I've always desired you even when I was thirteen and now..." She cleared her throat and stopped halfway to him. "Will you make love to me tonight? Make me a woman and I'll give you my virginity."

The feisty girl he knew so well vanished. Now she was solemn and he saw the terror in her eyes, yet there was passion simmering there as well. He didn't doubt she wanted him. It seemed they were both haunted by this unrequited desire between them. "Now, tonight, we still can't. Aidan, it's not because..." he needed a stiff drink right now. "I won't make love to you."

"Because...?" she prompted.

Holding his breath for too long, he let it out in a swoosh, roughing his hands through his hair, unable to think of anything to say. "Aidan, you're still a little girl. Look at yourself." He paused and watched as she looked down. "Your breast are barely there, nothing for a man to hold. When you fill my hands, then I'll make love to you. Not a moment before."

A sob tore through her. "I see," she grit out, seeming to look around the room for something, he wasn't sure what.

Needing to end this before the pain lasted one more second, he strode past her and grabbed a blanket off the bed. Wrapping it around her, he swept her into his arms and strode with her from his room into hers.

Before he set her on the bed, he touched her lips with a fingertip, wishing he dared kiss her, but if he drank from forbidden fruit, he might not be able to deny himself a second or third taste. "When you are a woman, sweet Aidan, and not a moment before. I promise you."

~ * ~

"Is that a baby I hear crying, Richard?" The Duchess sipped tea and nibbled on an orange scone. She didn't want to seem too obvious but really, Richard Rathen was taking no precautions to hide the fact that there was a child in his home.

"Yes, my grandson." Richard motioned for the woman standing in the doorway to come in. "This is Eliza, his wet nurse."

"Really, Richard, aren't you a bit old to be fathering children? Oh, your grandson?" The Duchess corrected herself then walked to the baby, extending her hands. "May I?"

Richard nodded and the girl let The Duchess hold the child. She cradled the baby and uncovered the face. Blue eyes, pert little nose and hair as blond as Christel's... "Doesn't look like you at all."

"Well, takes after the mother I suppose."

"And who is that? The mother?"

Richard cleared his throat and stammered something The Duchess couldn't understand.

"Who?" She leaned in closer to hear his mumblings better.

"My mistress, none of your business." His statement was almost as rude as her question.

"Thought you said he was your grandson."

"Don't want anyone knowing I have a bastard," the earl told her. "Since I disowned Richy, I'd like a legitimate heir."

She made a mental note to look into Richard Rathen's affairs. It was an easy task to ferret out such things. If last she heard was true, Richard's mistress was past child bearing age. Indeed, the babe looked just like a McLellan. Thank god for small favors.

The Duchess hummed and rocked the tiny child, determined to get this baby back to her mother and Ryder. She'd sent the letter a couple of days ago. Ryder should have received it by now. She prayed he would come for the child. Richard had no claim to this little boy.

"He must be hungry. He's sucking on my finger." She looked at Eliza who retrieved the boy and left the room.

"Where is your son, Richy?"

"I don't know and I don't really care. Last I heard he was in Scotland somewhere, squandering the last of his inheritance."

"You don't care about your son?"

"I thought he had more backbone, more character, but I gave him too much, didn't make him work for anything. Guess I made his life too easy. He's turned out to be a drain on my estate and worthless to boot."

"So, you plan on redeeming your character as a father with your new grandson? What's his name?"

"Brett."

"Ah, Brett, your grandfather's name. I like that." She would pass that information on to Ryder. He should be in London in a few days. "Where is the nursery?"

"Upstairs, why?"

"Just curious. You know that's one of the things my husband liked about me." Sure it was. She'd found herself in some rather delicate situations in her youth. But her inquisitiveness had given her some fond memories. How she missed the Duke and hearing his laughter when she recounted her exploits.

"Curiosity can be the downfall for some." Richard strode to the doorway and looked up the stairs. "He'll be napping soon."

"Is that my cue to leave?"

"Absolutely not. I was just wondering why you really came here." Richard drummed his fingers on the doorsill.

"Ah, good question. I haven't seen you around the city. I find as I grow older, I like to get out more often, go visit. I don't want to lose old friends. And Scarlet is so much fun to do things with."

"I suppose the dressmaker and shopping would bore someone like you."

"How many dresses does an old lady need? No one cares if I wear the same old dress to a party or even a recital." How she lied. There was nothing she enjoyed more than dress shopping. Although it had brought her more pleasure when the girls had been living with her. She reminded herself that she should ask for the fathers to send the other cousins to London. It would be so exciting. And perhaps she could prove to be a better guardian.

"You don't really expect me to believe that."

"No, I don't." The Duchess extended her hand. "I don't want to overstay my welcome."

"You could never do that."

"Oh, but I could. You give that little boy of yours a hug for me and take good care of him. I wouldn't want to see anything happen to that beautiful little boy."

Chapter Eight

The warmth of Ryder's body next to hers filled her soul. She wanted this moment to last forever but knew morning would come and they would leave her solar. She also knew he'd leave before the sun rose to protect her reputation. Not that anyone in his clan would care that the laird slept with her.

His hand cupped her breast and played with the nipple. She pushed back against him, reveling in the feel of his hard body nestled against her. Inside, a smile lit up her heart. He kissed her neck, bit softly across her shoulder.

Last night when he'd made love to her, she'd been confident and sure he would not hurt her. And she'd been right. A good fuck, she giggled, remembering the stories she'd heard when she'd come across some of her father's men talking about the tavern wenches.

Is that what she and Ryder had shared? Hmm...well the act was good. No, the sex they'd had was more than that. His hand settled on her belly then roamed lower until he caressed her most private parts.

"You're ready for me." Ryder pushed a finger inside.

"I am," she said and moved with the rhythm he set.

He turned her, his lips finding hers, his tongue delving inside her mouth as one hand explored every inch of her body and the other continued working its magic. The primal dance was magical, sensuous and mercuric. She moved against him, enchanted the lovemaking.

"Straddle me." With both hands he pulled her up then brought her down on his rod. "You set the pace."

She moved on him. He rose and sucked a nipple deep inside his mouth and worked to give her pleasure. Trembling, her movements grew jerky until she shook with the pleasure he gave. "Ryder, oh God. Ryder."

Christel needed to scream his name, but he covered her mouth with his and as her blood pulsed and her body climaxed, she cried out, but the sounds were silenced with his kiss.

He pulled her on top of him, caressed her back, trailed his fingers up then down her spine. She closed her eyes and marveled at how her world had changed. She loved him so much and she hoped someday he would return her feelings. She wasn't ready to share her thoughts with him but soon, maybe.

"Christel?" He pushed hair from her face and smiled at her.

"Hmm..." He'd managed to leave her speechless and boneless. She didn't think she could move.

"I have to go."

"I knew you would say that, but you don't, not really. No one would care if they saw you leave the solar." If she could, she'd spend the day right here with Ryder.

"I would." He kissed the tip of her nose. "I don't want our people talking behind our backs and whispering when we pass by."

But it was too late. "Ryder, you in there?" Blade pounded on the door.

Ryder groaned. "Go away."

"Can't, Owen said Richy's been spotted at the tavern in the village. He's sent men there, but we don't know what you want us to do with him. You have to come with us."

"He can stay in the dungeon until we get back from London." Ryder rose from the bed then slipped on his pants.

Christel watched, fascinated by his body, intrigued by the play of muscles across his back and shoulders.

He sat down on the bed and took her hand in his, holding it for a moment before he brought it to his lips and kissed the palm. "I don't want to leave you. I would stay if I could. Don't think for a moment I won't come back."

"You must go. There is no other choice. Will you see me before you leave for London?" Christel hoped she would see him again, but knew he wanted to leave as soon as he had Richy safely locked away. The thought of Rathen under the same roof sent a shiver down her spine.

"Yes, of course. I won't leave without a kiss and perhaps more if there is time. I crave memories to take with me."

"I'll miss you. It seems I wasted an entire week by locking myself in seclusion, afraid of my shadow. And now you have to go away." Thoughts of him leaving sent a deep despair within. She wanted to ride with him, needed to find her place by his side.

"Ah, but I will come back as soon as possible with your child and you will hold him and name him."

"Promise? I can hardly believe the baby is alive. What should I name him?" That was something she'd given little thought to. But now, "I want a good strong name." She prayed he'd be nothing like his father.

Ryder tucked a knife into his boot. "Just a precaution." Then, "Think on it while I'm gone. I'm sure you'll come up with something befitting your first-born. You know that when we're wed, I'll help you raise him, become his father if you let me."

"Thank you." That was more than anyone could wish for. He intended to raise this bastard child and keep him safe even when the babe would remind him every day of his life that she'd been violated. "Ryder," she rose from the bed and wrapped a robe around her, "I'd really like to go with you. I want to be there to see my baby. I won't get in the way."

He sighed and roughed his hands through his hair. "We've been over that. It's not safe for you."

"Is it safe here? Richy might be locked behind bars but he's conniving. What if he finds a way to get out?" Her mind reeled with the thought.

"He won't."

"What if you're wrong?" She cringed, knowing Richy would come straight for her if the impossible happened.

"Owen can stay in my room and guard you night and day. I trust him completely." Ryder sat down beside her again and pulled her into his arms.

The kiss was bittersweet. She didn't want him to go without her, and if he did, she didn't want to stay here with Richy in the castle. He couldn't understand the fear just his name triggered.

When he moved away from her and traced his finger down the column of her neck, she made up her mind. She'd convince Aidan to embark on an adventure. The carriage ride would be safe, and Richy would not be able to hurt her.

She smiled at Ryder. "Very well."

"What is that look?" He touched her beneath the chin, lifting slightly.

She knew he searched her eyes, wanted to know what she thought. She shuttered them, hoping to keep her newly forming secrets to herself. "One of a contented woman." Christel's mind raced with plans. She was almost eager to send him out the door so she could rush to Aidan's room. Convincing Aidan would not be difficult. Her littlest sister was always ready for adventure.

"I'm not sure. It seems there is something else there, something I can't quite read. Promise me you will remain on MacLaren land." It seemed he could read her mind, but she wouldn't let him know how close to the truth he'd come.

"Really, I understand all of your fears for me and your need to protect my life at all cost. But I'm a grown woman and the only thing I'm afraid of is Richy in this castle. I doubt if I'll get a moment's rest until you return. You'll undoubtedly find me an irritable shrew because of a lack of sleep."

"Are you trying to convince me to take you? If anything goes wrong with the kidnapping, I don't want you implicated." Ryder kissed her again, his tongue delving deeply into her mouth. She responded, kissing him back as if she could make him stay another few moments.

"Even if I stay here, I will be implicated no matter what happens. The earl will know we figured out his scheme. What would you have me do?"

"Remain at the castle, safely tucked away from harm. You fled to MacLaren land because you knew the people here would keep your secrets as well as your safety. "

She paused to think. She'd already given too much away. He seemed to understand her thoughts and know what was in her head even before she did.

"When do you think you'll be back?" Needing to change the subject, she wanted to reassure Ryder. Lying to him out right was not an option and if he pressed her, she would have to comply with his wishes. She didn't want to promise anything.

He sat down and pulled her onto his lap. "Bloody hell, I don't want to leave you, but I'm hoping this won't take more than a couple of weeks."

She inhaled a long deep breath. "Then we'll wed, in the church?"

"Yes, the banns will be read this Sunday. All the details have been taken care of."

"Do you know of a good dressmaker in the village? I want my gown to be of the latest fashion." She tried for a lighter tone, one that might convince him she planned to do his bidding.

He kissed her neck then ran his fingers through her hair. "Yes, Madam Adelle, she goes by her first name."

"Then she is French?"

"*Mais non*, but she likes to pretend. She grew up in the village and is very much Scottish to the core. But she says a French name is good for business," Ryder chuckled.

"And she gets so much here where most of your clan make their own clothes?" Christel laughed. "Well, Aidan and I will pay her a visit. We can hunt through the fashion plates and if she is good, we'll have fine gowns for the affair."

"Then you'll be so busy you won't have time to miss me or worry about Richy." His hands circled her waist. She turned in his arms, her robe slipping from her shoulders. For a moment, she wondered if she could seduce him.

"God, Christel, but do know how much you tempt me? My rod is hard against my pants. But I don't have time. Blade waits outside and is sure to pound on the door in another few seconds."

"You could make the time." One breast slipped free of the confines of fabric. She wasn't sure if she'd done this or he'd moved just right so the material would give way. He touched a nipple then lowered his head to suck it into his mouth. She squirmed against him, knowing where this could lead.

He turned his attention to the other breast. She slipped her hands inside his shirt and touched him, weaving her fingers through the hair on his chest. Her head thrown back gave him access to whatever part he wanted. Never had she been so openly brazen.

"I don't have a choice. Can't ride in this condition." Their mouths melded as one.

Nothing else mattered to Christel. "Ryder, one more time. God, how I want you." She unfastened his trousers and slid them down his legs.

"Wrap your legs around me." She did then he was inside her and she was pressed against the wall. Hard and fast and she'd never felt such pleasure as he gave her now. Her heart raced and her breaths were frantic.

They finished. "I can't move." Christel let her head fall on his shoulder.

"And I don't want to." Ryder ran his hands down her back then settled her on the bed. "Sleep."

"Not without you."

"You realize I have to go."

"Tomorrow." She pulled him down beside her, knowing if he wanted to resist, she'd have little power over him.

"Today," he murmured then ran more kisses across her collarbone. "God, but I can't get enough of you."

"Ryder, you comin'?" Blade pounded on the door.

"Go away." Ryder touched Christel's cheek then traced her lips.

"If that's what you want."

"No," then he turned to Christel. "I have to leave. I'm sorry." He kissed her and rose from the bed.

"I will miss you." Christel felt the smile in her heart melt. *I will miss you so much.*

"Take care, Christel. Don't do anything foolish."

"That's Aidan's agenda not mine." Christel laughed, understanding he wasn't going to like what she planned and he would consider it foolish as well.

"Wandering in the forest and looking for Richy with just a bow and arrow was probably not the smartest thing you've done."

"Any day soon?" Blade called from behind the closed door.

"I'm coming." Ryder gave Christel one last kiss then strode to the door and opened it to see Blade raising his hand to knock again.

"Richy is here in the dungeon."

Christel's heart leapt to her throat. A sickening wave of terror washed through her. She braced herself, holding on to the bedpost as she watched the door close behind Ryder. How could he leave her with that bastard in the castle? She could tell herself one hundred times and more she would be safe from him, but she knew when she closed her eyes to sleep even the magic of Ryder's touch could not wipe away the memory of her rape.

Frantic to get away from the castle, she dressed in pants and a shirt then tucked her hair beneath a hat. Standing by the window, she was able to see the courtyard below and the gate where Ryder and Blade would leave. Impatient, she drummed her fingers on the windowsill.

Seconds seemed like minutes and minutes as if hours had passed before she saw them canter their mounts through the gate and toward London. When she and Aidan showed up at The Duchess' home, he might be angry but he'd forgive her.

Turning, she raced to Aidan's room and knocked. Met with silence, she opened the door. "Aidan."

"Christel?" Aidan sat up in bed then stretched, her eyes red from what might have been crying. "What are you doing? Oh, you've come to plan the wedding." She sounded despondent.

"No, I've come to see if you want to see the sights that are London. What is wrong?"

"What? Yes... Why?" She swung her legs over the bed. It seemed Aidan wanted to avoid the question. "You're wearing pants."

"I'm not riding sidesaddle all those miles." Christel stood with her hands on her hips and one toe tapping on the floorboards. "Do you have trousers?"

Aidan grinned. "Of course. I'll be ready in a minute. What about the wedding?" She rummaged through a trunk, tossing clothes over her shoulder before finding the items she would wear.

"They're going to be furious, you know that," Aidan pointed out as she slipped out of her nightclothes and dressed in men's clothing.

"In time they will see my side. I can't stay in this castle with

113

Richy. When I think about him, I can't breathe."

"Blade won't understand ever and quite frankly at this moment I don't care a bloody fig what he thinks." Aidan looked in a mirror then turned to face Christel. "How do I look?"

"Not like a boy."

"Neither do you, my big sis, neither do you, but I'm sure at first glance we might pass. Even if we don't, this is much more practical. I'd like to flaunt my appearance in front of Blade. If I didn't have any curves, I'd pass as a boy despite what he thinks."

Christel regarded her sister closely then deciding she'd tell her when she wanted to, she set a map on the table and spread it out. "We can travel about eight miles between horses, maybe a bit more if necessary. I want to be able to stop at an inn every night. Don't like the idea of sleeping on the ground. So..."

The two charted a course and found places where they could trade horses for fresh ones. Christel had followed this general path when she'd fled London more than a year ago.

After packing food and extra clothes, Aidan and Christel were at the stable and mounting the horses.

"I hope I don't regret this." Christel blew hair off her face, yet she felt the exhilaration of doing something for herself and getting out of the castle.

"Well, I know I won't. I've lived for an adventure ever since Hunter disallowed us our journeys to our island. I lost so much freedom when he took over the reins. I don't think any of us understood how good we had it until it was jerked from us."

"I know and when the three of us went to London to find a husband, I felt as if I abandoned you. I didn't want a husband then."

"Do you now?" Aidan looked wistful.

"Yes. Are you thinking of yourself? You're old enough now and Blade loves you."

Aidan's breath wooshed out in a long sigh. "Blade might love me, but he hasn't figured it out yet. However," Aidan paused as if trying for the right words, "he doesn't seduce servant girls any more, and he hasn't raced off to a tavern for sex since he's been at the McLellan castle. That's been about two months and I am counting. After last night though, I've more doubts."

"I suppose that is good news." Christel joined in the laughter.

"But something happened last night," Aidan paused seeming unsure if she should tell her. "I went to his room and I...well I stood in front of him naked, and well," she moistened her lips, "he swore just before he wrapped a blanket around me and carried me to my room."

"I'm sorry. I think he's just confused." Aidan's story shocked her, yet she was glad he didn't take advantage.

"Confused at my expense. One minute he's acting like he might want to court me, and the next minute he treats me like I'm still a little girl," Aidan blew a lose piece of hair from her face.

A few raindrops hit the ground. Suddenly, thunder boomed from behind them and clouds covered the sun. Wind whipped through the trees, sending debris scattering around them. They had been so engrossed in conversation they hadn't observed the darkening sky.

"I didn't even notice the storm brewing. We should find shelter. The storm will pass and we can be on our way again." Aidan pulled the hood of her summer jacket over her head and kicked her horse into an easy gallop.

"I think there is an old hut set back from the road. It used to be owned by one of the MacLaren clan, but she passed away a few weeks ago. I came here sometimes to check on her and bring food."

"Good, because I'm getting wet."

"Me too, didn't plan on bad weather. I'll bet Blade and Ryder are tucked away safely at the inn." A lightning strike hit the road behind them. Aidan's horse whinnied and pawed the air with his hooves.

~ * ~

Rushing into the hut and out of the torrential downpour, Christel came to a complete stop as Aidan plowed into her back. "Ryder!"

"Blade?"

Terror for Christel ripped down Ryder's spine, emotions so high his hands shook. He could barely speak. "What are you doing here?"

"C-came to check on, Grizela." Christel shook out her cloak then hung it on a peg. "Didn't know you would be here. Expected you to be on your way to London."

"You must have known Grizela passed on a few weeks ago." Ryder had heard about the old lady as well as Christel's visits. He didn't like the fact she lied to him but decided she must have a good reason. So he would wait.

"Caught." Christel shrugged then sat down, her brows furrowed. "Ryder, I can't stay at the MacLaren castle, not with Richy under the same roof. I just can't. I won't. For me, there was no choice but to follow you and hope you wouldn't be too angry when you found out the truth."

"And you came along for moral support?" Blade turned to Aidan, his tone fierce. "What were you thinking?"

"Couldn't let her go by herself." Aidan slipped from her coat then placed it beside Christel's. "I'm hungry. Is there anything to eat?"

"You could have been the voice of reason." Ryder ran his hands through his hair then across his face. He didn't know what to do—couldn't send her back to a place where she was terrified. Didn't want to bring her along for fear of reprisals when they stole the baby. But he sensed if he took her home, she and Aidan would follow on their own. Perhaps he should be thankful he and Blade visited Owen before they left and were caught by the storm.

"I knew she'd go with me or without me." Aidan rummaged through the pack and brought out fried chicken and oat scones. She opened her water bottle and drank then wiped her mouth with her sleeve. "In this case, there was no such thing as a voice of reason, only a woman desperate to leave."

"Aidan, I swear you still don't have an iota of common sense. You flit about as if the world is a safe place and by now you should know better." Blade's gaze could have sent sparks flying Aidan's direction.

"Well, Christel made it here from London by herself." Aidan shot back at Blade. "She's quite capable and so am I. We are both grown women."

"Stop arguing and let it be. Now that we are all here together, we will continue on the trip—together—when the storm lets up. Probably

116

tomorrow morning." God, it would be hell to sleep in different beds. He'd touched her last night, loved her, and discovered how much he was going to miss her. Now he had to watch her sleep from a distance. Surely the devil danced around them, tempting him. "Just let it be." This last said for himself more than anyone else.

"Thank you. I'm glad you're not going to send us back." Christel slipped her arm through his and smiled at him. "You do know that would be a waste of time. As soon as the two of you were out of sight we'd follow again."

The expression melted his heart. He wanted to pull her into his arms and kiss her then he wanted to make love to her. But none of this was going to be possible, not tonight or any other night until they were married. Maybe they could find a small parish on the way and say their vows.

Thunder rocked the skies above the hut. Beside him, Ryder felt Christel's trembling and wished he could vanquish her fears. "Perhaps this happened for a reason."

"The storm or our chance meeting?" Aidan asked, nibbling on the food in front of her.

"Both." With Christel at his side, Ryder strode to a small window and watched the rain drench the earth and the lightning brighten the dark sky. He thought of Christel's child living with the earl, Richy's father, and shuddered. The babe would be ruined, could end up just like Richy if the earl raised him. He wouldn't let that happen.

"If the storm passes by, we could still get a couple of miles in tonight. Do you think we should try to make it to Kings Crossing?" Christel asked, hoping for a little more distance from the castle.

"No," Ryder smiled, understanding Christel's eagerness to be away. "The horses have been spooked and are in need of rest. We'll get up early tomorrow and try to make up some of the time."

The whinny of horses and men talking clattered through the window into Grizela's hut.

Blade and Ryder both drew swords. Ryder reached for a pistol he'd set on a small table before motioning for silence. He opened the door a crack. "Friend or foe."

"Friend," came the reply. "Not looking for trouble. We're searching for a dry place to stay the night."

"There is a barn around back. You can settle in there if you have a mind, but if the rain stops, I expect you and your friend to move on."

"Very well, we were looking for someone. Don't suppose you could help us out?" a man asked.

"Who?" Ryder didn't like the sound of these men nor the idea they would be sleeping in close proximity.

"Richy Rathen."

"Why?" That name at this time sent a chill down Ryder's spine and set him on guard. Neither he nor Blade would get a full night's sleep this evening.

"Owes us money."

"I know of him but not where he is. How did he come to owe you fellas money?" Ryder had no doubts Richy would be in deep trouble if he were to let on to these clansmen that Richy was in his dungeon. But Ryder didn't want Richy dead, he wanted him to suffer.

"He bet on the horses and lost heavy," one said.

"Then he borrowed money from me to pay Cameron, here." The Scotsman gestured to the hulk of a man sitting his horse next to him. "But didn't pay him back or me."

"Yeah, instead he bet on another loser of a horse."

Blade stood behind Ryder, blocking the men's view into the hut. Ryder wondered how Gizela had survived over the years. She wouldn't have been able to defend herself from vagrants and thieves. Yet she always seemed to do fine. Perhaps the hovel she lived in was far enough from the road people rarely discovered her or perhaps she had luck on her side.

"We've been to the tavern about six miles down the road. Heard he molested a serving girl there. The father kicked him out, but not before someone working for the Laird of the MacLaren clan captured him," Cameron spoke through clenched teeth, his hands fisted at his sides.

"We're just travelers in need of a dry spot to wait out the storm," Ryder said, glad of the fact the men didn't recognize him.

"Ya wouldn't know anything of Laird MacLaren, would ya?"

Ryder wasn't real sure where to go with this. Under different circumstances, he'd relish a good fight and he rarely lied, but he had the girls to think about. "If you found this Richy fella, what would you do?"

"Make him work off his debt. It's obvious he doesn't have the money to pay us anything." Cameron looked to the north. "Got land up there that needs a whole lot of farming and boulders that need clearing. I'd make sure he worked from sunrise to sunset."

Ryder held out his hand to shake and more politely greet this man. "I'm the MacLaren." Then he waited to see the men's reaction.

"Did ya lie? Do ya have him in your castle?"

Ryder nodded. "In the dungeon and I'd be happy to give him over to the two of you. But I have business in London. Won't be back to the castle for a few weeks, maybe a month. Would you mind waiting?"

"As long as the end result's the same. It wouldn't hurt the wastrel to spend some time thinking about what he's done and who he's hurt." Cameron looked to the skies above. "Time to get out of the rain. I'll see you in a month then."

Leading the horses, the men made their way to the small barn. Ryder watched until they disappeared from site then he turned to Blade. "Do you want the first or second shift?" His gut told him these men meant no harm, and he prayed they did not see the women, but he didn't intend to take any chances."

"I'll take the first. You get some sleep and I'll wake you in a few hours." Blade settled down near the door, pistol in hand, sword beside him and his dirk in his boot.

Ryder set about to use the pallet in the hut, spreading out the trail blankets the men had brought with them. The blankets had been a last minute thought because they both understood one could never foresee everything that might happen.

The girls stretched out on the bed, but Ryder sat, back against one wall, pistol in hand. He knew he should close his eyes and rest but fear pooled inside.

He felt the nudge on his shoulder. How long had it been? He had managed to sleep but he shook himself awake.

"What is it?"

"Shh..." Blade looked to the door then crawled back to his position in front of it, motioning for Ryder to do the same. In a whispered voice, "I'm not sure if there is anything wrong. The storm has stopped and there is no more rain. So, they may just be movin' on."

Blade was right. All Ryder could hear was the sound of the wind whistling around the eaves and the racing of his heart against his chest. He looked to where the girls slept. Christel was so beautiful, her hair spread across the blankets, her breathing even. He didn't want her to ever fear anything again.

"I'd like to confront them. Let those two understand we know what they are doing."

"All right." Blade stood and Ryder followed suit.

Pistols in hand, swords buckled to their sides, ready for a fight if necessary, they stepped into the darkness. "Leaving so soon."

Cameron nodded then let his hand rest on the hilt of his sword. "Thought we'd get an early start on the day. As you can see, the rain has stopped and the sun is rising over the eastern hills. We have a ways to go before we reach home."

"See you don't return here." Ryder's voice was calmer than he felt and his fingers tightened on his pistol.

"We don't mean you and your women harm."

He drew in a sharp breath. So they did know...

"We'll be on our way and see you at the MacLaren castle in four weeks." Cameron nodded then looked to the east.

"What is this?" Christel stood in the opening, her hand on the doorframe, her long blond hair falling in glorious disarray around her shoulders.

"Nothing, go back inside." Ryder's gut clenched and he knew his voice sounded tense.

"Ma'am." Cameron tipped his hat to her then mounted his stallion, the other man following suit.

Ryder would have given everything he owned for Christel to have not appeared in the doorway. He watched as the men rode from sight and when he turned, Aidan stood, hands clasped in front of her.

"Best we be on our way." Ryder strode inside, furious he had not been able to stop the past events and angry these men had turned up, yet hopeful Richy Rathen would get what he deserved at the hands of these Scots.

He prayed these men were good honest men.

"So soon?" Aidan asked, a weary sigh emanating from her lips.

"The men who rode in last night have gone on their way. We are all up and awake. If need be, we can stop when we get to the inn we were supposed to make it to yesterday."

Christel had picked up her backpack and had it slung over one shoulder. "No need to wash up. I believe we are only a couple hours ride from Stonybrook Inn."

Ryder smiled at his soon-to-be wife, enjoying her resilience. Aidan seemed happy to be on her way too.

"Perhaps a quick meal, a nap then another short ride will be in order." Ryder motioned for them to leave first.

Inside the stable, their horses had been watered and fed. Perhaps his fear should be put to rest, but on the other hand the gesture could be a ploy. They mounted and rode southwest.

As predicted, a couple of hours later Stonybrook Inn came into view. Chickens were scattered around the yard. A rooster crowed, an alarm to the animals that the sun was rising. Mist clung to the ground like a ghostly shadow the water from the storm last night evaporating as the air warmed.

Christel pulled her cape close and Aidan pushed her hair from her eyes. He knew they were excited and eager to make it to London, but he also knew by the time they reached their destination, they would be exhausted.

"I'm tired. Don't think I can ride another hour." Christel stretched her back and swung free from her horse.

"I'm famished." Aidan added her bit. "Could eat a horse."

"Don't get any ideas," Blade said, looking at her horse. "I don't think your little mare would appreciate her demise."

"The horses need to be exchanged." Ryder nodded to Blade.

"I'll take care of it." Blade helped Aidan dismount then grabbed the reins of all four horses and led them to the stables to make arrangements for fresh mounts.

Ryder and the girls entered the inn then he motioned for the innkeeper. "We would like rooms; two but adjoining if possible. After that we'd like breakfast sent upstairs." He pulled out a purse and handed the man a gold coin.

"Very well, anything you need, sir."

Ryder ushered the girls up the steps and to the rooms he'd rented. Walking inside, he looked over the space then opened the adjoining door. "We can eat. I know Blade needs sleep. I'll take the first watch."

"Do you really think that is necessary?" Christel plopped down on the bed and yawned.

"I won't let anything happen to any of us."

Ryder strode through the door and looked over the room he and Blade would share for a few hours then walked back to the girl's room. Aidan was asleep and Christel still sat on the bed, her hands folded in her lap. A lone tear dropped from one eye before she wiped it away.

"I truly don't want to worry. But I do. You have made everything seem so dangerous."

"This is dangerous." He gestured outside then toward the door, his emotions escalating when he thought of the peril.

"You must get some sleep." She rose and wrapped her arms around Ryder, pressing herself against him then letting her head fall against his chest.

"If you stay in my arms, I might lock the doors and let Blade and Aidan fend for themselves." He laughed and turned her, putting his arm around her waist at the knock on the door. "I believe that is our meal."

Ryder opened the door and Aidan, not asleep after all, sat up. "What is that wonderful smell?"

"Let's see." Christel peered under the checkered cloth covering the food. "It looks like we have strawberries, oatmeal, scrambled eggs and hot bread."

"I'm so hungry I could eat the whole cow." Blade stepped through the door, shaking water off his head like a wet puppy dog.

~ * ~

The Duchess sat in her parlor, waiting for all her efforts to come to fruition. Scarlet sat opposite her. Another servant brought in tea and lemon cakes then poured the Earl Grey tea.

"Two sugars." The Duchess held up two fingers then nodded her approval. "I adore lemon cake."

Scarlet smiled and sipped her tea. "Has everything been taken care of to your approval?"

Again, The Duchess nodded. "I called in almost every favor the late Duke was owed and a few of my own. I'm almost past favors and thinking about blackmail. I've information on quite a few of the aristocracy. Things they wouldn't like anyone to know."

"What happens next?" Scarlet sipped the tea, looking pensive yet ready to do whatever might be necessary.

"We wait. These things take time. Patience is a virtue my late husband always said, but I never believed him."

"I'm not too good at waiting, Duchess. I can hardly breathe thinking of that tiny babe who will be in the upstairs nursery any day now." Scarlett set her cup on the table before helping herself to one of the lemon cakes.

The Duchess settled back, leaning her head on the chair behind her. She didn't remember ever feeling quite so tired as she did now. For the last week she'd visited the Prince Regent and various lawyers until she found Master Heathrow. He was known for his intelligence but mostly his cunning. The Prince had given her the go ahead and said the crown supported her and her efforts. Master Heathrow had provided the legal knowledge. She'd found a legitimate way to procure Christel's child. No one had to revert to kidnapping.

Thank God.

The noises in her home made her heart swell with warmth. Upstairs she heard the sound of Ravyn and Amorica giggling. It wouldn't be too long before Allura and Christel joined the girls, Aidan too.

Perhaps she would finally be able to plan a wedding, one out of three was not what she'd hoped for two and half years ago. But Amorica and Ravyn had wed wonderful men. Now she had to make sure Ryder and

Christel would end up as happy as her cousins.

"Duchess?" Mr. Finkbiner, The Duchess' butler, stood in the doorway of her parlor, a grim expression on his face.

"Yes?" Her heart felt like a lump in her throat. This could not bode well for her plans.

Then the sound of a screaming baby filled the room. "He's here." She leapt to her feet and raced to the front doorway. "I cannot believe the babe is here. He's really here."

The wet nurse stepped from the carriage, holding the child who squirmed in her arms, seeming to want to get down and walk. The Duchess put her arms out, needing to hold the tiny child who had such a tumultuous first year of life. She didn't think she would ever forgive the earl. But then, if there were any justice in this world, he'd spend the rest of his life in Newgate prison for the horrendous crime he committed.

"Ma'am, I believe master Brett here is hungry." The wet nurse held out her hands to take the boy back.

"He's on solid food, right?" The Duchess did not give the boy back but turned and walked up the steps to her home. Once she entered, "Scarlet, go see Cook and find some suitable food for the young man here. "I'm going to take him into the kitchen and put him in the highchair we procured.

Suddenly the girls, Amorica and Ravyn, hovered around The Duchess. "He's so cute." Amorica squealed, touching the top of his beautiful blond head. She was holding her little girl, Lyssa and Jessie, her little boy, hovered close by.

"Oh, and he's got the look of Christel, her eyes, anyway." Ravyn ruffled the boy's hair and cooed in delight while her first-born clung to her skirts.

"Give the poor little fella room to breathe." The Duchess laughed, feeling happier now than in a very long time.

"You will not get away with this, Duchess!" The earl stood in the parlor of the house glaring at them. "The boy is mine. I will be back, you can count on that."

Chapter Nine

"There he is! Is that really my baby?" Her heart pounding, hands sweating, Christel raced up the steps, arms extended. "Oh my God, he's so handsome. Such a little man and he looks just like my father." The journey lasted one day longer than they'd expected, but she never thought The Duchess would have her baby so quickly and without a fight.

The Duchess handed the boy to his mother who hugged him tight. "Your arrival has great timing."

"How did you pull this off?" Ryder dismounted and walked to the chatting group of women.

The others followed suit, Aidan and Christel enjoying group hugs from their sisters and cousins then cooing over the child then all the children.

"I called in most of the favors owed my husband by the late Duke. He was an extremely intelligent and cunning man and he had a lot of friends—good friends. He also knew a lot of secrets."

"I thought Blade and I would end up sneaking into the country home of the earl," Ryder said. "We were prepared to kidnap this little one."

"Don't forget us," Damian stepped forward then nodded back to the door way as Aric marched into the sunlight.

"We would have been on your heels, friend," Damian, Amorica's husband, said.

"And I'm heartily glad no one had to resort to kidnapping in order for this happy day to come about," The Duchess smiled.

"Amen to that," Ryder said.

"Come, let's go inside." The Duchess spread her arms wide as if to herd everyone where she wanted them to go. "Help yourselves to whatever you want to drink and there are plenty of lemon bars for everyone."

Christel walked to the kitchen, intent on feeding her child. Savoring every moment with the wee little man was so important. He grabbed onto her finger and smiled at her as if he had waited a year for this moment, as if he knew she was his mother. "You are just the sweetest little thing."

In the highchair, he banged the top with the spoon he'd been offered. Cook set a plate of mashed peas, applesauce and ground up chicken on his tray.

"Does he have teeth?" Christel tried to look inside his mouth then laughed at herself. The wet nurse hovered behind her as if she was jealous of the new mother. Perhaps the young woman had grown overly fond of the child. She couldn't chastise her for that.

"He has two," the woman said.

"I'm sorry. What's your name?" Christel asked, hoping she could make friends with the woman.

"Elizabeth, you can call me Beth."

"You must think I'm a bit overbearing, but I'm not sure you know the truth about what happened." Christel inhaled a deep breath while she tried to think of the needed words to explain the situation to Beth.

Beth nodded. "You gave him up to the earl. Said you didn't want to raise a bastard child."

Christel sucked in air, astounded at the falsehood the earl had passed on. "That's a lie. He stole my baby and told me he was stillborn and a girl." Christel could barely breathe, realizing all the lies that had been told.

"The earl wouldn't do such a thing. He's a kind man. Loves the little boy dearly." Beth persisted in her support of the horrible man.

"Only when he gets what he wants." Christel held a spoonful of peas in front of the boy's mouth.

"He likes the applesauce better." A lone tear slipped down Beth's cheek. "He's going to want to nurse soon. He always does after he eats then he goes down for a nap."

Inside, Christel bristled, but her rational side recognized the fact Beth knew more about her child than she did. "I will listen to all of your advice, Beth, but you need to remember I'm his mother. As long as you do this and continue to put this handsome little man first, you can remain here. If you cannot do that then leave right now."

"Thank you, ma'am. I will. I want Brett to grow up knowing how much he's loved," Beth said, her voice filled with emotion.

Christel recoiled, anger simmering deep inside. She didn't want to recall any of the past, had needed to put it behind her. "His name isn't Brett. I'm not sure yet what I will name my little boy, but the name will in no way carry on any part of the Rathen lineage."

"But..."

"There is no discussion here. You'll do what I say and in addition respect me. I won't have you gainsaying my every decision." This woman could be dangerous. Christel intended to speak of this with Ryder in private as soon as she could find a chance.

"How are we doing?" Ryder appeared beside her, one hand resting on her shoulder. "This is all new to me, but I think I'm going to like being a father."

She felt the reassurance all the way to her core. "Just fine, I think he's finished." Christel wiped his mouth and hands with a damp cloth then after lifting him from his high chair, handed the boy to Beth.

"Thank you, M'lady." She held him on one hip as she walked through the room.

"Beth."

"M'lady?"

"When he is finished, I want you to bring him to me." She needed to name the young man but couldn't remember any of the names she'd thought of when she'd been pregnant. Had she thought of any or had she just been too busy running and hiding from Richy?

"He usually falls asleep when he nurses and I just set him in his crib." Beth's voice sounded contrite.

"This time you can set him in my arms and I'll take him to his bed." Frustration swept through her, eating at her core. How could she make this woman understand that she was the little boy's mother.

Beth stiffened. "Very well."

Christel wondered if the earl had any contact with his grandson. At first glance it appeared Beth thought of the child as hers. Her way of thinking would have to be changed quickly.

"Is there a problem here?" Ryder looked from one woman to the other, his eyebrows drawn together in apparent concern.

"No," Christel smiled at the man she loved and the child she'd never held until this day. "All will be fine. Won't it, Beth?"

Beth curtsied then strode from the room her back ramrod stiff. "Of course, ma'am."

"Were you a bit harsh with the woman?" Ryder helped Christel from the chair then touched the tear that slipped from her eye.

"No, I'm afraid of that woman. She terrifies me and thinks of the baby as hers. I won't have that." Christel had no other words for this new situation that was making her hands shake.

"Really? She is an employee."

"Beth is loyal to the earl. I'm afraid she might turn on us and take the wee one back to him."

"The earl will be in Newgate by sunset. If she wants to remain part of this child's life, she will become loyal to you and only you." He kissed her on the cheek. "What are you going to name the lad?"

"I don't know. Any suggestions?" she asked, looking to him for answers.

"I think he should have a good and strong name. Something that will instill a sense of character in him," Ryder said.

"We have a lot of work to do." Christel thought on raising a child. She hoped Ryder would embrace this boy as his own. Even though he said he would, she knew it was a lot to ask of anyone. And she also understood if Ryder had a boy, that child would inherit. Bastards just didn't have much of a place in this world. Perhaps, this boy would inherit from the Rathen estate instead. If there was anything left of it after Richy ravaged it.

"He will grow up just fine." Ryder smiled at her. "We will make sure of that."

"And you know this how?" Christel understood there were no

guarantees where parenting was concerned. "I'm scared to death he might become a wastrel like his father."

"Time will tell. I believe the parenting has a great deal to do with the development of the child not just lineage." Ryder strode to the window and gazed outside. At one moment he moved the curtains aside and leaned closer to the glass pane. "He won't be raised in London but on our land, on MacLaren land, where he'll learn what it is to be responsible and to know the love of a mother and a father. Unlike his father, he will understand what a good day's work entails."

Christel saw his back stiffen, his finger tightening around the lacy curtain. "What is it?"

"I'm not sure but I do agree with you we must carry on cautiously. We can't take any chances nor can we believe the earl gave up this easily."

"Would the earl have favors to call in too? The Duchess isn't the only member of the ton who has friends." Christel rose and walked to Ryder's side, looking out the window in hopes of seeing what concerned him.

"Of course. They all do. His friends would be on the seamier side, and they would most likely hate the duke and his family."

"I'm done. Brett is here." Beth brought the child back to Christel. Christel ignored Beth's use of the name and took him into her arms then up to bed, rocking him as she walked.

The nursery had an adjoining door to her room on one side and to Ryder's on the other. Ryder strode beside her.

Beth had the boy ready for bed, so Christel set him in the crib with a hug and kiss to the forehead. The tenderness in her soul filled her with such fierceness. She wanted to protect this precious child from any harm that might come his way, including Beth.

Ryder placed one hand on her shoulder. "I promise you nothing bad will come to this boy."

She turned to Ryder as he pulled her into his arms for a long and loving kiss. When they parted, "Thank you."

"For what?" he asked, pushing a wayward lock of hair behind her ear.

"Your support and care. I don't think I would have recovered my child without your help and the fact you want to help me raise my son goes beyond anything that would be expected."

"The Duchess is the one who managed that," Ryder reminded her. "And the boy belongs to you and so he is precious to me."

"No." Christel shook her head in denial. "No, you discovered the truth and set the events in motion. The Duchess would have never guessed the earl's grandson was my child." She realized the validity of those words. Ryder had done so much for her she could never repay him.

"Come, now it is our job to protect and nurture this little boy to become a good man."

"You're right, of course. Are you as tired as I am? And famished?" Christel felt the need to change the subject. So much had happened she needed time to think and plan. She needed a new name for her little boy, and the sooner she came up with one the better.

"You have thought of only your child. Now, for his sake, you must take care of yourself," Ryder said. "An exhausted mother cannot cope as well with her child as one who has had a tiny bit of sleep."

As if someone had read their minds, a tray of food was brought to them. "The Duchess thought you might be hungry. Cook prepared food, and when you are done, pull the cord and I will see to a bath for you." Scarlet looked to the nursery. "The Duchess has men to stand guard outside his door."

"You're so kind," Christel said, her mouthwatering at the scent of the heavenly food. As if on cue, her stomach grumbled.

"I love The Duchess. She has been very kind to me, and I would do anything for her. I believe she has a plan in place that will eliminate Beth as a threat to you and your baby." Scarlet smiled at them. "Eat and rest. You have nothing to worry about."

Christel dipped her finger into the strawberry jam. "Yumm..."

"You need to eat more than jam." Ryder sat down beside her then grabbed a plate and prepared a meal for Christel.

On the table were meat pies, peas, hot bread with homemade butter, lemon cakes and to top it off, The Duchess had included a bottle of wine.

"I cannot possibly eat all that food." Christel stared at the plate then picked up a fork, digging into the meat pie. "Delicious."

Ryder prepared a plate for himself then poured wine. "How long has it been since we ate?"

"I think I forgot." She waved the fork in the air for a moment then bit into another piece of the pie. "This morning around six o'clock, maybe."

"And it is past six in the afternoon. No wonder we both feel as if our belly could touch our spine."

They ate in relative silence. Christel listened for sounds coming from her child's room while she searched her mind for a name. She thought it so strange the child had not been afraid of her. She had expected him to cry at separation from Beth. Strangely, he did not. It seemed to Christel the baby knew who she was from the first moment she held him.

"A penny for your thoughts?" Ryder sipped the wine then grinned, settling back in his chair with an easy nonchalance.

"I love my child more than life itself." Christel realized at that moment she wanted Ryder to love her just as much. Was she selfish? She wanted to be his first priority in life. Perhaps that would be asking too much.

"I didn't doubt that for a moment." Ryder took a last bite, looking replete and ready to move on to something else. After a moment, he rose and walked to the bell cord. "You ready for a bath? I'll scrub your back." He winked at her.

"As much as I'd like to tell you yes, I believe The Duchess would not look favorably upon those actions. Despite all I've been through, she is still my chaperon and I respect her too much to bring any scandalous rumors down on her good name." Christel laughed then slanted him what she hoped was a flirtatious look.

"Do that again and I won't care what The Duchess thinks." With that said, a knock at the door took their attentions away from each other.

"That was quick."

Scarlett stood outside the door, servants with pales of water behind her. "We anticipated your needs and we were ready." She turned and motioned the bucket brigade to the room and the tub, which sat behind a privacy screen. The men poured the steaming water.

Ryder bowed to the two women. "I will see you when your baths are finished."

"We have prepared water for you too," Scarlet said. "It is already in the tub in your room."

A boom echoed through the room, coming from the outside. It sounded as if a cannon had been shot in front of the house.

"What is that?" Christel felt as if she'd jumped out of her skin. She watched Ryder stiffen, saw the change of expression on his face, noticed his hands fist at his sides as he turned.

"Go into the nursery and stay there. Scarlet, do you know how to use a pistol?" Ryder appeared ready for a fight. "Where are Aidan and Blade?"

She nodded. "Aidan talked Blade into taking her to Vauxhall Garden."

"Good, one less person to worry about." He pulled a pistol from an end table in the room and handed it to Scarlet. "Stay with them and shoot if necessary."

Ryder raced from the nursery.

Christel's heart lodged in her throat as she rushed to the baby's room. He slept, his little thumb in between his lips, oblivious to the noise. What on earth was happening? No one would get to this room because the house was filled with people who would keep harm from anyone here.

Gunfire echoed, men cried out. Damian barked orders and Aric shouted to Ryder. So much noise and confusion reverberated through the house. Christel could not understand the words that were said.

A scream filled the air then an all-consuming silence.

~ * ~

Ryder reached the foot of the stairs to find the parlor in shambles. Desks and chairs had toppled to the floor. Blood stained the carpet. Outside, Aric and Damian barked orders to the servants.

A fight had been brewing in Ryder's soul since he'd learned of Christel's rape and loss of her baby. He'd hoped this tussle would include Richy but hell, Richy was safe and sound in his dungeon. *Bring 'em on.*

His blood pulsed and energy leapt through his veins. He swept the front door open with his free hand and stepped onto the porch. Sunlight blinded him for a moment. A bullet whipped by his shoulder, tearing into his shirt.

"Bloody hell."

"Take cover," Aric called out.

"Don't have to tell me twice." Ryder jumped over the porch railing and found Damian beside him.

"'Bout time you got here. Are Christel and the child safe?" Damian asked as he took aim.

"As long as no one goes inside the house." Ryder looked up and his breath caught in his throat. Christel had pulled the curtains aside and was peering out the window. He motioned for her to move back, but she didn't see him or she chose to disregard what he tried to say.

A bullet splintered wood on the window frame. Christel ducked down. God, he felt thankful she didn't get hit and prayed she'd just learned she shouldn't be so curious.

"It's Lord Rathen. I'm guessing these are a few favors among the aristocracy." Damian moved in a sideways fashion and gazed around the porch. A shot imbedded in the brick near his head. "Remind you of the good ol' smuggling days?"

"You can think of that at a time like this?" Ryder did remember and he didn't want to go back. They'd had a few too many close calls. The thrill of the chase had been exhilarating. Outwitting the local constables had never been difficult. And all had been for a good cause. He couldn't count how many people seeking asylum for religious and political reasons the three of them had helped.

"We haven't seen the earl, but I'm guessing he didn't spend much time in prison." Damian looked around the barrier he'd taken cover behind.

"Where are Ravyn and Amorica and The Duchess?" Ryder searched the surrounding area once more, his focus riveted on a spot across the street.

"Ravyn and Amorica are not here. They have gone to our respective homes for safety. Aric and I decided to come back. As for The Duchess, I can't say."

"Damian! Ryder! A little help, please." Aric's voice boomed from nearby. The gunshots seemed to have died down, and Ryder guessed everyone was out of bullets and swords were the weapons of choice.

He grinned at Damian. "You ready for a bit of swordplay?"

"Child's games against these ruffians." Ryder pulled his sword from the scabbard and Damian followed suit.

Swords drawn, the pair stepped forward, but two men blocked their way. Ryder felt the grin inside. Exhilaration spun through him. He'd been anticipating this, needing to let go his pent-up emotions.

Swords up, the men paired off. Rapiers clashed. Ryder thought to play longer than need be but remembered Christel upstairs. What if this was just a diversion? Both men, seeming to think as one, finished the unequal duels.

"I'm going to find The Duchess," Damian said, heading inside the house.

"Good, I'm going to make sure Christel and the boy are still safe." Ryder checked the surrounding area. No one stepped forward. He took all of the steps three at a time, skidding into the nursery in time to see the elder Lord Rathen, gun to Christel's head, his beefy forearm around her neck. Beth had the child in her arms and Scarlet was on the floor, blood pooling from a wound on her arm.

"Did you think I would be so stupid as to let you win?" He sidestepped with Christel in a semicircle toward the door. "The boy is mine."

"You have no claim to Liam." Christel spoke with such calm determination it surprised Ryder.

"Brett."

"The law is on Christel's side. You were sentenced to Newgate. How did you get out?" Fury flowed through Ryder, yet he knew he had to control the anger.

"Promised one of the guards a home in the country and property." Rathen shrugged. "It was as simple as eating cake."

"You have nowhere to go." Ryder stepped forward but stopped when he saw Rathen pull back the trigger.

"I hear America has a lot of untamed land and there is always

Australia." Closer to the door, in order to exit he was forced to let his guard down. "And of course, South America."

Liam cried out, "Mama."

"You are worse than your son. Do you care what fate is about to befall him?" Ryder was appalled at the lord. Even if Richy had been a deplorable son, he was Rathen's son. With this knowledge, Ryder felt no pity for Richy. A man was responsible for his deeds. And Richy raped Christel. He had to pay, but first his father was about to learn he was at death's door.

Liam was safe. Beth had exited the room with him and was no longer in danger of catching a misguided bullet. He had only Christel to think of. What he needed was a diversion.

"Richy deserves whatever fate has befallen him. I plan on a second chance with his child," Rathen said, his voice too calm.

"No, I will find you wherever you go. There is nowhere you can run." Ryder held his sword at his side. But knew it would be useless as long as Rathen held the gun at Christel's head.

"I could put a bullet in her brain. What do you think of that?" The earl sneered, his hand moving a fraction.

"It would be the last thing you did." A calm settled over Ryder even though he knew Christel's life was still at risk.

"But I'm in control here." Rathen's back was at the open door. He pulled Christel through.

A shot filled the air, shattering Ryder's composure. Ryder's heart fell to the floor and his breath caught in his throat.

Christel stumbled inside, blood covering her back and hair. He pulled her into his arms. Moisture welled in his eyes as he held her tight and prayed. He wanted to touch her everywhere, hold her, never let her from his side. But he pulled back and looked into her fear glazed eyes.

Damian stood in the hallway, a smoking gun in his hand. The earl lay sprawled on the floor. Damian knelt, touching a finger at the pulse of his neck.

"Liam—"

Beth had the boy. Even with Lord Rathen dead, she could find a way to elude them. The wet nurse was strange, and she hadn't been able to let go of the child, accept that Christel was the mother, not her. Ryder had meant to find a child for Beth, one to replace Liam, but he hadn't had the time to tell her. There were so many illegitimate children—babies—who ended up in work homes.

"Christel." He held her by the shoulders and gazed into her eyes. "She cannot be very far. I will find her. She cannot get away with your child. Please stay here. See if you can find The Duchess and help tend to wounds."

She looked at Scarlet who nodded while she held a sheet to her arm. "I'm fine."

Eyes glazed over, Christel nodded. He needed to know she would be fine, but he had to find the baby before Beth disappeared into the hellholes of London. If that happened, she might never hold her child again.

A ghost appeared in front of him, motioning for him to follow her. Sounds of weeping came to him, yet he sensed this was the crying ghost from the MacLaren castle. She was with Christel to protect her and help retrieve the child.

Damian and Aric stood beside Ryder. "I believe she is on foot. So, she cannot get very far."

"I will search the gardens. There are places to hide, but with a child in tow, her travel will be slow." Aric disappeared through the iron gate that led to the gardens.

"I'll head north. The streets are not too busy right now around the townhouses. Does anyone know if she has family?"

Ryder shook his head, unable to answer the question. "The Duchess might but we've yet to locate her."

"Here I am." The Duchess waved at the group of people. "I saw her with the baby. She got into a carriage about a quarter mile that way. I've sent the butler to the Bow Street Runners as well as the constables for help, and I've a man trying to follow the carriage."

Ryder put his fingers between his lips and whistled. The sound echoed around the area. He hoped Aric would hear and return from the gardens. "Where would she go?"

"I don't know," The Duchess said, "but I mean to find out soon. I won't have Christel without her child for a second longer than necessary. I'd meant to fix Beth up with a little boy of her own and a home in the country where she could stay safe and happy. But she's ruined her life by kidnapping the babe."

"I'm not going to sit by and do nothing." Ryder strode to the stable along with Damian and Aric who had heard the whistle and returned. In a matter of minutes, they were mounted and riding.

A ghost floated in the air in front of Ryder, seeming to lead him. He prayed the ghost had only good intentions. His gut feelings rarely let him down, and this time it was telling him to follow this apparition.

"Do you see it?" he asked Damian and Aric. "The ghost?"

"Bloody hell," Aric said. "A ghost? No. Have you gone daft?"

"Me neither." Damian looked at Ryder as if he thought he was crazy.

"Just checking, but I swear there is something very ghostly leading me. And I'm hoping she somehow knows where the child is. There is a ghost at the MacLaren castle who seemed to befriend Christel."

Through the streets of London vendors were closing and going home. Daylight faded and still they rode, searching, listening. But they heard nothing that would lead them to the child they sought. Soon it was dark and a few street lamps were lit.

"Let's go to White's and see if we can get information." Ryder turned his horse in that direction. The apparition seemed pleased at his choice, because she continued to float slightly ahead of him. Frustration as well as fear raced through Ryder. Every passing hour could mean more danger for Liam.

In silence they rode on. "It will be a cold day in hell if we don't find the boy." Aric seemed impatient and had now taken the lead. As if on cue, the threesome picked up the pace.

Prostitutes lined St. James Street and waved at them as they passed. What seemed an eternity later, they arrived at the private gambling house.

Inside, the room buzzed with conversation. Gaming tables were set up throughout and the booze flowed. Talk of the earl and what he'd done seemed to be prevalent.

"Lakeland, Andrews, it's been a long time. Come join us." The three strode to the table.

"We're not here for pleasure." Ryder's words surprised the men at the table. They looked up from their cards.

"Then why?" one asked.

"We're looking for a child, a one year old. He was kidnapped out of The Duchess's home this afternoon. Have you heard anything?" Ryder asked, impatience guiding him.

One man laid his cards on the table face down. "Heard of a child being auctioned down in the hells."

"Where?"

The man gave a brief description of the place. Aric, Damien and Ryder raced from White's. Ryder felt his heart in his throat then energy sped through him. Nothing was said but the ghost leading them wept as if they were on a fool's mission.

I'm not too late.

Ryder had never felt such fear. Sweat beaded on his forehead, sliding down his face. Christel had been through so much, she deserved more than a few short minutes with her child. Bloody hell, but he didn't want to think what could happen to Liam. The medical underground was evil. They sold children and worse. Why had Beth taken this little boy she seemed to care so deeply for to be auctioned?

Inside the bowels of the earth, darkness surrounded them, water dripped down concrete walls. They strode around a corner and the light nearly blinded Ryder. He put his hand up to shield his eyes.

Beth stood in the middle of the room holding Liam. An auctioneer called out bids.

"Stop this now, I say cease this nonsense." The Duchess walked in from the other side of the room. She pointed a sword cane at the crowd and flanking her were two Bow Street Runners as well as five more constables.

Whistles blew, pistols were out and pointed at the men. As if on cue, the bidders sprinted for the openings that led to the tunnels. The police gave chase.

Within seconds, everyone had made a mad dash for freedom.

"Well, that was easier than I thought it would be." The Duchess flicked the lever on her cane to bring the sword back inside.

"What are you doing here?" Ryder strode forward to reach for Liam. And giving his attention to Beth, "You have some explaining to do."

She handed the boy to Ryder. "I had nothing to do with this." Her voice shook with emotion.

"But you kidnapped the boy." Ryder snuggled the boy close, but he waited for an answer.

"I did but—"

"But? As I said, you have a lot to answer for. We need to know why." His gut churned as he rocked the sleeping child in his arms.

"I owe money, lots of it."

"You could have come to me." The Duchess pointed her cane at Beth. "I would have taken care of you. I planned on taking care of you until you did this."

"Why? I worked for a man you despised, a man who stole the baby from its rightful mother. You must have hated me."

"I didn't always hate Lord Rathen. There was time when he was not so self-absorbed and cruel."

"Let's get out of here." Liam woke up and let out a loud wail. "I bet you're hungry, aren't you little man?"

Tears slid down the little boy's face and he clung to Ryder as if Ryder were his lifeline.

"I will get you to your mama."

~ * ~

Richy Rathen paced the confines of the tiny cell in the MacLaren castle. With a tight fist, he hit the side of the slime-ridden wall. They could at least have the decency to keep him somewhere warm. He wrapped his arms around his chest, trying to ward off the chill.

He'd asked to write a letter to his father but was met with laughter from the guards. The only person with empathy was the cook's daughter who brought him a tray twice a day. Practicing a few lines to help ensnare her help had been all he'd thought of the last seven days.

His stomach grumbled. He was sure his belly button hit his spine. Famished was how he'd spent the week, and he hadn't been granted a sip of ale, just tepid water.

I'm a lord of the realm. Someone will pay.

"Rose, my darling girl. You have brought food. Is it dinner or breakfast? Without a light, I cannot keep track of the time." His voice purred even while he whined about his circumstances.

Rose curtsied. "M'lord, it is supper time. Cook has made you a fabulous dinner. Here it is. And I managed to steal a pint. I could be in grave trouble if mama discovers what I have done."

"You are a darling for it and I will tell no one." This little fool was going to be his way out of this place. She was an innocent and an easy mark.

She pushed the tray through the bars then sat down on a stool, her head tilted slightly to one side. "Why are you here?"

"No one has told you? It's because I've been wrongly accused. I'm innocent." He had a plan and he hoped it was a very good one.

"Mama says everyone claims they are guiltless." She ran her hands down her skirt then smiled at him. "She also told me you'd lie to get your way."

His eyes focused on her beautiful and very large breasts, cupid's kettledrums. He could almost taste them. *Pull a little farther sweet darlin' and I'll see your pretty pink nipples.* She looked up and her hands fell to her sides.

"Well, this time she's wrong. I'm in here for gambling debts. I've funds to pay if they would let me retrieve them. I just have to get to London and my bank." One step closer to convincing Rose, he had been misjudged.

"Mama says you are a wastrel and you did something terrible to M'lady Christel. Nobody knows what you did, but Mama says the deed was so horrible you are not to be forgiven."

"Christel is here?" Bloody hell, but that was the first he'd heard of that. "I did nothing to her. I've been searching for her. How long has she been here?"

"She arrived nearly eleven months ago today. But she left, went to London with the laird, her husband to be."

"Bloody hell, I have to get out of here." Richy paced the small confines of his dungeon cell thinking of a plan. Perhaps Rose could find a way to get him out. The keys hung by the huge door. All he'd have to do was get her to empathize with his situation and perhaps hand over the means for him to find his way out.

Maybe he could find a way to take Rose with him. He shook off that idea. If he did something like that, he'd have the entire castle after him, although the idea spurred pleasant fantasies in his head.

"There is no way for you to get out," Rose told him as if reading his mind. "This dungeon is secure. No one has ever escaped."

"The keys are hanging over by the door. You could get them for me." He watched the horror on her face and knew he'd approached this too quickly. "I promise you I've been wrongly accused."

"I don't know." Her gaze shifted from him to the keys then back. "I'd get into a lot of trouble."

"No one will know. I'll wait until after dark and slip from the castle. You can discover me missing when you bring food tomorrow morning. By then I'll be halfway to London." He could see she wanted to help him. It was just a matter of time and a bit of patience before he'd win her over.

"I will know and I'm not sure I could live with myself if something happened to M'lady Christel." She wiped her hands on her skirt again then looked up at him. A tear slipped from one eye.

"Nothing will happen to the lady. She is my wife, and if anyone has told you different, they have lied to you." He felt pleased with this falsehood and the sudden shock he read in Rose's expression.

She gasped, her brown eyes growing wide. "She is not married to you. M'lady and M'lord are making wedding arrangements as we speak. They seem very happy."

"Ah, but if I had my satchel and if no one has stolen the marriage certificate, I can prove the truth of my words. Be a dear and go get it for me. It's on the floor." He pointed to a brown leather bag in the corner of the dungeon. "If you look inside, you will find the truth. The marriage certificate will rest inside."

Rose got up from the bucket she was sitting on and retrieved the bag. When she opened it, she rummaged around inside. "There is not but clothes."

"Cursed be the day. They have stolen the proof of my words." He tried to put anguish in his tone. "I will never have the evidence. Now it is up to you to help me prove the truth. You must help me."

"Are you really married to Christel?" Rose now was pacing. She walked to the key that hung beside the door then walked away, eyeing it then looking back to him. It seemed she wanted to believe in him and help.

"We were wed over a year ago," he told her, trying for at least one teardrop but failed.

"Promise me no one will know." She reached up, grabbing the key from its holder then tossed it to him.

She was gone before he could say thank you, not that he would have bothered. A few seconds later, Richy Rathen made his way from the MacLaren castle. He was headed to London.

Chapter Ten

When Ryder strode into the nursery with Liam, a sliver of a moon hung in the sky, competing with the rising sun for dominance. Christel sat in the rocking chair, baby blanket in hand, her head lolling to one side.

He knelt down beside her and touched her cheek with a fingertip. "Christel, my little one?"

She snuggled in deeper with the blanket. "Hmm..."

"Wake up, darlin'. I have Liam."

She stretched, his words reaching her dreams, head pounding from the tears she'd cried during the night. The gentle voice next to her ear brought her halfway to awake.

I have Liam.

Those words opened her eyes. She swiped away the hair that had fallen in her face. "Liam?" She sat up. "Liam is here?" Her heart pounded, racing with anticipation. She felt as if it might truly explode with happiness.

"Yes, with a little help from The Duchess we retrieved the little man and he is no worse for the adventure."

"Adventure! Where did you find him?" Christel held out her arms, tears falling freely as she cuddled with her son.

"Perhaps it would be best not to know." Ryder touched Liam's forehead.

"Ryder."

"After a short discussion at White's, we were led to believe he was in one of the gaming halls in the bowls of the city. We raced there to find Beth and your child on the auction block. Thankfully, The Duchess arrived with two of the finest Bow Street Runners as well as five other men to back them. The people there scattered in every direction imaginable."

Christel brought Liam in closer for another hug. "It doesn't matter. We have him back. Nothing more will happen. And Beth, what of her?"

"She was a pawn in this game. None of it was her fault. The Duchess has vowed to help her out and find a child for her. Then she will purchase a small home and land where Beth can live in peace."

"She should find a husband then a child will not be an issue." Even though she did not want to let go of the little boy, he stretched then yawned just before his eyes closed shut. Christel set him in his crib and covered him with a blanket.

"Come, you need your sleep. There is a guard at each door into the house and one in front of the nursery, but the earl is dead, and we should have no other troubles."

"Richy is in your dungeon." Christel stood beside the crib. She didn't want to leave, didn't want to sleep, and intended to watch Liam breathe. She needed to stand here and make sure no one would ever harm her child again.

"Christel. Come." Ryder wrapped his arms around her and held her, rocking her as if she were a child, yet the movement comforted and gave hope. She let him guide her to his bedchamber.

He turned her and raised her chin as he lowered his mouth. Their lips met, tongues melding together. She leaned into him, pressing her body against his, reveling in the feel of his warmth and the security she felt at the moment. He made her feel cherished and loved.

Wrapping her arms around him, she wound her fingers into his hair and pulled him closer. His hands on her back were large and warm. He ran them up her spine then down to her derriere where he squeezed.

"Ryder," she gasped, pulling away for a moment.

"Christel, I want you now." Ryder slipped the sleeves of her gown down her arms, lingering on her shoulders for a brief moment. He quickly unlaced her corset and her breasts were freed. He kissed her down to one nipple then sucked the bud into his mouth.

Her knees weakened and she felt spineless as she let him hold her up. His hand found her other nipple as he rolled it between his fingers.

She undid the laces to his shirt and pushed it up, forcing him to release her nipples from mouth and hand. He pulled her leg up to his waist then ran his hands down the inside of her thigh and back to her knee.

"Liam..."

"He is asleep and we are in a different room."

"I know but..."

"But he will be fine." Ryder kissed her again then rid her of her gown. She stood before him, naked.

"I want to see all of you." Christel loved the way he looked with nothing on. His belly was rock hard, his shoulders well-muscled as were his legs.

He disrobed then his hand once again found her breasts before he buried his face in her cleavage. Nipping then soothing with his tongue, he sent shivers of pleasures racing throughout.

Yet her mind was not focused. She kept thinking of her little man sleeping in his crib just outside the door.

Ryder seemed to sense her conflicting emotions. "Do you want me to stop?" His gentle query made her think.

"Yes...no...I don't know." Tears gathered in her throat. "I want you but..."

"It doesn't seem right." He finished for her. "It's your choice."

Christel felt the tug of her emotions, but she also knew she could not deny herself the pleasure of his lovemaking every night just because a child slept in the nursery nearby. She wanted more children, Ryder's children.

She responded by pulling his head down and sealing her decision with a kiss. For a moment she was aware of the pounding of her heart then she felt his kisses across her collarbone, butterfly soft, tender but intoxicating too. Leaning back to give him more room, it was her silent way of applauding his attentions and asking for more.

I love you so much.

One of his fingers traced her nipple then squeezed. She couldn't keep a tiny moan of desire from slipping out into the silence of the room. Dear God, but this was heaven. He gave her so much she intended to make him happy as long as he would stay with her and if he decided he needed adventure, perhaps she and her son could go with him.

With his mouth, he traced his way up her neck and to her ear, alternating nips and kisses. Against her skin his tongue felt warm, rough and it provoked every part of her then heated to a mercuric level. The rough stubble of his beard further reminded her of how different they were. The feelings were hot and primal, the dance as old as time.

"My petite one," he whispered in her ear then his tongue whirled inside, delightfully tracing the lobe.

She thought she'd just jumped from her skin. Her hands roughed through his soft hair then down his back to his muscled tight butt. She pulled him to her, reveling in the feel of his shaft nestled against her belly. She didn't want to think about right from wrong. They weren't wed yet, but she was promised to him. She wanted Ryder MacLaren more than life itself, and she needed him with an intensity she'd never felt before.

He swept her into his arms and strode to the bed then spread her legs and settled between them. Kissing his way from her ear to her mouth then down her neck, he finally settled on her nipples. With teeth, lips and tongue he paid tribute to each one. Her body spiraled out of control as she arched her back. She summoned more from him. He bit and kissed each nipple then ran his tongue around each one. Renewal of life, safety, and security was what he brought to their lovemaking this night.

One hand slid down her belly then to her feminine folds. He worked his enchantment, touching her as her walls clenched and tightened then wept for more.

"You are so wet and hot. I want to taste you. But not yet," he told her through tender kisses.

"Please," was all she could manage to say.

"You don't have to plead. I'll always give you what you want." He continued, gently nipping then sucking a nipple deep into his mouth, one finger still manipulating her then pushing inside.

Heat soared through her body. She suddenly bucked and moaned, the climax building as he pulled back gazing into her eyes.

"Ryder," she shouted his name.

"Keep your eyes open, my petite one. I want to watch when you reach that peak I'm taking you to."

Suddenly he was inside her and he drove into her again and again as they both sought that pinnacle only true love can bring.

She slid into blinding sensations, heat spiraling through her as she trembled with the force of the climax. She moved with the rhythm he set.

"Ryder," she called out again then almost spoke of her love for him. She bit back the words, unable to give him her heart.

He drove one more time then slid to his side, bringing her with him to lay on top of his chest. When her body finally slowed, he grinned at her. "You are so incredibly gorgeous, and your sweat sheened body calls to me. I want to kiss every part of you, love every inch."

"Good lord," she moved a lock of hair from his eyes. "My heart still races and I can barely breathe. It seems you unravel me one tiny strand at a time.

He set the palm of his hand above her heart. "I feel it and the racing of your breaths. You will..."

"Mamma!" The cry startled Christel but she reacted instantly. Maternal instinct overpowered every thought and emotion.

"Liam, I'm here." She pushed away from Ryder and grabbed her chemise from the floor. Slipping it over her head, she rushed to the nursery.

Did he just call me mamma?

"Hush..." She lifted him from the crib and snuggled with him. His tear stained face made her heart break. Yet he responded to her, placing his cheek against her. "Everything will be fine," she cooed. "What is it? Did something frighten you?"

He sniffed. "Mamma?" he asked.

"I'm your mamma." She told him. "I know you don't remember me but..." Christel looked at Ryder for help. She wanted to vanquish all of his fear as well as the terror of the night.

Ryder smiled at her. "You are doing fine."

"I don't feel as if I'm doing anything right." Then she looked at her little man. "Are you hungry?"

He nodded, "No."

"What does that mean? Would you like some banana or eggs?"

Liam nodded again, "No."

Ryder laughed outright. "He must like the sound of the word no." Ryder had slipped on his pants and shirt when she rushed to Liam's crib. Now he held out his hands. "I'll take him to Cook. She'll know what to give him. Get dressed and meet us in the kitchen."

Christel handed the boy to Ryder. "I'll be down in a minute." She watched Ryder walk from the bedroom. Emotions overwhelmed her as she sat on the bed, her head in her hands, and sobbed.

This won't do, Christel McLellan. Wipe your tears away and be a mother to that little boy. She heaved a huge sigh then managed to dress and race down the back steps to the kitchen.

She stopped short when she saw the spectacle in front of her. Laughter slipped from her. Covered in mashed green beans, Ryder held a spoon in front of Liam who was blowing green bubbles from his little pursed lips.

He turned, a broad grin forming. "This is fun."

"Really?" Christel stepped into the room, unable to believe the sight in front of her or his words. "I think I might have to let you do all the feedings after this. I'm not sure I'd like to be covered in green beans, and I'm not sure I would think it was fun."

Ryder shrugged his broad shoulders. "That's what baths are for." He turned back to give Liam another bite.

"Nanas," Liam said.

Cook had cut a banana into tiny bits so Ryder put the plate on the highchair table top in front of the boy.

Liam reached for the slice, squishing it between his pudgy fingers then putting the banana in his mouth before smearing the remains on his face.

"Was that good?"

Liam grinned then banged his spoon on the highchair tray.

"He's most likely done." Ryder took the spoon from Liam and accepted the wet rag from cook.

"I can do that."

Ryder handed the cloth to Christel. "He's all yours."

Well, that much was certainly true. "Thanks." She shot him a cocky grin, so pleased that what he said was true. He was all hers and no one was going to take him away from her.

Aidan tore into the room, skidding on mashed green beans that had found their way to the floor. Arms whirling, she came to a halt, seat on the floor and legs spread, as if they could stop the slide into Ryder.

By the time she stopped skidding, Ryder was on the floor too.

"Well, that was an entrance I hope you never duplicate." Christel shifted Liam to one hip and watched her two favorite people extricate themselves from each other.

"I'm in agreement there. Could you hand me that wet cloth? I'm in need of some cleaning." He strode to the sink and pumped water then washed his face and hands.

"Wow!" Aidan stood then shook out her dress. "I didn't want to miss his breakfast."

"You did, but I'll make sure you know when he eats next if this is the way of it."

Aidan smiled and held out her arms. "May I?"

Christel handed him over to her sister then helped Ryder rid himself of the mashed beans.

"A man is here to see you. Says his name is Owen."

Christel shot a questioning glance toward Ryder, fear rolling in her stomach. She needed this to be over, but it seemed there was always something else they had to contend with. She reached for Liam, and Aidan, seeming to sense the change of mood, quickly gave the little boy back to his mother.

"I'm sure it's nothing." Ryder turned to Christel. "Come into the parlor when you're ready.

~ * ~

"Owen?"

"We've trouble brewing." He stood with his fists clenched at his sides, a grim expression on his face

"What is it?" Ryder felt the same fear as Christel. He knew Owen would not make the trip unless the reason was of utmost importance.

Ryder motioned for Owen to sit. He shook his head. "Not before

I give you the news. Richy Rathen escaped."

"Bloody hell, how did he manage that? He was locked in the dungeon." Ryder paced the room, his mind whirling with the implications and the knowledge they still had to guard both Christel as well as the child."

"It seems the cook's daughter let him go. She fell for his sob story of innocence and his marriage to Christel. But I warn you, if there is any truth to the tale, then you have favors that will need to be called in. I know you will need to find him soon."

"I believe The Duchess has done that. I'm not sure she has any more to expect." Ryder's teeth clenched. Christel walked into the parlor, as did Aidan and The Duchess.

"I didn't hear that—"

"Yes, M'lady you did. Rathen escaped. Don't know where he's headin', but I informed the Scots who wanted him and they are looking for him as well as the MacLaren clan."

"He's too evil to get caught. I doubt if Satan could hold him in hell. Wouldn't want to." Christel moved to the window and stared out at the street below.

The Duchess poured tea for everyone before she sat down. She sipped the hot brew then set her cup on the table. "I haven't called in half of the late Duke's favors. Besides, there are many who would help regardless. For now, we must guard Christel and the wee one night and day and..." she paused long enough to take a bite of the lemon cake in front of her, "...we have a wedding to plan."

"I wonder what he thinks to gain by returning to London." Christel turned from her musings to address the room. "He owes too many aristocrats here, and I believe he also owes Prinny. Now wouldn't that be interesting if the prince regent caught him in London."

"Off with his head!" The Duchess gave a chop in the air.

"The MacLaren dungeon would be preferable to Newgate. Unless he believes that with his father's passing, he will come into the fortune left behind."

"Liam has that money in trust," Christel offered, "surely Richy must know."

"Richy has always felt it was his right. He never thought to earn his way." Ryder's gut tightened because he knew Richy could cause a great deal of trouble and waste a lot of time.

Christel yawned. "Good God, even with all this going on around me, I can't seem to keep my eyes open." She wavered on her feet.

"We have a wedding to plan, girls, but Christel, you need to get your rest. I've hired a new nanny for Liam. In deed she has come with the finest endorsements."

"Who is she? I'm not sure I want to leave him with anyone. I could just sleep in his room."

"But darlin', your little boy takes one nap a day, the rest of the time is play time. Now if you are going to make up for a sleepless night and all the stress that went with it, then I suggest you trot on up to your room and go to bed."

"You didn't tell me who—"

The Duchess waved a hand in the air. "Pshaw...the nanny is my littlest cousin. She's lonely and would like nothing better than to play with your child. I promise you she will take good care of the boy."

"Oh...then I suppose I'll go then."

"Aidan and I will get started on the wedding plans. It will be so much fun. What's your favorite flower?" The Duchess asked.

"Forget-me-nots."

"Then the wedding will be done in blue and white. When you wake, we'll take a trip to the dressmakers and plan your gown. Shoo now." The Duchess turned to Ryder, "You and Owen go on up to the study and figure out what you think Richy is up to and what you will need to keep him from getting his hands on Liam's trust and Christel as well. You know he'd like both."

Ryder left with Owen, following Christel up the stairs but turning into the late Duke's study. Ryder wasn't sure the room had been touched these last five years since the duke passed away and The Duchess' son, Richard was seldom home to take over the duties.

He walked to the window and pulled back the heavy velvet draperies. The scene below caught his attention. The duke must have been able to keep track of all his neighbors just by standing in this spot.

"Do you have any idea where Richy has gone?" Ryder turned from the window and walked around the room. He picked up a tiny ceramic dragon breathing fire, blew off the dust then set it back.

"My contacts have told me he's heading for London. He might be here now since he set off before me. However, I traveled nonstop."

"And he has his addictions..." Ryder knew that soon this would come to an abrupt halt. Richy would either end up in prison or dead. Cameron and his clan would not get their money back.

He strode back to the window, hoping he would see Richy walking down the sidewalk, but to no avail.

Owen stood beside him. "I've brought five men with me. They are all loyal. I do believe that with the men The Duchess has hired and your men we can keep Liam and Christel safe from any foul plans Richy Rathen can dream up. Remember he has no money and can't hire help."

"Liam was abducted from inside this home," Ryder reminded himself. Yet he understood it was the earl's doing, not Richy's.

"Maybe you should try and draw him out," Owen suggested.

"Perhaps, I do not play the waiting game well."

"We know he likes to gamble and whore," Owen said, "we could set him up, draw him into a game he can't refuse."

"I'll send messages to Damian and Aric. They will be happy to help, particularly if I let them visit White's. I'm not sure the establishment will allow Rathen inside its doors. He owes too many of the patrons small fortunes."

"Then we need to go to the seedier parts of town," Owen said.

Ryder rocked back, arms crossed, "The gaming hells where we found Beth and Liam might be the best place to begin our search."

"I will send men there." Owen waited for Ryder's consent. "We must make the bait sweet or he will not come."

"Wait until evening. I'll take Christel for a ride in Hyde Park as soon as she wakes."

"Very well," Owen said before leaving the room.

He wasn't sure he should risk Christel, but waiting created an even greater threat. Taking the offense would be the best strategy in this cat and mouse game. He wanted this to be over with so they could return and begin a life of peace and serenity, perhaps start of a family of their own.

"We can meet here in a few hours when everything has been planned." Ryder strode to the nursery and looked inside, reassuring himself all was as it should be.

Liam woke with a quiet murmuring in his crib. He seemed intent on playing with his toys. Ryder found himself drawn to the little boy in a way he didn't really understand.

Bending over the crib, he ran his hand over the child's baby soft hair, enjoying the way Liam looked up at him with a cherubic smile.

"Mamma?" He held onto his ball with a tight grip while he grinned at Ryder.

"She's sleeping." Ryder pulled him from the crib. "Ah, but I think you need changing."

He looked around the room and quickly found the nappies then debated calling for help or changing the boy himself. He decided to do it himself, even though he wasn't sure how to go about it. He didn't think it could be too hard.

He set Liam on the changing table, quickly ridding him of the wet diaper. As he lifted Liam's body, the boy let out a stream of pee, catching Ryder in the chest. "Bloody hell!" Then he let out a long roar of laughter. "You little devil." The explicative as well as the laughter brought the upstairs maid to the nursery.

"Let me finish for you," she said with a grin on her face. "And I'll order you a bath."

"I can order my own, but the little tyke must be hungry as well."

She curtsied and bobbed. "I'll see to it."

"Good." But Ryder decided he didn't need a full bath. Striding to his bedchamber and to his washstand, he poured a basin of water. After slipping free of his shirt, he washed his chest and face.

Shaking his head and laughing to himself, he wondered about the care of children. They were certainly fun to play with, but he decided he would leave the diapering to the servants or Christel.

A few moments later he was in the kitchen. Liam was proceeding to repaint the room with food so Ryder sat down to watch and not participate in the feeding of the little man.

With that done, he took Liam into the parlor where The Duchess was reading. Ryder set the boy on the floor along with a few toys. But it wasn't long before Liam had scooted on his bum across the room to a table. He pulled himself up then waddled precariously around the perimeter of the furniture.

"Look at him go. Why he'll be walking in no time." The Duchess set her book down to watch Liam.

"And then we'll all be in so much trouble."

Liam gurgled happily. "Mamma?"

"Why, there you are my sweet boy." Christel walked into the parlor. "Look at you. You're walking."

He turned sideways to the table and reached out his arms. "Up..."

Christel knelt down and held out her arms to the boy. "Come on, you can do it."

Liam seemed to understand. On unsteady feet he took two steps and it was enough to reach his mother. "Up..."

"Of course," she swept him into his arms and twirled him around in circles.

"More."

"Oh, but I'm quite dizzy. Perhaps Ryder will toss you into the air." She brought him to Ryder and set the boy into his arms.

Ryder was quick to toss him above his head, over and over. Liam laughed and clearly enjoyed the playtime.

"Enough," The Duchess said. "You are wearing me out and much more of that will surely have the little man throwing up his dinner."

After the nappy fiasco, Ryder didn't want to risk anything else ending up on him.

As if on cue, Scarlet entered the room and picked up the child. "I'll take him back to the nursery and play with him, if that's all right."

"That would be nice. I need to talk with Ryder and The Duchess." Christel poured herself a cup of tea and sat down.

Ryder cleared his throat, searching his thoughts for a way to tell Christel he meant to make her a target. "Christel..."

"I know Owen was here. Scarlet overheard some of your conversation and warned me. I'm prepared to do anything you think we need to do in order to draw Richy into the open."

Relived Christel had the same ideas, Ryder said, "That was my plan."

She tilted her head and the smile on her face gave Ryder pause. "Which is..."

"We are going for a ride in Hyde Park. I think it would be nice to let Richy know we are in town."

"If he's read the London Times, he knows you'll be wed this coming Saturday," The Duchess interjected.

"And we will need to be on guard for his trouble making," Ryder wondered what the odious man would try. He knew there would be something.

"We have the Bow Street Runners and the constables informed as well as my men, Damian and Aric," The Duchess said. "Blade of course will also be on hand."

"Damian's crew will surround the church," Ryder added, "and they'll be joined by Owen."

"What could he possibly think?" Christel rose then looked up the stairs as if she wished she could be with Liam. "Truly, he wouldn't try to stop the wedding, would he?"

"Owen said he convinced Cook's daughter that he had been wronged. She gave him the keys and he left unnoticed."

"What?" Christel whirled, the look on her face was one of astonishment then rage, her fingers winding into the fabric of her skirt.

"He told her that you were married to him and he had the papers to prove it," Ryder said, trying to keep his voice calm while his insides were in turmoil. He watched the color drain from Christel's face then the anger that began to surge.

"And she believed him?"

"She is young and foolish, easily swayed. It seems she fancied herself in love with Richy."

Christel inhaled a long breath then let it out as a whoosh of air. "There might be more to his claim than I'm able to remember."

Ryder felt his gut tighten. "It has to be a last minute ploy or his father would have known. What do you remember?"

"He drugged me." He saw the tears slip from her eyes. "It's more what I don't remember. There was a period of time I don't remember anything."

"I wouldn't dredge this up unless I felt the knowledge was absolutely necessary. Believing his claim as truth would be counterproductive. If a marriage to you had any validity, we would have heard about it a long time ago." Ryder wanted to ease every ache in Christel's soul. At the moment, he caused her more pain.

"After he...after he raped me and I kneed him, a man appeared from the shadows and kept me from running. I'd forgotten until now." She held her head in her hands, "But I just don't remember." She looked up. "Could he have married us? It would have been against my will."

"I can't imagine a legitimate man of God marrying you to that rake and in a drugged state. No, there has to be something about this that isn't right," The Duchess sat up straight, slamming her teacup so hard on the table it shattered into tiny pieces.

"If he has a marriage document, we must discover the truth." Ryder looked to The Duchess for direction. "Do you have someone who can take care of this?"

"I have an idea and will look into his claims. I'm sure he is grasping at straws, so to speak, and his statement is false." The Duchess rose from her chair and pointed at the shattered porcelain. "Scarlet, I'm so sorry for this. Can you find someone to clean this up? I didn't mean to break the cup."

Scarlet curtsied. "Yes, M'lady. I'm sure you thought it was Richy's head." Then she disappeared.

Ryder held out his arm, beckoning Christel. "Shall we?"

"To the stables?"

"Yes, and do you need to change or are you going to ride sidesaddle."

Christel beamed for the first time this morning. "I think I will set the gossip mills going if I don't. I'll be back." With that said, she raced up the staircase.

~ * ~

"I'll put a hundred on Born With the Wind." Richy handed over an IOU to the man he spoke with.

"You sure? He's the long shot."

"Bloody hell, do ya think I was born yesterday? I know what I'm doin'.'" Richy wiped the sweat from the back of his neck with his embroidered pocket-handkerchief. He'd resorted to sneaking into the Rathen Estate to find some way to pay off his debtors. A few trinkets wouldn't be missed, and the little boy would never know what had been stolen.

His body shook with rage when he discovered what his father had done with his inheritance, given it to his bastard grandson.

The nerve...

Now he'd lost the money he'd stolen as well as a thousand pounds more. He rubbed his temples in an attempt to stop the horrific headache pounding on his brain and between his eyes. Nothing could be set right because his father had the nerve to get shot and die.

Arghh...

The horns signaling the beginning of the race reverberated in the afternoon sky. His heart pounded against his ribs. "This is do or die," he muttered. "Do or die."

He'd watched this horse many times. The stakes were always against him, but he always ran well. Never in the top three, never to place. This time he'd picked him for the winner. Bloody hell, but it was almost too much. He didn't want to watch, but he couldn't help himself.

The horses were off and his start was bad. Known as a come from behind horse, Born With The Wind had better find a tailwind or Richy was going to be hung from his toes. Richy found himself bobbing his head in time with the horse's strides and trying to push him along.

Suddenly, Born With The Wind was in front. God, but Richy had never felt the rush of energy through his body as he did now.

I'm going to win. He's going to win. He won. I won!

His body shook.

"Sir, your wife has been spotted in Hyde Park with the MacLaren."

Chapter Eleven

"Do you think this will work and we'll find Richy?" Christel put her head back and let the beautiful warm sun reflect on her face. She loved to ride and this couldn't be a more perfect day. Birds chirped in the trees above, squirrels ran along the ground to find a tree to climb. It seemed most of the aristocrats in London had decided to enjoy a ride this day.

She leaned over and stroked her horse. "Arturo, you are strong as a bear and as fleet as the wind."

"Look." Ryder pointed up the trail.

"Ravyn," Christel urged Arturo forward while she waved at her cousin. "It's so good to see you. What are you doing here? Did The Duchess send someone out to tell you what we are up to?"

Ravyn laughed, "Guilty."

"We wanted to enjoy the day," Aric said while he seemed to look adoringly on his wife.

"I could say, liar, but he's right about that also. With no threat of rain in the air, everyone should be out, and perhaps we can find someone who has heard of Rathen and his whereabouts," Ryder said.

"I'm not thinking that's going to happen. Hate to get my hopes up." Christel knew a lot rode on what they heard. She wanted to be optimistic, but she needed to lean toward realism. Richy was always hard to find.

The girls dropped behind Ryder and Aric. "Have you and The Duchess made plans yet for the wedding?" Ravyn asked as her horse sidestepped, seeming eager to run.

"No, we haven't done anything since the day you and Amorica helped. I don't care about anything except finally being Ryder's wife."

Christel let out a petulant sigh. "If we'd stayed in Scotland, all would be done but I wouldn't have Liam."

"I know you had to take care of the most important item first, your child. But now we are going to plan a grand celebration." Ravyn beamed from ear to ear. "I do love a party."

"You haven't changed."

"No, and as much as I love my life with Aric, it is equally wonderful to be in London again for a few months. I've missed all this, and he was a dear man to bring me when he really wanted to stay home. It's hard to drag him away from his land and all we've built."

"I've never cared for the balls or the social stuff that goes on here. It all seems so frivolous and expensive." She watched the road ahead as well as Ryder as he sat his horse, tall and strong. When she met Ryder, luck must have been on her side.

"Always my practical Christel, and I will take heed of your wishes and not plan something Ravyn style and you must find a way to control Aidan. One never knows what she will come up with. We need to keep it simple. Thank you for reminding me."

"Thanks," Christel said, smiling and happy for the first time in so long she couldn't remember. Even her fears for Liam were put aside with the beautiful day and thoughts of her family.

"You are very welcome. Now if I remember correctly, your favorite flower is the forget-me-not, am I right?" Ravyn asked.

"Yes, and...what was it I was going to say? I've forgotten." Christel felt as if she were going a tad bit crazy.

"Don't worry, it's just the wedding day jitters," Ravyn laughed.

"Did you have them? Were you nervous too?"

"It all happened so fast I didn't even have time to think. I was betrothed and wed before I could say no. Don't you remember?"

"Yes, you lied so you wouldn't have to wed that wastrel, Lord Dickens. What did they call him? Something..."

"Dicky," Ravyn cut in with a sneer in her voice. "I couldn't have ever imagined a more horrible life. I wonder what happened to him."

"Do you care? I would give anything to never hear from or see Richy again, but I'm afraid my wishes will not come true."

"Ryder will do everything humanly possible to keep him away from you. Look," Christel pointed down the trail. "It's Damian and Amorica."

"Come to help plan my wedding, no doubt." Christel laughed through the happy tears forming in her eyes.

"Of course, and I'm sure The Duchess is expecting us back at the townhouse. She really is a dear, and I know she was disappointed when she didn't get to help plan Amorica's and my weddings. If we don't return, Aidan will take over the arrangements."

"Well, The Duchess did have a hand in your marriage whether you believe it or not. She was the driving force in bringing you and Aric together. I think she knew the marriage would never happen unless she gave you a bit of a nudge." Christel wanted to laugh at Ravyn's shocked expression.

"She manipulated us?" Ravyn asked then paused, seeming to think, "I guess I always knew what she did, but the first time I saw Aric I lost my heart so nothing underhanded she might have done concerned me overmuch."

"What, so you did know?" Christel was even more pleased at this new revelation and she loved the shocked expression on Ravyn's face.

"Was Aric a part of it too? I'll, I'll..."

"You'll what? Amorica asked as she turned her horse to ride in the same direction.

"I'll kill him. Well, maybe not since I've never been happier and it would seem foolish to get rid of someone who is the best thing that ever happened to me. Don't you think?"

"Absolutely," both girls said.

Christel turned to Amorica, "And your little boy, Jessie, can be the ring bearer."

"Who shall be the flower girl?" Ravyn asked. "Lyssa?"

"I don't know, not sure she's old enough. I'm sure The Duchess will know of a suitable little girl," Amorica said.

Christel drew in a long deep breath. "I will be the happiest when the wedding is over and Ryder and I are back on MacLaren land." It seemed strange how the ghostly apparition from the MacLaren castle had followed them to London. She'd seen the woman weeping several times and wondered if it was some type of foreshadowing of the events to come.

"Where do you want the ceremony to take place? I'm sure you would not like Westminster Cathedral."

"Oh my God, no!" Christel was horrified. "The Duchess hasn't booked that church, has she? That's where I draw the line."

"Then where?" Ravyn asked.

"A small church in the outskirts of London, nothing fancy. I'm sure Ryder will agree." Ryder would go along with anything she decided, but she also knew he would prefer something private, very small.

"And I know he will give you whatever you want," Ravyn said with a smile.

Christel felt a rush of color to her cheeks. "The men have stopped and they are talking to someone."

"Do you know any of those men?" Ravyn asked.

Both Christel and Ravyn said, "No."

"Maybe they have news of Richy," Christel urged her horse to a quicker pace then pulled up beside Ryder.

"These men have seen Lord Rathen at the race track. Word is, he won a sizeable amount of money on a long shot." Ryder looked worried, his brows furrowed and his lips thinned. "If he has funds, we've a great deal more to worry about."

Christel felt a surge of fear spiral within. "Does that mean he's in town?"

"I believe it does. The question that arises is where did he get the funds to place a bet?"

"He probably thinks he is heir to his family's estate," Ravyn said. "He's likely gambling with money that isn't his. Now, however, it doesn't really matter if he did win big. He can afford some of the nicer places to stay."

"But it's Liam's and if he's taken anything, he is stealing from his son," Ryder said, rubbing the back of his neck as if in deep thought. "We have to find a way to put a stop to this before he escalates."

"Could he be arrested for that?" Plots began to take shape in Christel's head, ideas she could pass on to The Duchess.

"Yes, if it can be proven. If he was smart, he would have taken items that cannot be traced back to the inheritance."

"Yes, valuable bowls, jewelry, statues, and the list can go on." Christel didn't like to think Richy would steal from his son, but where else would he get the money? From all she'd heard, there wasn't a bookie in town who would accept an IOU from Lord Rathen.

"If he doesn't have them on his person, there is no way to know. If they cannot be found, there is no way to prove anything," Ryder said.

"How did he get inside the estate? They've guards around it to keep him out." Christel's fury rose another notch. Would Lord Richy Rathen plague her the rest of her life?

"It's his family home," Damian said. "Even I know ways into the home that are not through the front door."

"Really?" Amorica asked. "Then why aren't the guards there? Where they will do the most good."

Ryder grimaced then whistled through his teeth. "Good point, Amorica. As soon as we get back, I'll make arrangements. Damian, you'll have to help."

"My pleasure," Damian laughed, a grin spreading across his face. "I'd like nothing more than to help rid London of the now infamous Lord Richy Rathen just as we took care of his father."

"I'm sure London will pin a hero's medal on your shirt too," Ryder said.

"And I will humbly accept it." Damian bowed in front of Ryder with a broad smirk on his handsome face.

"How did we go from wedding plans to ridding London of Lord Rathen in a matter of seconds?" Ravyn asked. "I enjoyed the previous conversation much better."

"Can't really have one without the other." Christel knew that for the truth. A marriage between her and Ryder could never exist until all threat from Richy had vanished. Suddenly, the joy and the beauty of the day vanished.

"Come, let's leave the men to their diabolical strategizing and meet The Duchess for lunch. I for one would like to have the wedding planned," Ravyn said.

"We're to meet her at the dressmakers," Amorica said, smoothing her skirts then looking at the other girls.

"Whatever for?" Christel asked, clearly baffled. "I don't need anything new."

"Your wedding gown," Ravyn said.

"Oh, I have..." but she'd left the plans for the unfinished gown in Scotland.

"You deserve a beautiful dress and if you don't want one, you'll have to fight The Duchess, because she is determined to make this a gala event," Amorica said. "Even if there won't be a lot of people in attendance."

"And we will help tone it down so you will remember the day with happiness and no regrets." Ravyn reached over and rested her hand on top of Christel's. "I promise, nothing too fancy."

"Thank you." Christel was truly awed by her cousin's determination to make this a good day for her. Even though she knew every fiber of Ravyn wanted a large and very extravagant event, something she'd been denied with her hasty wedding in The Duchess' parlor.

They broke into a canter, the men following, and headed for the dressmakers. She envisioned the dress she planned, the one she'd left behind. Its simplicity was its beauty. Perhaps it could be replicated. The gown certainly wouldn't take very long to create.

Carriages zipped by on the busy London streets as hawkers cried out their wares. The hustle and bustle was far different from the laziness of Hyde Park. As they rode through the streets, Ravyn's grin stretched across her face. Christel wondered how she fared living in the wilderness of America. The social butterfly had not wilted though. She seemed to thrive and radiate. Amorica the same, she was beautiful and the two of them clearly loved their husbands. And the love was reciprocated. Christel supposed that where one lived didn't really matter if one was happy.

Christel watched Ryder with wonder. Did he love her or just feel sorry for her? Perhaps the need to protect had overcome his personal desires, for he was a man who rarely stayed in one place longer than a month. The month had come and gone.

Ryder was still here, still trying to find a time and a place to marry her. But he was fighting a foe and she knew he would remain with her until he won. After that..." she had no idea what would happen when Richy was no longer a threat.

"See, we are here." Ravyn said, and in a second, she'd dismounted.

"And is that The Duchess peering out the window with Aidan beside her?" Amorica laughed. "She is so cute and headstrong. I wonder where Blade is. He rarely leaves her side."

"Take care, Christel, and be very careful. We know Richy is in the city and we know he is evil. I see The Duchess has taken precautions. Those are her men." Ryder pointed at the two men standing guard at the door to the dressmakers.

"I will," Christel promised, a feeling of dread pooling in her stomach. "See that you are careful too. I have a sick feeling about all of this."

"All will be fine." With that said, Ryder turned his horse and Damian and Aric following suit, headed north out of town.

"I do wonder what they are up to," Amorica said as she and Christel dismounted and tied their horses to the post.

"There you girls are. We've been waiting." The Duchess wrapped her arm through Christel's and hustled her inside the room where fashion plates and fabric adorned several tables.

"Good afternoon," they seemed to say in unison.

"First, we will work on Christel's dress, but you girls also look for suitable bridesmaid's dresses." The Duchess clapped her hands together, an angelic expression gracing her face, "This is going to be so much fun. I've wanted to do this for so long. When my Richard decides to get married, I won't be able to do this for him, so I have to enjoy this moment with my nieces."

Christel had been in dress shops before, this one included, but she'd never felt this overwhelmed. She turned around then again, wondering where to start. "I..." she began.

"I'm Madame Bernadine, but you may call me Bernadine." She

motioned to a table at the far right. "These plates are for the bride to look at and the fabrics on these two tables are quite suitable to the patterns. After you've had a few moments to peruse the stack, we can see what colors will make the bride glow."

Ravyn did a little jig. "I'm so excited. Look at all of these." She held up a dark blue velvet. Against her porcelain skin, the shade was gorgeous.

"Remember, this time is for Christel." Amorica spoke in older sister mode even though the girls were not sisters.

"Of course, it's just that someone has to be excited for Christel. She is so solemn. I'd like to put a rosy blush on her cheeks," Aidan put in her thoughts. "If I could think of something bawdy to say, I wouldn't hesitate a moment."

Christel smiled at her cousins, knowing she should be at least as enthusiastic as they were, but it was hard. Moisture threatened in the back of her throat as she tried to put on a happy façade. She sat down at the table meant for her and sifted through the fashion plates but not seeing anything through the tears in her eyes.

"Perhaps a bit of nourishment would help." Bernadine carried a tray of tea and some little strawberry tarts to the girls, letting each one help herself.

"This is perfect." The Duchess said, seeming to take in everything that was going on around the room.

Christel sat up straighter and once again smiled. "I was famished. Thank you so much."

"You're welcome." Bernadine appeared pleased with herself as she set the tray down. "I believe this one would be nice with your figure. It is more conservative than some of the others, and I'm sensing you do not want to have anything gaudy. Am I right?"

Christel felt a wave of relief wash through her body. "Yes, how did you know?"

"Can I say a little bird told me? Now I want you to know that some of these we have already sewn for you to try on. The Duchess told us to go ahead and stitch them up just for you. We guessed at your measurements, and if I say so myself, looking at you, we came quite close."

She motioned to a rack where some premade dresses hung. "If you would like to try any of these on, please feel free. You're not obligated to purchase any. We already have buyers for a couple of the gowns if they don't appeal to you."

"Oh my, I think I need another cup of tea."

"Take your time. If you find nothing you like today, we'll try again tomorrow." Bernadine looked to the backroom. "There are hundreds of patterns. But I do hope you find what you like. Dress shopping can be time consuming as well as exhausting."

Well, Christel couldn't agree more, but she wasn't sure if she was exhausted from all that happened the last few weeks or just the idea of sitting in this shop. She looked through the gowns hanging on the racks and three she thought she'd like to try. "I like these a lot."

"Fine choices." Bernadine plucked them from the dress rack then carried them to a fitting room.

"You'll be so beautiful." The Duchess clapped her hands, a smile spreading across her face.

"Gorgeous." Amorica set her tea on the table.

"Perfection." Ravyn threw her arms wide. "All of those fit your personality."

"Absolutely beautiful," Aidan echoed their sentiments.

"Now, to the fitting room." Bernadine pointed the way, "Who wants to help?"

~ * ~

Ryder, Damian and Aric rode through London and toward the late earl's estate. The filth and dirt of London gave way to a picturesque landscape. Sun beat down and a few clouds dotted the blue sky.

Energy surged through Ryder, nerves seemed to vibrate within while he anticipated the night to come. "Richy has piled up more debt than ever before. I wonder if what he won will come close to paying it all back."

"He has a black mark etched on his name he won't be able to rid himself of," Aric said.

"That's good for us. I'm willing to bet he'll try to get inside the estate sometime in the next few days. Otherwise, he could end up in Newgate prison. We can't forget the prize money from his long shot at the racetrack."

Ryder smiled then laughed loud and hard at the irony. "Newgate is where he should have ended up months ago, but alas, he was in my territory and my clan let him go. I'm responsible but I do hope Cameron and his clan find him. A life of hard work is just what he needs."

"It was an infatuated young woman who didn't have the sense god gave to her," Ryder said, "but I'm not giving the girl a pass. She needs to be held accountable for what she did too."

"As you say, doesn't excuse anything. She knew he was locked up for a reason," Aric said.

Ryder didn't like the arguing and he understood just how persuasive Richy could be. "He's a charming devil and always prided himself in his ability to woo a lady. This was a lass of just sixteen. She had no experience to help her make the decision."

"My apologies. I know you don't want to think about what could've been," Aric said.

"No apology needed. For now, we need to concentrate on the task at hand." Ryder looked over his shoulder at Damian. "Where is this entrance?"

"Actually, there are two. That's why The Duchess sent men ahead of us. We thought we should secure each one."

"And they are?" Ryder lifted one eyebrow as he stared at his friend.

"One is in the stables, the extra room for the groomsman, in the closet. And the other is a bit farther from the home. It's located in a small hut about a mile east of the house. They were built when the castle was burned to the ground in some war. But the escape routes have been there for centuries.

"Bloody hell, if we are to catch Richy, we cannot afford to be too obvious. If he sees any sign that someone is watching the house or the escape holes, he'll bolt. If that happens, we might never see him again."

Ryder wiped the sweat from his forehead. Different strategies congealed in his brain. He knew he was far too personally involved in this to lead. "Damian, I need you to take charge of this mission. I will help out but I'm afraid my head is too muddled and the fear in my gut is not about me but about Christel and Liam. What if we have this all wrong and he's at The Duchess' townhouse right now, taking Christel or her son?"

"Ryder, he wants money not extra baggage. The only reason he would take Christel would be for leverage against you," Damian pointed out, regarding him closely as if he was testing him.

"They are well guarded as is the house," Aric meant to give reassurances.

"That doesn't put me at ease. If I can't see Christel and Liam, I'm in constant terror." Ryder swallowed hard, his nerves stretched thin and he stared at the horizon as they rode.

"I understand that feeling all too well. When Amorica was taken by the pirates...God I never thought I would see her again. She was so strong and determined she would come home to me, or die trying," Damian said.

"It's the last part you said that has me terrified. I think Christel would die trying to save her child." The sun hung low in the sky, and Ryder knew they would arrive at the estate soon.

"I understand too. I vividly recall the night Ravyn left me and set off for Baltimore. She'd talked Damian into going with her," Aric said.

"And I was sure you meant to kill me, "Damian laughed, "but I knew if you'd taken her, he would have murdered you the moment he saw you and not waited for an explanation.

"Yes, if I recall, she asked me first." Ryder gave a snort. "You didn't know how wonderful your wife was until you almost lost her."

"I admit it. I was a fool," Aric said. "And, just as Damian concluded, I would've killed you."

"That's why I refused." Ryder shifted in the saddle, straining to look down the road. "I'm not a stupid man and I was thinking of Christel but even that explanation would have never kept you from killing me."

Damian put his hand up to stop the others. "We need to split up here. I'll go to the cabin with Ryder. Aric, you go to the stables. Try to find a place to conceal yourself and the horse."

Aric nodded. "What do you want me to do if I see him."

"Grab him."

"And let the Bow Street Runners take him in? Those are the other men The Duchess has surrounding the place."

"Bloody hell, I'd like to catch the idiot and wring his neck." Ryder didn't want to miss his capture. He'd fight pirates, storms, anything that might keep him from marrying Christel, but he didn't want his love placed in any kind of danger.

"She'll be fine," Damian said. "Aric, God speed."

Aric nodded then turned off the main road to make his way through the forested area that skirted the estate.

"So..." Ryder began then stopped. "Where are we going?"

"The opposite direction. I found this broken down hut on a stormy night. Amorica and I needed a shelter from the rain. The entrance to the tunnels is in the stables. Bloody hell, but Amorica threatened to shoot me that night."

"She didn't though," Ryder laughed.

"No, but I discovered how much she despised smugglers."

"With all the good we did?" Ryder found little humor in the memories. On several occasions they'd nearly been caught. Smuggling French brandy had been a ruse to cover up what they were really doing, smuggling political and religious refugees from European countries.

"I did enjoy the brandy and I like to think we saved lives or changed them for the better," Damian said.

They turned off the road and followed a narrow deer trail through the woods. Cobwebs seemed to jump out and attack them. Ryder would brush one from his face to find another wrapped around him.

"Were you and Amorica the last ones to ride through here?" Ryder asked as he wiped a spidery web from his face for the umpteenth time.

"It's possible."

"What if..." Thoughts raced through Ryder's head, and the lighthearted banter of the last few minutes vaporized.

"What if this hut is where Richy is staying?

"How far away are we?" Ryder didn't want to believe they'd lost this battle before the fight began. If Richy saw them coming he'd know...

"Not far."

"We need to go the rest of the way on foot, Damian."

"We can leave the horses and come back for them." Damian dismounted, leading his horse off the path and found a safe place where they could tie their mounts and walk to the hut.

Darkness enveloped them, tree trunks even darker than the night, their shade masking the sunlight above. "Bloody hell, I can barely see my hand, Damian."

"It's only a few more yards."

As they emerged from the thick forest, a faint light flickered behind dilapidated walls. "Damian put his hand out to hold him back. Shh..."

"He's there?" The mission couldn't be this easy. "Something is wrong."

"Yeah."

Staying to the rear of the house they cautiously approached. Ryder inhaled a long breath as he clenched his fists, ready for a fight. "What now?"

"There is a window in the front. Let me go first."

His back pressed against the frame of the house, pistol in hand, Damian slid toward the front. Bathed in shadows, he moved slowly. At the window he peered inside.

"Good God, Ryder."

Ryder stepped next to Damian. Inside the dimly lit room he saw Rose, the cook's daughter. "Do you think he kidnapped her?"

"No, you would have heard when Owen came to town. He said nothing. Perhaps no one knew she'd left with him."

"She followed the bastard. And what has he done to her?" Ryder's anger grew. "I'll see she gets home. She can go with Owen when he leaves." Ryder threw open the door, hearing Rose's gasp.

"Careful," Damian's words of caution came too late.

Horses' whinnies shot through the night air. "He knows we're here."

Ryder let out a loud whistle, Damian followed suit. This time the sound of hooves pounding the earth came to them on the night breeze. Ryder's horse stopped then rose on hind legs, pawing the air.

"Bastards!"

Ryder whistled through his teeth. "Guess Richy didn't count on us retrieving our horses."

"A trick one needs when smuggling." Damian laughed.

"We missed our chance," Ryder said. "Rose, you have to come with us. Richy won't return here for you."

"But he loves me," Rose said, standing. "I want to stay here with him."

"The rake doesn't love anyone. He doesn't know the meaning of the word." Ryder gathered Rose's belongings.

"I'm not going with you. He will be back." She stood with her hands balled, a determined expression on her face.

"What will you do if he doesn't? Can you take that chance?" Damian asked. "You'll starve."

"I don't believe you," she said but her voice was weak and quivering.

"I think you do." Ryder held out his hand for her to take. "If he truly loves you, he'll know where to find you. Come on, lass."

She gave what seemed to be one last look at the tiny one room hut and walked toward Ryder, accepting his hand. "Where will you take me?"

"I'm sure The Duchess will find a room for you and you can help Christel with Liam. We'll take you back to MacLaren castle when we leave."

"She did have a baby?" Rose followed Damian and Ryder from the hut and accepted a hand up to ride behind Damian.

"Yes, and we were all pleased to find him happy and healthy." Ryder knew he couldn't talk about their plans for Richy. He didn't understand how the girl could have such faith in the bastard.

They retraced the trail they rode in on, finding the main road. The moon was a sliver and stars sprinkled the sky with tiny lights. A few hours later they arrived at the townhouse.

"Aric? Is he back?"

"He hasn't returned." One of The Duchess's men told them.

"Do you think Richy tried to get inside through the stables?" Damian asked.

"I didn't think he would be that foolish but..."

"He's a desperate man, Ryder. He'd try anything for money. We both know he's in debt to most of the ton."

"But tonight? After he was almost caught?"

"I'd bet on it."

~ * ~

"Bastards!" Richy had not expected anyone to find Rose, but the burning question was whether or not Ryder knew of the tunnel to his estate that exited in the barn.

He heaved a long sigh. He'd enjoyed Rose, sex with the young lady anyway; losing her did not make him happy. And he'd thought when he let the horses go, Ryder and Damian would be on foot. Leave it to those two...they always landed on their feet. With one whistle their horses had returned to them.

His heart had been in his throat when he'd seen the Bow Street Runners skulking around the estate. He'd meant to make a quick clean entrance to the house but the risk was too steep, so he rode back to the hut only to find Damian and Aric there ahead of him.

Luck had been on his side though. At least they hadn't caught him, but now he had nothing to pawn. No one would take an IOU from him, and he'd spent all his winnings.

"What now?" He needed to take a moment to figure this all out, but he didn't think he had the time. The law seemed to be bearing down on him.

Voices floated along the road, a surge of fear shivering down Richy's bones. He veered off the road and into the forested area. Dismounting, he walked his horse as far from the road as he could before the men drew abreast of him.

"We keep lookin'."

"Hate reporting bad news."

Ah, that was Aric Lakeland. So, they had everyone looking for him. Richy smiled. Despite all of Ryder's efforts, he'd eluded every one of them. He'd bested Damian Andrews and Ryder MacLaren once again. He puffed out his chest, his ego for a moment getting the better of him.

He drew in a quick breath and let the sensation glide through him. Damian, Ryder, Aric, they didn't have anything he didn't. Well, except money and the girl. But he intended to get both. He'd best them if it was the last thing he accomplished.

The forest provided a measure of security, but he needed to find shelter. London wasn't going to work out. If anyone spotted him, they'd ferret out The Duchess or Ryder.

Where then? The Half Penny Inn came to mind. The inn's usual clientele consisted of cutthroats and prostitutes. But he didn't think anyone would look for him there. He pulled the document from his satchel and read it over. It certainly looked authentic to him.

Oh, yes, he had a surprise in store for Ryder MacLaren and the bitch, Christel.

Chapter Twelve

"It's here!" Aidan flounced into Christel's bedroom and plopped on the bed. "Aren't you so excited?"

Christel couldn't help but grin at her littlest sister and the exuberance she portrayed, yet her heart wasn't in the same place. "I would feel better if they'd caught Richy. I don't see how one man can elude so many for so long."

"You always thought of him as a weasel. He's just living up to his name." Aidan grabbed a berry from a plate. "You know Ryder will find him. It's just taking him longer than we hoped."

"I'm beginning to have doubts, but I'll be happy if he doesn't show up at the ceremony and claim me as his wife. Who knows what he'd intend. The girl, Rose, said he showed her a marriage certificate and it looked real." Christel thought of Liam and the others affected by this scandal. And it wasn't gossip. Everything was true.

"The Duchess has a plan for that. Your wedding will not be ruined by the likes of Richy Rathen, that scoundrel."

Scarlet appeared at the door and bobbed a curtsy. "Your bath is ready for you."

"Thank you, I'll be right there."

Aidan waved her on. "Go relax, and I'll see to Liam and my bath. The Duchess bought a special darling suit for the little man. It's in the height of fashion."

Another knock on the door and Bernadine's girls swooped through the room with her wedding dress. Christel touched the fabric, sliding her hand down the length. "It's so beautiful."

The gown was made of pale blue over a silver sarsnet slip. The body was cut low and square around the bust and was tight to the shape. It was trimmed around the bosom and the back with a silver rouleau of crape with sapphire beads. The bottom of the skirt was cut in broad scallops, the edges of which were ornamented with silver trimming and an embroidery of crape roses. The headdress was a long veil and an elegant silver ornament consisting of a rose and an aigrette.

"Thank you," the girls nodded.

"We worked all week on this one and your bridesmaids' dresses too."

"Well, you did a wonderful job."

"I can't wait to see my gown." Aidan rushed from the room then suddenly peeked in the door. "I'll be right back to take care of Liam."

"Oh, don't worry about the babe. I've got him." Rose stood in the doorway; Liam perched on one hip and playing with her hair.

"Thank you so much." Aidan dashed from the doorway in a swirl of petticoats and red hair flying.

"Where does she get the energy?" Christel laughed as she slipped from her day dress. "I'd like half of it."

"She's still young and the weight of the world has not landed on her slim shoulders. Now enjoy your bath, let it wash away all of your cares." The Duchess stood inside the room, hands folded in front of her. "If I have any say what so ever, Rathen will not find his way inside the church. You need to be ready in an hour. We will pack your dress and you can put it on when we get there."

With that said, The Duchess left the room almost as abruptly as Aidan had a few minutes earlier.

Suddenly alone, Christel let one tear fall, wiped it away then smiled. She stepped into the bath. Warm water eased all of her aches and pains. With eyes closed, she dreamed of the conclusion of the day, the happiness she found with Ryder. He'd never told her he loved her. But then she'd never said the words either, at least not to him. Perhaps it was about time to do just that.

Her clothes for the carriage ride were laid out on the bed. Amorica and Ravyn would meet her at the church. Aidan and The Duchess would ride with her. Amorica helped her with her makeup, a tint to her eyes, something to darken her lashes and a light tint to her lips.

Precautions had been taken to keep the carriage from falling into Richy's hands, but really the man had no money. If Richy had hired ruffians to waylay them, he would have to have given the men promises, and if any knew of him, they would not risk their lives for a cause that would fail.

No, if Richy meant to ruin her day, it would be in a subtle manner. Again though, The Duchess had told her he would not be able to get into the church. There were posted guards, but she'd also been told he'd never get out of the castle.

A keening wail above her, she sat up and opened her eyes. The MacLaren ghost hovered in the corner of the bathing room and wept. Her tears were not of joy but sorrow. Christel felt as if a dark shadow possessed her. She inhaled a long deep breath, closing her eyes and saying a quick prayer.

"Are you here to frighten me?" Christel held a washrag across her chest as she spoke to the ghost who didn't answer but faded into the woodwork.

Enough, the water had turned cold and her fingers looked like prunes. Christel rose and grabbed the large bath sheet that had been set nearby. She dried herself quickly and pulled on her chemise. Ringing the bell, Scarlet appeared in a second as if she'd been standing by the door waiting.

"You're ready?" Scarlet asked.

"I believe so." Yet in truth she wasn't because she understood now that something bad was going to happen.

Her carriage dress was beautiful. The Duchess had given her best instructions as to the construction of this dress. It was made of lavender Merino with gigot sleeves. Christel picked up the little pink kid gloves then set them down.

"It is beautiful, Miss Christel."

She ran her hand down one of the two deep flounces, which were made from the same material as the dress, beaded and edged with a shawl pattern border of roses. "It is. But the gown is far more elaborate than what I'd imagined."

"Look at the cloak," Scarlet unhooked it from its hangar. "It's just a bit darker lavender than the dress."

Christel knew the color would bring out the color of her eyes and highlight her hair. "It's lined with ermine."

"For the chilly night when you leave your celebration," Scarlet said. "You'll be going to your wedding night. It has to be very special."

"Yes..." she picked up one of the shoes, which was a dark chestnut kid, then turned it over in her hand.

"You ready?"

Christel swallowed hard, determined to see this through. The marriage was what she wanted, but what did Ryder want? She still didn't know the answer and the weeping ghost had put a horrible damper and a decided chill on the upcoming festivities. She prayed the apparition did not cry because she was about to wed the MacLaren or because Richy was going to appear and create havoc at her wedding.

A while later, Christel sat at the dresser, wearing her carriage dress but not the cape. Scarlet arranged her hair, pulling it up and decorating it with a string of emeralds.

Scarlet stepped back, "You are so beautiful."

"Thank you, but I'm frightened, no terrified."

"Don't be. All will turn out as you wish. The Duchess—"

"Has everything in control. I know." But her heart fluttered in her throat and goose bumps rose on her arms. "There are guards. No one will ruin my wedding day. So, why don't I feel better?'

"It's up to you to enjoy and put your fears to bed."

With a deep breath, Christel walked from the room and down the stairs. In the parlor, The Duchess and Aidan sat and waited, both with expectant looks on their faces.

"Come," The Duchess rose and Christel followed. "The carriage waits outside. You are beautiful."

"Oh..." Aidan clapped her hands together while she jumped up and down like a schoolgirl.

Aidan had a way of always making her laugh. "Thank you." It seemed to Christel she said those words so many times.

"It will take about twenty minutes to get to the church. The

177

ceremony will follow as soon as we are ready."

This was it. Christel closed her eyes for a second then opening them, she followed The Duchess from the townhouse and into the carriage.

For Christel the minutes to the church ticked by in a cloudy haze. Everything passed by in a blur of colors. The Duchess and Aidan chatted nonstop while her heart beat a rapid staccato.

"Christel, honey," The Duchess said. "Christel..."

"What? Oh my, we are here."

"It's about time you joined the land of the living." Aidan smoothed her skirts and adjusted her cape. "You're about to marry a bonny Scotsman."

"I have a lot on my mind besides the wedding. I wish it wasn't so, but it is."

"Aren't you excited though? Aidan asked. "I know I would be if Blade was waiting in a church to marry me."

"Yes, yes I am, but my knees are shaking so hard I don't know if I can walk." Christel massaged her temples. "And my head aches. This last week has been..." she inhaled a huge breath of air, hoping to calm herself, but it didn't seem to work.

Liam stood on the seat, his hands on the window while he peered outside and pointed. He gurgled and laughed seeming to enjoy himself.

"Come, Liam, you can go with your uncles Aric and Damian. They will take care of you while we get Christel ready." The door opened and Aidan handed the little boy over to one of the guards who then handed him to Aric. Aric tossed Liam into the air.

Liam giggled. "More."

Aric obliged the little boy, tossing and catching him for a few more minutes.

Christel stepped from the carriage. "Where is Ryder?"

"You know it is bad luck to see the groom before the wedding." Aidan tapped her sister on the hand. "Now we'll go in that side door. I believe there is a room where you can change clothes. Ryder will be here. Don't you worry."

One of Bernadine's girls carried the gown and another girl the accessories that were made to go with it.

Christel pulled in a deep breath and tried to smile. "Still, I would feel better if I knew he was here, if I could see him."

"I don't know where he and Damian are, but they will arrive shortly I'm told." The Duchess set off for the church without looking back, her steps crisp, her back straight as if she didn't have a care in the world.

Aidan giggled then picked up her skirt so she could run to catch up to The Duchess. "We better get going. If we don't, I'm sure there'll be hell to pay."

Christel grinned. The one thing her littlest sister had always been able to do was make her forget any troubles she had. Nothing had changed. In a more dignified manner, Christel followed.

Inside the church it was dark, but a woman entered and lit several candles. Bernadine's girls hung the dress then set their attentions to Christel. Aidan quickly dressed in her gown of lavender silk. Scarlet had fixed her hair, but in Aidan fashion, some of the locks had come undone.

"Christel, do not worry about your little sister. Come..."

"Hold up your arms," one of the girls said.

Christel did as was told, and the pale blue gown slipped over her head.

"It's beautiful. You're beautiful. Ryder will be beside himself." Aidan clapped her hands, bouncing in her seat and another errant lock of hair fell from its pins.

"Thank you." For the first time since this crazy ride had started almost two years ago, Christel felt as if her life would be good. She heard a soft noise and in the corner of the room the MacLaren ghost hummed.

She didn't weep.

She looked at her dress; the perfection, the skill, she'd never seen anything finer. It must have cost The Duchess more than a few pounds.

The Duchess touched up her hair. "I believe you are ready to say your vows. I've never seen any bride more lovely than you, Christel. You and Ryder will live a long wonderful life together. I'm sure of it."

Amorica and Ravyn entered the room. "Are you ready? We need to get you married so we can celebrate."

Christel nodded then smiled as she inhaled a deep breath. "The two of you are so beautiful. Is everyone here?"

"You mean Ryder?" Amorica asked, grinning.

"He is waiting for you at the altar." Ravyn smiled and motioned for Christel to follow them.

"Come." Dignified and not bothering to hide the smile on her face, The Duchess led the way.

They walked around the church to its front. The Bow Street Runners surrounded the building. A sense of relief washed through her. Richy could not get in to create havoc. He could not ruin this beautiful day. For the sun was shining brightly and it wasn't too warm but just right. The MacLaren ghost seemed to be pleased with the events transpiring.

Inside the church The Duchess gave a nod of her head and music began to play. Aidan started down the aisle, then Ravyn, then Amorica and to Christel's surprise, Allura was beside her, giving her a hug before she too walked down the aisle.

Jessie, Amorica's little boy, the ring bearer, and Lyssa, the flower girl, followed them. When Christel stepped up and looked inside the church, the pews were filled. She knew very few of the people, and she could only assume they were friends of The Duchess.

The Duchess took her arm and they started a slow march to meet her groom. Ryder stood in the front, a broad grin across his handsome face. He didn't appear nervous, but she knew her anxiety was enough for both of them.

Once again, the events seemed to pass in a blur. She stood beside Ryder and handed her bouquet of forget-me-nots and white roses to Allura. On the other side of Ryder, Aric, Damian and Hunter, Allura's husband, stood in attendance. Allura and her family had arrived unexpectedly that morning.

Except for her father, her family was all here. A gut feeling sent her gaze to the corner of the church. Yes, her MacLaren ghost was in attendance too. She almost burst out in laughter but held herself in check.

Richy Rathen was not here. Relief swept through her. Once she wed Ryder, he would have no hold over her, save the child they shared. The only interest he held for the boy was his trust fund, his inheritance and that terrified her because he didn't need Liam alive to regain the fortune left to her little boy.

"Do you take this man to be your husband?" The priest asked.

Allura nudged her in the back. "Christel," she said.

"What? Oh!"

"Do you take this man, Ryder MacLaren, to be your husband?"

"Yes." She looked up at Ryder, her hands held in his, the ring on her finger. Where had she been?

Lost in thought and she'd missed most of the wedding.

"You may kiss the bride."

Ryder lowered his mouth to hers and lightly kissed her on the lips. The marriage was sealed now. Forever and for always.

"I pronounce you husband and wife."

They turned, Allura handed her the bouquet and they walked down the aisle. She smiled as her heart raced with happiness.

~ * ~

Ryder had spent the better part of the day chasing down leads that went nowhere. He had raced to dress for the ceremony. As he stood at the altar watching Christel walk down the aisle, The Duchess holding her arm, he knew he'd never been so in love.

She was a vision that made his heart catch in his throat. Weak at the knees, he wanted to hold on to something to steady himself, instead he straightened and smiled at his bride.

When he was finally told he could kiss the bride, he felt the world had come full circle and everything was right. The kiss was sweet, a daytime kiss that held the promise of so much more.

"Christel, you are so damn beautiful." His whisper made her open her eyes and smile at him. With that said, they turned and walked down the aisle to greet family and friends then on to the townhouse for the celebration.

They stood outside the church and hugged and kissed all who walked by. The sun shone down on them, a slight breeze ruffled the leaves on trees that shaded them. Birds sung in the sky overhead.

Once all the guests made it through the receiving line, The Duchess took charge again and signaled for the carriages. Theirs was decorated with flowers and streamers. The driver hopped down and opened the door.

Ryder helped Christel in then followed and shut the door. Cheers rang out as the carriage began to move.

"We made it," Christel inhaled a long deep breath, before letting it out slowly. "Finally."

"We did." Ryder pulled Christel into his arms. His lips found hers then he traced the seam with his tongue. He wanted nothing more than to sweep her into his arms and carry her to the bedroom.

She opened for him, their tongues dancing an ancient rhythm of passion and love. His fingers inched their way into her hair, a wisp falling free as the kiss deepened. Christel gave a tiny little moan of pleasure, her hands winding around his neck, pulling him closer.

Tracing kisses across her cheek to her ear, he explored the column of her neck.

"Ryder..."

"What, my wife?"

"The Duchess will have your hide if you ruin my hair and everyone will know what we were doing."

He moved away from her, his heart filled with pride and love, "Everyone will know anyway."

"But it doesn't have to be quite this obvious." She laughed, enjoying the expression on her new husband's face.

"All right then, I'll wait." He moved away from her, a silly grin forming on his lips.

She tried to pull the loose pieces back into place but couldn't. "Damn."

"Do you need any help?"

"Yes, and why do you look so smug?"

"Because your lips are swollen from my kisses," he put his hand on her breast. "Your heart races and I know you want me as much as I want you."

"Are you going to help?" she asked, turning away from him for a moment as if to assess what he'd just said.

"Of course." In a matter of seconds, he had the hair back in place and secure. "See, when you have me, you don't need a ladies' maid."

She laughed. "Arrogant."

"Am I right?"

"Yes..."

"Then I'm not arrogant, just honest." He laughed outright at the perplexed look on her face, wanting to start all over again with kisses and sex and passion filled nights. Yet he understood all too well that he couldn't relax, at least not until they returned home or Richy was found.

"No, you're the least egotistical man I've ever known." She touched his lips with a fingertip. "What are you thinking?"

"Do I dare tell you?" His laughter filled the carriage.

"Do you dare not?"

"When you say it that way, I was thinking about you naked on my bed, your hair spread out around you."

"I, well I didn't, wasn't...I'm speechless."

"You're blushing," he said, softly nipping at her ear then running his tongue around the tiny shell.

"I don't mean to..."

"We're here," he announced, placing another kiss on her mouth.

"Thank God, I do believe I'd melt if this went on a moment longer."

The door was opened and The Duchess and her cousins and sister stood in a line toward the door of the townhouse.

Upstairs in the ballroom, musicians played. A feast complimented the tables, the aroma fabulous. Then the sound of bagpipes filled the air. Ryder couldn't help but grin. He pulled Christel into his arms and danced with her, spinning her until she sounded breathless.

She pleaded, "I cannot breathe." He slowed the dance and brought her tight into his arms, loving the feel of her breasts pressed against his chest, the movement of her body in sync with his.

"Ah, Christel, this is heaven." He bent over and whispered close to her ear.

"I want this moment to last forever, but I'm famished."

"Then it is food you'll receive," he told her.

He helped her with a plate then prepared another for himself. They found the table where The Duchess, Allura and Aidan sat eating. Hunter was on his way to the table with two servings.

"Ummm... This is good." Christel popped a bite of roast beef into her mouth and chewed slowly.

Conversation seemed to vanish as they ate their meal and watched their friends celebrate.

Ryder stood and held out his hand to Christel. "Come, let's go for a walk."

She placed her hand in his, smiling. "I'd like that."

His heart turned over. He wanted more than a walk. They made their way down the stairs to the first floor then onto the terrace behind the townhouse. "Alone at last."

"Not entirely."

Shadows moved through the trees, and Ryder supposed they were the men The Duchess had hired to guard the house. "No, but for now this is the best it's going to get."

The night air was balmy and a slight breeze sifted through the leaves on the trees above. Ryder wrapped one arm around Christel's shoulder as he guided her through the grounds toward the little gazebo. Roses bloomed and their scent filled the air.

Christel rested her head on his chest then put her arm around his waist. "Are you happy?"

"I've never been happier," he turned her then bent to kiss her.

She moved into him and gave him what he sought. His hands found the small of her back, and he pulled her to him. Sighing with the pleasure and the passion he felt for this beautiful woman. His wife.

"And you?" he queried softly as he placed kisses down her neck and across her collarbone. "Did I tell you how beautiful you are?"

"Not lately."

"You, my sweet one, are beautiful." He found his way back to her mouth then deepened his kiss, pulling her closer and letting his hand settle on her breast. He squeezed gently as his tongue traced the seam of her lips then entered. He wanted her naked. Soon...

They'd have to say their good nights upstairs, and of course the jests that would follow but the sooner the better.

"Ryder, Christel, where are you? All hell is breaking out in the ballroom. You have to..." Aidan pulled up at the gazebo, bent over at the waist, heaving air. Her elegantly styled hair was in disarray around her shoulders. Blade followed. "I ran..."

Ryder sat back his arm falling from Christel's shoulder. "What is it?

"It's Richy..."

"Oh, my God," Christel said.

"I'll kill him," Ryder clenched his fists at his sides then ran his fingers through his hair.

"No," both girls said as one.

"He says he's married to Christel. Can that be true?" Aidan asked.

"No, we never wed. I fled before he could rape me again."

"He's gone crazy and he's waving what he claims to be a certificate of marriage to you. And he wants the child." Aidan seemed to get her breath back.

"That's what it's all about. The inheritance and becoming the trustee of his father's estate." Ryder waited a moment, thinking. "I want the two of you to go back to the house, but I don't want you anywhere close to the ballroom. Go to my room and wait for me."

"But..."

"Check on Liam and make sure he's fine and that Richy hasn't found a way to spirit him from the townhouse." Ryder raced toward the house and hoped Christel and Aidan would follow. He wasn't worried about them. Richy was obviously in the ballroom trying to convince everyone Ryder's and Christel's marriage was a fraud.

Two steps at a time brought Ryder to the ballroom in just a few minutes. He burst into the room to see Richy in the center, turning circles with the paper above his head.

"There you are." Richy seemed to finally notice him, spittle flying from his lips, his eyes dark sunken pools.

"What are you doing here where you are not welcome?" Ryder stepped closer to the man, wishing he could strangle him and be done with this pompous ass.

"Come to claim my bride and my son."

"You have no wife. You never married Christel, and I'm sure a thorough search of church documents will prove this. And you have no son. You abandoned him over a year ago."

Richy turned in circles, his arms waving. "I demand Christel and our son come with me tonight."

"You raped her and your father lied to her, telling her the son she bore was stillborn." Ryder's fists clenched tightly, his body tensing for a fight. "You deserve nothing."

"I married the slut." Richy held out the certificate, shaking it at Ryder. "See this. It says she's mine."

"Christel will never be yours. And if for some ludicrous reason this is valid, which I don't believe, then I will have it annulled."

"I will have to agree to a disillusion of the marriage, and I will never do that," Richy shouted.

"If necessary, you will." Calmness settled over Ryder. This man would never touch his Christel. He was a coward and the tiniest confrontation would send him on his way. At the moment Richy believed he had the upper hand, but he didn't.

"Let me see that." The Duchess stepped forward and grabbed the paper from Richy before he could keep it away.

She studied the document for so long sweat beaded on Ryder's forehead and slipped from his neck down his back. "Duchess?"

"It has a seal, a very official looking seal but...I will have this checked out. There seems to be something wrong."

"No!" Richy grabbed the certificate from The Duchess' hands. "You will not. Where is she? Where is Christel and my son? They will come with me now."

"As I said, she is not going anywhere with you." Ryder towered over Richy, his tone so menacing Richy stepped back.

"Then I will return in the morning with the constables. I will have everything that is mine."

"I am not yours." Christel appeared in the room. "And neither is Liam. We were never married and if you try to take me, I'll kill you."

"You have no valid and legal claim." Ryder said, wanting nothing more than to kick him from the room and wishing Christel had done what he'd asked and stayed downstairs.

Aric and Damian made their presence known, and one man on each side of Richy grabbed his arms then ushered him from the room and Ryder assumed from the townhouse.

"How did he get in here?" Ryder turned to The Duchess who appeared just as perplexed as he felt.

~ * ~

At the top of the porch, Aric and Damian shoved Richy Rathen down the steps. "Don't come back," Damian said. "If we could legally haul you back to the MacLaren dungeon, we would."

Richy picked himself off the concrete and dusted his hands on his pants, a sneer on his lips. "You'll regret this."

"No, I doubt it," Aric said. "If you want to leave London in one piece, don't bother Christel and Ryder again. For that matter, any of the MacLaren clan, including little Liam."

"You can't get rid of me that easily." Richy looked at the certificate then set off down the street. He needed to get back to the Inn and figure out how he was going to convince them this piece of paper was authentic.

You idiot. Richy called himself every name he could think of. *You didn't expect them to just hand the chit and the boy over, did you?*

He pulled a few coins from his pockets, staring at them for a few seconds. He made a bit of money gambling in a tavern outside the city. It had been enough to rent a horse and pay someone to fake the certificate. Now he had to find a roof over his head.

He was tired of living in poverty. The slums just didn't work for him. He was used to servants and his women, well, one who didn't have lice infested hair and beds. Damn the earl for disowning him. Bloody hell, his estate and wealth should have been his.

As he walked toward the Thames, he felt a few fat drops of rain hit him. Before he knew it, a downpour had him soaked. He ducked inside a tavern and found a seat in the corner. He didn't dare spend a single coin on food or drink. If he did, he wouldn't have funds for a room.

This wasn't supposed to be happening to him. He was meant to be the lord of the manor.

"Can I get you anything?" A serving girl stood in front of the table. It was clear to Richy she might be willing to share herself if he bought a pint. He felt in his pockets for the coins and pulled one out, knowing he might spend the night outside in the elements.

"A pint of ale and you?" he asked, trying to use all of his charm. Bloody hell, but he wasn't sure he had any charm left. It certainly hadn't been working lately.

He wondered if he could sneak into his father's townhouse, or would that home be guarded as diligently as the country home?

He closed his eyes, rubbing his temples and wishing for an answer.

"Scum! You've eluded us far too long."

Three burly Scotsmen stood over him.

Chapter Thirteen

Christel cuddled Liam close, hoping he would not sense her fear. She wiped tears from her eyes.

"How many times?" Ryder questioned, striding to Christel and pulling both her and the child into his arms. "How many times must I tell you all will be fine?"

"Dinna worry," Christel laid her head against Ryder's chest. "I believe in you and in the power of trust. Good will win over evil."

"It doesn't always—win," Ryder said. "But good will win this time. I promise you." He kissed her on the cheek then did the same with Liam before stepping back.

The morning sun had risen an hour earlier. Christel meant to discover how Richy had forged the document that caused so much pain. She hoped he had to sleep in the gutter.

"Look at this." Ryder held their wedding certificate in his hand. "I saw the other one briefly last night. But there was something different. I close my eyes and try to see, but it just isn't coming to me."

"Did the paper have my signature?" Christel queried.

"I'm not sure. But there was something in the space." Ryder turned and hit the wall with his fist. "I cannot remember."

Christel felt the pain and frustration deep in her heart. She knew how much Ryder needed to rectify this and put her fear of Richy in the past where it belonged. "I didn't marry him so there are no records. He cannot keep up this facade for long. Richy has no money, no home and a plethora of men wanting the money he owes."

"He has no friends, only enemies." Ryder crossed the room, his long strides carrying him to the door. He flung it open just as Damian's hand rose in the air to knock.

"Good morning," Damian stepped into the room. "How are you all holding up?"

"Good morning to you, too, and we are doing our best." Christel smiled at her friend. "Do we have a plan?"

"As soon as they are open, I will go to the registration office. They will have the records there. If they are not in the files, then we can put all this aside and carry on with our lives."

"It won't be. There will be no verification of Richy's claims." Christel knew there could be no official documentation of a marriage that never took place. Still, Richy was capable of so much and he would stop at nothing. There could be paperwork at the church, but there was no church and each parish was supposed to send copies to the registration office. Her heart felt as if it were in her stomach. She had never expected this turn of events.

"Liam is hungry. I'm going to the kitchen. You two can figure out what will happen next and how you will find Richy." Christel turned and fled the room with Liam. She hurried through the townhouse to the kitchen where she set Liam in his highchair.

"Cook, what do have for Liam?"

Rose appeared from a side door. "Good morning M'lady."

"What are you doing here?" Christel was curt, too curt and immediately regretted her words. "I'm sorry."

"It's all right. I would feel the same about me. I've learned a horrible lesson and at another's expense. I should be doin' the apologizing." Rose curtsied then set about getting food for the child.

"Is that fresh bread I smell?" Christel had not expected to feel a bit of hunger, but the aroma wafting her way had her stomach growling.

"Yes'm." Rose set a plate of scrambled eggs and a few pieces of cut up strawberries and sausage in front of the boy.

Liam dug in with his little fingers, avoiding the small fork Rose had set beside him. "Me want more."

"You can have as much as you want, little man." Christel loved the way her son took her mind off Richy, and she was so glad he didn't look like his father. The constant reminder would be more than she could bear. He actually looked like the McClellan, her father, Liam's grandfather. If he grew up to be half the man his grandfather was, he'd be a fine man.

Rose brought more of everything. "He has a good appetite."

Christel smiled then laughed as half the food found its way to the floor. "He certainly does."

"Is he walking?" Rose asked.

"Yes, a bit wobbly but I'm sure he'll be running circles around all of us in a short while."

Rose set a plate of fresh bread and strawberry preserves in front of Christel. "This is for you."

"Thank you." Christel broke off a chunk then smeared it with butter and jam. "Umm...this is heavenly. Give my thanks to Cook."

"Yes'm." Rose left the room and the two of them to their own devices.

Christel ate and watched her son. He was so remarkable, laughing and talking gibberish as he ate.

"Done, mama." Liam pushed the plate off his tray and watched with seeming curiosity as it landed on the floor, its contents falling then rolling around in a congealed muddle.

Before Christel could gather a rag to clean up the mess, Rose returned. "Don't, it's my job."

"Very well." Christel lifted Liam from his seat. "We'll be in the parlor if anyone comes looking for us."

Rose bobbed a curtsy then went back to work.

In the parlor The Duchess was sipping tea and staring at her certificate of marriage to the Duke. When she looked up, "We really need to correct Liam's birth certificate. I've sent Scarlet to do just that. I'm not sure what it says, but I'm pretty sure it will list the late earl as father. The birth may be harder to rectify than the marriage."

"My God, I never thought of that." Christel set Liam on the floor and gathered a few toys around him.

"Duchess, what am I to do? I cannot..." She was at a loss for words. What had she done to deserve this entire trauma? "Why do people hate me so?" Tears welled in her eyes.

The Duchess reached over and put her hand on top of Christel's. "They do not hate you. No one does. You have just been a victim, a person in the wrong place at the wrong time."

"I don't like that word, victim." Christel sat up straighter. "I refuse to be a victim or let Liam be one." For the first time she did not feel powerless. She'd let everyone else fight her battles.

"That's what I like to hear." The Duchess sat back, crossing her arms over her chest and stared at Christel. "So, what are we going to do?"

"Find Richy. That cannot be too hard. He has no one and has left a trail of gambling debts that should not be too hard to follow."

"Finding him might well take you into the seedier parts of London," The Duchess said with a smile forming.

"And you are planning on going with me?" Christel knew The Duchess relished excitement, but this? What had she started by proclaiming her independence? But she understood, once The Duchess made up her mind, nothing and no one could stop her.

"We will have escorts. It will not be dangerous. Go get dressed appropriately and we will be on our way. I'll make sure Scarlet takes care of Liam and keeps a watchful eye on him at all times."

Christel wondered what she meant by appropriate, and when she looked back before starting up the stairs, The Duchess winked at her. Well, that sent her head spinning. In her room a set of clothes was laid out on her bed, but they weren't her usual attire.

"Men's clothes..."

What did The Duchess have in mind? She'd worn men's clothing on numerous occasions, but with her hair and curves she didn't look much like a man. She inhaled a swift breath of air as if that would give her the needed courage.

Rose popped her head around the corner. "The Duchess sent me up here to help. I have a set of instructions."

"Oh my," was all Christel could say when she looked at herself in the mirror. She didn't look like a man but a boy, maybe in his early teen years. Aidan had helped her bind her breasts and her hair had been braided and pinned on top of her head. The hat was the finishing touch to her new look.

"Duchess." She called out as she ran down the steps to the parlor. "I'm ready."

The Duchess rose with a smile on her face. "I see that. You are quite fetching as a young man. We will create less of a disturbance with you dressed this way."

"I feel so free and light." Christel picked up Liam and kissed him on the cheek. "Be a good boy. We will return as soon as we complete our little mission." Then she set him back down.

Once inside the carriage and watching the townhouses go by, "Where should we go first?"

"If you were Richy, where would you be?" The Duchess asked, a pensive looking frown forming between her eyes.

Christel sat back on the seat, "Oh, I believe Newmarket."

"With no money to bet and no one to take his IOU?" One of The Duchess' eyebrows rose as if in speculation.

"All right then perhaps a tavern down by the river."

"There are a few on the seedier side that might serve him. He did not appear too well-kept last night when he stopped by to deliver his mouthful of lies. He smelled too."

"So, we are going to look at places of ill-repute." That thought gave Christel pause, and when she peered out the window, she wondered what Ryder would think and say when he discovered she and The Duchess had set out on this adventure.

"Those too." The Duchess touched her on the shoulder. "Are you afraid?

Was she afraid? Silence followed as Christel wondered at the undertaking she'd embarked upon and mused about the hellion The Duchess must have been in her younger years. Now she had a spark of light in her eyes and a rosy blush to her face.

The first stop garnered them no information, same as the next four. Christel began to feel as if she was on a fool's mission. "This is not getting us anywhere." Her frustration was not something she handled well.

"One more place then I don't know what to do. Perhaps we should find our way to Newmarket. Although I doubt if anyone there would do naught but give him a swift kick to the curb."

Escorted into the tavern, Christel turned up her nose at the stench. It smelled of vomit and cheap perfume. As they approached, a man stepped from behind the bar.

"Can I help you?"

"We're looking for a man. He's—oh, I think that is him." Christel walked to the corner table in the back of the room. The man was slumped over, his head resting on the table. She gave the chair a kick in hopes of waking him. A deep snore reverberated from the man as he turned his head.

"It's not him." The Duchess grabbed Christel by the arm then turned to the tavern keeper. "We are looking for Richy Rathen. Perhaps he has been here."

"You can pay his debt if you're a relative." The man's face had turned grim, and he'd stopped wiping down the bar's counter.

"We are not. He owes this young man here, and we were looking for him to collect."

"He was here last night. He can't be far," the man said, looking toward the door. "But you aren't the first to be looking for him."

A prickle of fear swept down Christel's spine. "Who? Who was looking for him?" They had to find him, had to set things right.

"A man came into the bar, found him he did. Didn't give a name but the man said Rathen owed him and he intended to collect every pound—one way or the other."

"What did he look like?" The Duchess stepped forward. "Perhaps you can remember something."

Using his hands, "Well, he was about this high and this broad. I wouldn't want to be on his bad side, and it seemed this Rathen fellow had brought down his wrath."

"Was he a Scotsman?" Christel remembered the pair from the Grizela's home that first night she left the MacLaren castle with Aidan. "Cameron?"

The tavern keeper shook his head. "Didn't give a name."

"Were there others with him?"

"Yes, another fellow was with him. He didn't say much."

If Cameron found him first, she didn't think Richy would survive the work Cameron meant to give him. Richy was a wastrel. He wouldn't be able to survive anything that was exertion. "And they were looking for him."

"We should try Newmarket. If he was down on money, he might have slept in the stables there and if not, perhaps someone there could help us find him. I do want to find him first."

The keeper ran his fingers through his hair and looked as if he had thought of something. "You know, he did mention to one of my serving girls a place outside of town where he'd been staying. But it wouldn't be safe for you two ladies, ah...well it wouldn't be safe."

He knew. Her disguise wasn't very good. She hadn't thought she could fool anyone. "Where is this place?"

He gave the name. "Horn's Creek Tavern."

"Thank you," The Duchess said then took Christel by the hand and rushed her from the establishment. Once inside the carriage, she gave directions to the driver before she leaned back on the seat laughing.

"He knew," Christel let out a belly laugh. "I didn't think..."

After the laughter finished and the tears dried, "No one is going to take him in. Let's go to Newmarket and look in the barn. If he isn't there, we can always follow his path to Horn's Creek."

"I almost feel sorry for him. If he hadn't created so much misery, I might have a penny for him."

"Don't! Never go there in thought. He is not worth a penny, and everything he is he has done to himself. He does not deserve anyone's sympathy."

"I understand. But—"

"But nothing. We will find him or find out what has happened to him."

~ * ~

Exhilaration raced through Ryder as the sound of his horse's hooves beat the earth. Earlier in the day they had heard rumors about Rathen and his whereabouts. He'd been left penniless.

Indeed, he'd fallen far to take up with this crowd of ruffians. He'd also learned Cameron had been searching for Richy. He didn't care who found him first. Either way Richy Rathen would get what he deserved—a life of honest work but for Richy. That life would seem as if he'd entered the gates of hell.

He pulled hard on the reins, slowing his horse then leaned down and rubbed him on the shoulder. "Good boy."

"I've seen better places to herd my cows," Damian said.

"This tavern wouldn't do for anyone's cows," Aric added as his horse reared on his hind legs.

The Horn's Creek Tavern roof sagged, moss grew on the siding and the door hung loosely on its hinges. Three men staggered from the establishment, arms wrapped around each other's shoulders. Each had a cup in his hand.

They stopped. "What can we do for you fine gents?" one asked.

Ryder leaned forward, resting his arm on the horn of his saddle. "Any one seen this man?" He held up the portrait Stewart had drawn of Richy.

"He's been here. Owes me several pounds. Lent them to him to bet on a horse at Newmarket. But he lost and now he says he doesn't have the money to pay me back."

"You aren't the only one who's lookin' for him."

"I'm not?" Ryder watched the men who appeared as if they'd just as soon cut their throats as talk to him.

"Tell you all about him for a price," the first man said as his gaze seemed to rake over the trio.

"Nah..." Ryder started. "Understand enough already."

"You do? What does the likes of you know?"

"Well, I know the Scotsman. If he finds this man first, all is good." Ryder sat up straighter and let his hand rest on the sword at his side.

"It ain't only the Scotsman who came here lookin' for him." One man broke free and stepped closer to Ryder. "It's a lady masquerading as a boy. Didn't make a damn good one though, too many curves."

Ryder inhaled a sharp breath. *Christel.*

"Yeah, had an old lady with her, carried a cane and waved it at us."

"Where are they now?" Ryder's heart felt as if it exploded in his chest.

"Wouldn't ya like to know?" He rubbed two fingers together, a sneer on his face.

"Whether you tell me or not, I'll find out." Ryder dismounted, Aric and Damian followed suit.

"Where ya goin?"

Ryder didn't acknowledge the question. He tethered his horse and walked inside. It was dark and smelled of spilt ale and urine. Even knowing what he did about Richy, it was hard to believe he'd fallen so far.

Just inside the door he had a three hundred sixty degree view of the tavern. Tables were on end and chairs broken.

The tavern keeper appeared from a side door. "Don't want no more trouble."

"Looks as if there was a fight. Anyone hurt?" Ryder fists clenched, thoughts of Christel rumbling through his head. *And The Duchess.*

"What's it to ya?" The keeper rocked back on the balls of his feet, seeming to prepare for a fight.

"Where are they?"

"Got a lot of clean up here." The man looked over his shoulder. "Gonna cost a pretty penny to fix this."

Ryder reached into his purse and tossed him a gold coin. The man bit down on it then grinned.

"Well, ya see this here old lady showed up with this wee little lass. She didn't fool me none. Knew it was a woman from the start. They was askin' about a man called Richy Rathen. But he wasn't here. This huge Scotsman got to him first."

"The fight?"

"Oh, that. Well some of the men here haven't seen such a fine lookin' lass in a while and they thought they should get somethin' from her."

Ryder's gut clenched. "I'll kill anyone..."

"She means somethin' to ya?"

197

"My wife."

"Then ya' ought to be teachin' her what she should and shouldn't be doin'. Not to worry though. The old lady whipped out her cane and started a swingin', but it wouldn't have done any good."

"She did what?" Ready to hit some heads together, his anger bubbled while his stomach churned.

"Hang on," Aric put his hand on Ryder's shoulder. "I don't think she would've taken Christel on a mission of this sort without protection."

"You're right," he turned his attention from Ryder. "Before I could blink, whistles were blowin' and men rushed into the tavern. The brawl was something to see. I stood behind the counter and enjoyed it. Only took a few minutes and fightin' men were hauled off. Don't know what's goin' to happen to all of them."

"Bloody hell!" The explicative rolled off Ryder's tongue.

"You can catch up with them."

"My wife or the Scotsman?" Ryder wasn't sure he wanted to see Christel, at least not until he cooled down.

"Either. They've only got a few minutes on you."

"Think we should check on Richy first," Damian said with a grin on his face.

"Thanks for the information." Ryder strode from the tavern, not wanting to ever visit this place again.

"Nasty business. What do you think The Duchess and your wife were doing?" Damian mounted his horse and turned him down the road.

"Just what we were. I don't want to know what brought them here. I know where we've been and can only pray they haven't been in the same places."

"You got to admire them," Aric said, laughing at Ryder's vexation.

"No, I don't." His gut told Ryder something was not as it seemed. The hair on the back of his neck stood on end and sweat beaded across his forehead. They mounted.

"I don't think he's told us everything." Damian urged his horse down the road.

"He hasn't." Ryder pushed his horse to a canter.

"They're only a few minutes ahead of us. We can catch up to the Scots and see if they've got Richy."

"What if they don't?" Aric asked.

"Can't make any decisions until we talk to Cameron. I'm worried about Christel and The Duchess. Bloody hell, whose idea was this?"

"Then why aren't we going back to town?" Damian asked.

"Because." Ryder spurred his horse harder, hoping to make up the distance in the shortest amount of time. Because the innkeeper said no one was hurt, because he might do something he'd regret, because... And the list appeared infinite.

Minutes seemed like hours before Ryder finally saw the three men traveling, two on beautiful sleek stallions and the third on a donkey. He smiled for a moment at the sight of Richy on top a donkey.

"Whoa..." Ryder called out to the Scotsmen in front of him.

Cameron turned and stopped. "Didn't expect to see you."

"Heard you picked up Lord Rathen and had to make sure he was in your capable hands before I headed home." Ryder leaned over, resting a forearm on his saddle horn. "Wanted to hear what happened at the tavern."

Cameron went on to explain the events pretty much the way the innkeeper had told them. "Heard a young lad took a shot in the chest though."

"A lad or a lass?" A wave of darkness passed through Ryder. He needed to turn and ride hell bent back to London.

"Well, that's the thing. There was talk of a disguise. Don't know. Weren't there."

"What happened to them? The innkeeper said no one was hurt." Ryder needed answers, and he knew The Duchess would take care of Christel if she were hurt in the fight.

"Heard they headed back to London under armed guard."

He breathed a bit easier yet his heart still thundered against his ribs. "What are your plans for Richy?"

"He's going to work off his debt then he's free to go," Cameron said, looking at Richy as if he were the scum of the earth.

"And free to harm my family."

"Don't think he'll work it off anytime soon." Cameron let out a belly laugh. "Maybe in the next twenty years or so. By then he'll be too old for foul play."

"Guard him well. He has a silver tongue and it seems he can convince any young lass to his side. He's done it before and I'm sure he can do it again. He wormed his way from my dungeon with his lies."

"I'll take heed and make sure the only ones of my clan who come near him are old men."

"Before you go, I want the forged marriage license."

Richy spat in the dirt. "I don't have it."

"Look in his satchel." Cameron tossed it to Ryder. "I saw some papers there when my men searched for weapons." Cameron dug into the bag until he pulled a batch of papers from it then handed them to Ryder.

"Thanks," Ryder held the papers aloft. "These will be burned."

"She is my wife and the child's my son." Spittle flew from Richy's lips. "I will return for them."

"Liar. If the law had its way, you'd be in Newgate. You're getting off easy. You'll be fed, get clean clothes and in perhaps twenty years free to move on to a different life. You should be thankful for your head."

"I'm thankful to no one."

Cameron tugged on the donkey's rope. "Time to move along. We've a great distance to travel before we can rest."

Ryder watched the Scots disappear around a corner in the road then turned his horse toward London. Finding Christel and making sure she was safe was paramount on his list.

Hours passed by in a blur before Ryder reached The Duchess's townhouse. Leaping from his horse and racing up the steps three at a time had him in Christel's room in a blink.

He stood in the doorway, trying to control his breathing, his heart racing. A doctor sat at the bedside, bent over. Damian and Aric stood behind him.

The Duchess met him. "You shouldn't be here." She tried to escort him from the bedroom.

"I wouldn't do that." His voice was a low growl and made The Duchess step back for a moment.

"You shouldn't be here. Christel is fine." The Duchess persisted.

"A doctor would not be here if that were so." Ryder stepped forward, peering over the man's shoulder but to no avail.

From the nursery, Liam let out a bellow. "Mamma..."

"Really, see what you have done." The Duchess berated him. "You woke the little man."

"What I've done?" His body shook with anger and fear. He'd never felt so helpless. Someone would pay for this travesty. "You took her on a fools' mission with no regard for her safety."

"You're wrong about that. We were heavily guarded; now go see to your horses or the baby or whichever you prefer."

"That is what the stable boys will do and I'm sure Aidan or Rose will be happy to take care of Liam. Tell me what happened and why the two of you went to that inn. Bloody hell, but that was the most foolhardy notion. And where else were you? Masquerading..." What hadn't they told him?

~ * ~

Sweat beaded on Richy's forehead and slipped down his face. The back of his head was slick with moisture as well as his back. His muscles bunched and strained as he hoed the rocky land. He'd give anything for a cold pint of ale.

"Get back to work."

The harsh voice brought Richy back to this horrible reality. "You get on with work." Richy wiped the sweat from his face with his sleeve. "I'm not doing anything more 'til you bring me water."

"You'll get water when you finish this row. Bloody hell, but I've never seen anyone as lazy as you. Shoulda' been finished with this plot yesterday."

I will kill Ryder MacLaren if I ever see him again, if I ever work my way out of this hellhole.

"The harder and faster you work the sooner you'll be done."

"You readin' my mind?" Richy asked. Lord, but he wanted to be done, but what did he have to go back to?

I have a son who needs a trustee. I'd have all my father's money at my disposal. But I'd have to get rid of Christel to claim it.

"When you finish with Cameron's land, you got three others you owe. They're linin' up." The man cracked a whip and Richy jumped. He'd never hit him, but the sound made him cringe.

Chapter Fourteen

Christel fought the fog in her head and the searing pain engulfing her. Ryder's voice pounded in her brain. She tried to speak but she heard nothing, her throat raw and parched.

"Ryder," she thought she mouthed the words. Evidently, he heard. "Christel."

She knew he was close but she couldn't see him, couldn't open her eyes no matter how hard she tried. *Ryder...*

"What happened to her, Duchess?" Ryder's voice was harsh, condemning.

Duchess sighed heavily and Christel heard the hesitation as The Duchess tried to tell Ryder her foolishness. "She stepped in front of me, took the bullet meant for me. I..."

Fighting the muddle surrounding her, the fire consuming her arm where the bullet ripped through her skin. She would be fine, nothing life threatening, so bloody hell why couldn't she open her eyes?

"She's unconscious." Ryder picked up her hand and the warmth sent a feeling of security through her.

"She'll wake up soon. It's the laudanum."

Christel heard the doctor's voice and silently thanked him for answering her question. Once more she tried to form words, needed to tell Ryder what had happened.

If her head would just stop aching, she could open her eyes. She needed to reassure Ryder and to find out what happened to Richy. She didn't remember and was so worried he might have escaped Cameron and his men.

A moan escaped her lips.

"She's in pain." Ryder smoothed the hair from her forehead. "Wake up, my petite one, please."

She'd never heard Ryder plead for anything.

I want to see your face, want to tell you how sorry I am and how foolish The Duchess and I were to search for Rathen.

The fire in her arm had turned to a dull throb; she moaned again then opened her eyes. "Water." She wanted to speak her husband's name.

His hand settled behind her head and gently lifted her. He held a cup of cool liquid next to her mouth and helped her to drink.

"How are you?"

She nodded, not wishing to tell him how she really felt. "I will live, I think." She sipped more water. She understood he must want to yell at her for not staying safe. He probably ranted at The Duchess.

"The doctor here says you have naught but a flesh wound, your arm. And The Duchess says you are a heroine and should be applauded."

"But you don't think so." Christel tried to smile. He'd set her head back on the pillow and bent to brush a light kiss on her lips. Exhaustion seemed to engulf her, and she prayed she could keep her eyes open long enough to explain.

"I didn't say that. I'm more than ecstatic. After all that happened and what the two of you did, you are both alive. But if you had stayed at home, the outcome would have been the same, and it would not have been necessary for you to protect The Duchess with your life." He sounded too calm.

"But we did not—stay at home." She reached out to touch his face but didn't have the strength. "You can yell at me."

Ryder lifted her hand to his cheek then kissed the back. "No, I don't intend to lecture or yell. Rest now and promise me you'll never again do anything so foolhardy. No, don't. I'll pray that you can accept my protection, but I fell in love with you and this is who you are."

"Really?"

He smiled then inhaled a long breath. "I would change nothing about you."

The door to their room closed. Liam's cries for his mama had ceased. She wasn't sure when but someone must have gone to him. The

Duchess and the doctor had left them alone.

Ryder walked to the other side of the bed then stretched out beside her, propping his head up with his hand then traced one finger around the bandage on her arm.

"You shouldn't worry so much about me. If Richy is with Cameron—"

"He is."

She swallowed searching for words. "If Richy is with Cameron, then he won't be around to hurt anyone I love."

"Or hurt you and Liam."

"Tell me, did Cameron take Richy?"

"Yes, we met up with the Scots and they'd put Richy on a donkey. His hands were tied and he looked damn uncomfortable."

"Good." She wanted Richy to be reminded daily of the horrible things he'd done and of all the people he'd hurt.

"Good?" Ryder laughed long and deep. "My sentiments too, however, Richy will not be easy to keep as a captive."

"We both know how cunning he is." She didn't want to believe he might be able to wile his way out of Cameron's confinement.

"And he will not waste any time searching for a way out. I've retained men to work for Cameron and to send a message if Richy escapes."

"Can you help me to sit?" Her head's pounding had changed to a dull throb. She thought if she could get her brain above her heart, the blood would flow downward and stop hurting.

"Do you think that is a good idea?"

He looked so concerned for her. "Yes, I wouldn't have asked."

"Oh..."

Taking his time, he fluffed the pillows behind her then helped her. She sat back with a long sigh, feeling better the moment she'd relaxed into the softness.

"Thank you," she said. "You know we discovered a lot about Richy." They had and she vaguely remembered a moment of empathy for the horrible man. Everything he held dear had been wrenched from him, but at his own hand.

"Where did you and The Duchess go?" Ryder's face took on a solemn expression she wasn't sure how to figure out.

"I'd rather not say, but the people we spoke to sent us in the direction of the inn and well, after that..."

"You were shot."

"Yes, but we are all safe. Ryder, I don't want to argue." She rubbed her temples, the pain ebbing with the massage. As each moment passed, she felt more normal.

"Neither do I, but I cannot help myself. I need to know everything you did, all I was unable to protect you from."

"It's not your job in life to protect me." She wanted to yell at him but chose to remain calm, understanding she'd never be able to convince him otherwise.

"I can't agree with you." His eyebrows slanted together, his eyes darkening.

"I would rather you..." She didn't know what to say. She wanted to tell him how much she loved him and she'd die if he did not return. But there was still, in the back of her mind, the thought once this was all solved and he knew Richy could cause her no more harm, he would leave. Giving him her heart to have it ripped from her chest was a real fear.

He had the power to break her heart and condemn her soul to a life of loneliness and despair. She and the MacLaren ghost would spend their hours weeping together for their lost loves.

Not if she encased her heart in steel and surrounded her soul with armor so strong nothing could break through.

"Yes?" he asked. He'd walked to the door and opened it. "What would you rather?"

"We thought you all might be hungry." A servant stood in the hallway with a platter of food.

She was thankful for the diversion. The scent of roast beef filled the air. "I am famished." Christel sat up straighter but grimaced as pain shot through her arm.

Ryder looked at her then held out his hands for the tray. "Thank you," he said then he walked to the table and set the food down.

"What is there?"

"Let me see." He lifted the red and white-checkered cloth that covered the tray. "Besides the roast beef we both smelled, there are blackberries and cream, fresh from the oven hot bread, steamed green beans covered in butter and boiled potatoes."

"Oh, I don't remember when I last ate, and my stomach just roared to life, begging me to appease it."

"Then let's eat." Ryder piled a plate for Christel, putting a sample of every item from the tray on her plate for her to eat.

"This looks so good." Christel dug into the food as soon as Ryder gave her a fork. She tried to savor the first bite of meat but found she was so hungry she could not. She tried the beans then ripped off a piece of bread from the loaf. She didn't even wait to slather it with butter before eating it. "It's as good as it looks."

Ryder sat back in his chair, arms crossed, watching her, a smile on his face even though his brows were drawn together.

"Aren't you going to eat?"

"I'm enjoying watching you, but yes, I'm hungry too."

For a few minutes they ate in silence. Christel sat back, replete and closed her eyes, taking pleasure in the feeling of satisfaction the food had given her. "Was it as good for you?"

"The food was excellent, but I believe you appreciated it more than I." He laughed as he held out a bowl of berries and cream. "Dessert."

"Hmm... Don't know if I saved room."

"I'm sure it will wait."

"Are we truly married?" Christel folded her hands in front of her. "Everything The Duchess and I discovered says we are. But I need to know."

"We are wed. There are no papers, nothing that would indicate Rathen wed you. The clergy must file records and give them to the registration office. I procured the fake document from Richy and your name was forged. The Duchess was able to have your name put on Liam's birth records. There is no mention of the father."

"Good, I'm so happy there will be no recriminations about Liam's birth. He is safely mine. Then are you going to stay?"

"What?" He sounded confused and incredulous and once again his brows furrowed together.

"Stay in Scotland, with me?"

"I had no intention of leaving you." His words sounded sincere, but there was always a chance he'd change his mind.

She hoped they were from the heart, pure and true. "I want to go—"

The interruption surprised her. "Ryder... A moment please."

He walked to the door but glanced back at Christel. She couldn't hear the whispered words between Ryder and Damian. A wave of fear began with a slow tremor then escalated. She breathed in a deep lungful of air in hopes to calm herself.

Several times Ryder looked back and each time her terror grew. A horrible thought of Richy escaping the Cameron's swept through her. This could not be happening.

You are a dunderhead. Do not think the worst before it has happened.

Ryder clasped hands with Damian then they hugged as if saying goodbye. *They are leaving without seeing me first?* She sat up in bed and winced.

"What is going on?" She'd had enough questions to last a lifetime. They could have included her in the conversation.

Damian stepped around Ryder but then was overshadowed by the rushing of footsteps. Amorica and Ravyn were suddenly beside her. Ravyn clasped her hand then tried to hug her.

"We are going home and wanted to make sure you were well enough to see before we left."

"No..."

"Yes," Amorica said. "It is time. Our visit, although wonderful and memorable, has to end. There is much to do at home. We have crops to plant and harvest. Then there are the horses."

"I see." She knew they must miss their homes and their friends. Loneliness enveloped her, and an emptiness of her soul invaded her heart. Tears pooled in her eyes, but she found a way to push them back. She'd done enough crying for a lifetime. It was time to stop and look at everything positive.

Ravyn hugged her, as did Amorica. "We don't know when we will be back. You and Ryder can visit anytime."

"I know, but I'm not sure if Ryder..." She looked at him. He was talking to Damian, their heads bent together as if sharing a secret. She could only imagine what it might be.

"You are not sure if Ryder what?" Ravyn asked, glancing at the men.

"He married me, but I don't know if he loves me or if he will even stay once he knows I'm safe from Richy. He likes to wander, and how does a man like that change?"

"You're wrong," Amorica said, looking at her as if she were crazy. "He loves you and not the sunrises you so often talk about. You must put that notion from your head and look to your future with this wonderful man."

"Am I wrong? Ryder has never been one to stay in one place for long. He likes to chase sunrises."

"Has he told you he doesn't want to stay in Scotland?" Ravyn asked, picking up her hand in an effort to console.

"No." Christel pushed the moisture forming in the back of her throat away, trying to stay strong. "He has said he will stay, but I don't want him to feel tied down or obligated to me in anyway."

"He loves you. All I have to do is watch him look at you." Amorica's smile was warm and sincere. "He's not going anywhere without you."

"He has not told me he loves me." Christel had prayed to hear those words for such a long time. Until this moment she'd given up hope of ever hearing them.

"Have you told him you loved him?" Ravyn asked. "You know it's something that should be shared."

"No," Christel hung her head, feeling guilt sweep through her. "No, I'm afraid to give him my heart." She didn't want to feel as if it had been ripped from her body. But if she voiced her love openly and he didn't reciprocate, she would be heartbroken.

"Well, I know from experience that honesty is important," Amorica said. "If I'd spoken of my feelings sooner, Damian and I would have had a much easier time finding happiness."

"That was also true of Aric and myself. We never told each other the truth but danced around it until I thought I had to leave him to make him happy. What I didn't know was that he wanted me more than life. Don't be so stubborn."

Christel closed her eyes for a moment, thinking on everything Amorica said and wondering at the risk. Perhaps speaking her feelings would erase the fear. Or speaking her feelings would make that terror damn real. In any case she would know the truth and what he felt for her.

"I will think about what you told me. I know in my heart you're right but..." there was always a but.

"Trust me in this. Not knowing is worse than all the fears that go along with it. Honesty is too important to forego. Once you discover the truth, you can get on with your life." Amorica hugged her and blew her a kiss.

Ravyn did the same then they were out the door. She watched as Damian left with Amorica.

They were alone.

"Ryder, we need to talk."

~ * ~

"What's on your mind, sweetheart?" Ryder sat down beside her bed and picked up her hand. He placed a kiss on the back of it then turned it over and lightly traced the lines.

"You and me. Our future, my future. What you plan on doing next." She looked at him, her eyes large and shimmering with passion and something else he didn't understand.

"What is it you need to talk about? You're scaring me." His heart felt as if it would break. He had been so concerned with Richy, the baby, the false wedding papers. He'd left her alone. He'd not paid attention to her when she most needed him.

She looked down for a moment then at him, her eyes penetrating his heart. "I'm afraid too."

"Afraid of what?" His concern turned to fear. "Of Richy? He

cannot harm you anymore. He's a broken man."

"Afraid you do not love me enough to want a life with me and children of our own." She'd turned a deathly shade of gray. "I can survive by myself if I can stay on MacLaren land, but I'd rather you remained and we could build a life."

"Christel, I'm so sorry. I love you with all of my heart. I'm a fool for not telling you sooner but I do love you." He watched her relax back into the pillows. "I did tell you earlier that I want to live at the castle. I want to build a life with you and Liam and have children of our own. Is that so hard to believe?"

"And children of your own?" She parroted his words.

"As many as you want," He had been afraid she would tell him she was leaving. Terror that now Richy was no threat she'd go home or stay in London. But how did she feel about him?

She touched his cheek with the palm of her hands. "Ryder, I love you with all of my heart."

Relief swept through him. "Thank God." He held her face in her hands and kissed her. Then he rose and walked to the door, bolting it from the inside. "How is your arm?"

"It only hurts when I laugh." She grinned at him.

To Ryder, it appeared she knew what he thought but he wasn't sure. He didn't want to hurt her, but he did want to reaffirm his feelings. He needed to make love to his wife and show how much he loved her, but he damn well didn't want to cause her pain.

He slipped in beside her, pulling her close, reveling in the feeling of her body next to his. "I want to make love to you."

She kissed him lightly on the lips. "Please."

"You will tell me if anything I do hurts, your arm..."

"Yes."

His lips found hers. They kissed then kissed again, each one a little deeper than the last. He traced the seam of her lips with his tongue and she opened for him. He'd never made love to his wife and it seemed as if he'd waited a lifetime for this. Thoughts whirled through his head. A lifetime would not be enough with her. She was his soul mate. If he had his way, they would love each other through eternity and a few seconds later they were both naked.

Heat, sexual need and a rising desire replaced thoughts. His body hardened against her softness. She ran her fingers over his face touching the stubble that grew there. She was so soft; all of her save the nipples pressing against his chest. God, but he didn't want to hurt her.

She stroked his back and neck with one hand. He rubbed his face lightly against hers then trailed kisses down her neck then between her breasts, circling her belly button with his tongue. She moved against him, her sweetness an aphrodisiac to his soul. He continued, laving kisses as he made his way ever lower. She was wet with need for him and that made his heart soar.

"You want me." He looked up and saw her stomach, her breast with beaded nipples and her face. Her hand encircled his head. He wasn't finished. He moved lower still, pushing her legs apart so he could see all of her, the pink folds that guarded her woman's secrets encompassed in her cream.

Nipping his way down the inside of her thigh to her knee then down to her tiny ankles. She was so fragile and so soft but she was tough as nails too. He looked at her again; the view so enticing it was explosive.

"Ryder."

"Yes, my little one." His grin whirled from the inside out. He knew what she wanted, needed, her voice told it all. Yet he wasn't about to end his seduction yet. He continued up her other leg, kissing, sucking, nipping until her hips writhed with need.

He reached her folds, so pink, so wet, then tasted her, massaged her clit with his tongue. Nipped in places then laved the spot reveling in the heat emanating from her and the tiny moans of pleasure.

"I swear I will torture you like this when my arm is healed." Her breaths came in tiny little pants.

He laughed and slipped a finger inside her, felt her body convulse around him and continued his ministrations until her hips bucked, until she quivered and shook, "Ryder, please." Then calmed.

He moved upward, letting his body slide against hers, enjoying the soft nakedness against his hardened flesh. He kissed her then kissed her again. They weren't' finished yet.

"How do you feel?"

"Hot, winded, satisfied."

"Not for long. Your arm?"

"It doesn't hurt. I don't even know it's there."

He sucked on one nipple the other he rolled between his finger and thumb. She massaged his shoulder muscles then his biceps. Running her fingers through his hair, he basked in the feelings swamping him.

She would never be enough. He would never have her enough times.

And yet it wasn't the physical part of their relationship that drew him and made him want to stay. It was the embodiment of Christel, her beautiful nature, the serenity that usually encompassed her and what he loved the most was her impulsive nature.

His hands rested on her belly, and he felt her quiver. She wanted him again, needed him as much as he needed her.

He was inside her. She pulsed around him, sucking him deeper inside with each movement. Her fingers wrapped in his hair pulled. He delved inside, deeper and harder until he could hold back no longer.

"Christel!" her name tore from his lips. He pumped harder until all of his seed was released inside her body. "Christel," he said more softly than he could ever remember saying her name. "Dear God, I love you."

"I love you more," she told him then tugged on his hair, bringing him closer for another kiss.

He moved up behind her, holding her nakedness against him. He loved the way the soft curves of her butt nestled his cock with such endearment. Cupping her breast with one hand and sleeping beside her was heaven.

He wanted her again.

Yet he held back, touching her bandage, guilt washing over him.

"It doesn't hurt," she told him.

"Little liar."

"Ryder, I want to go home."

Epilogue

Two years later

"Are you happy?" Christel watched Ryder cradle his newborn son in his arms.

"Never been more pleased. I'm glad this tiny little cherub came into our lives." He placed a kiss on his forehead then stroked her cheek with his finger.

"He smells so clean and sweet. See, he's smiling." Christel knew that would delight Ryder. He was such a perfect daddy. He'd always been good with Liam, but neither one of them had known Liam as a newborn. All their skills were put to a test.

"I'm his favorite." Ryder laughed.

"No, I'm his favorite, right mamma." Liam looked to Christel for confirmation.

"You're his favorite big brother and no one can take that away. Ryder's his favorite daddy."

Ryder laughed again then ruffed Liam's hair. "Am I your favorite daddy?"

"Of course," Liam looked as if that was a stupid question.

Ryder handed the baby to Christel then rose. Picking up a ball, he tossed it back and forth between his hands. "Want to play?"

"Yes, I do." Liam ran and Ryder kicked the ball to his son. Liam kicked it back giggling. "I like this."

They played while Christel nursed the little boy. He was such a sweet angel. Their lives had been good the last years. Richy still labored in the Cameron fields. Talk was that he grew stronger and he'd changed.

Still Christel didn't believe he could ever change enough that she wouldn't be terrified of him getting away and stalking her again.

Owen appeared in the glen where they picnicked. He stood watching them for a minute or so before walking closer.

"I've news," he said, the look on his face terrified Christel. "No, it's nothing bad; in fact, I think you might be a bit pleased."

Ryder strode to Owen and they shook hands. "What is it?"

"Richy has wed one of Cameron's servants. They are expecting."

"Shotgun wedding or love?" Christel wondered if this was something Richy had wanted or if he'd been forced.

"Rumor has it, they love each other." Owen shrugged. But I don't think it's prudent to let down our guard too soon."

"One way or the other, I hope he stays put and has tons of children." Christel stopped nursing the tiny child then placed Kenzie on his back. The soft coverlet she was sitting on served as a nice resting spot for the infant.

Ryder laughed. "You think that will keep him busy?"

"No, but I pray it will make him forget about our son." She looked in Liam's direction. He sat on top of the ball, watching something on the grass.

"I'll be leaving now. Don't want to interrupt your pleasant afternoon, and I'll keep a few men at the Cameron's fields just to make sure Richy stays put."

Ryder nodded then sat down beside Christel, wrapping an arm around her. He kissed her. "I love you, Christel MacLaren, more than any sunrise I've ever seen and more than all the adventures in the world"

She sighed and leaned into his warmth. "I love you, Ryder MacLaren, and someday I want to chase a sunrise or two with you."

Also by Christine Young
Available at Rogue Phoenix Press

Storm's Passion
The fifth book in the Twelve Dancing Princesses Series

Chapter One

The Year of our Lord: 1818

"No! I'd rather jump off hell's cliff north of here." Storm's hands were fisted at her side, her insides churning. What could her father be thinking? But it was her father, and she knew he thought only of himself.

"What?" Bradford appeared stunned at her revelation, his eyes narrowing. His cheeks turned red, and a small drop of saliva slipped down one corner of his chin.

"You heard me father." She turned from the old man who thought to call himself a man unable to look at him, yet resigned to see this through to the bitter end if that's what it took. She would find a way to thwart his plans.

"You can't refuse. I have a signed contract." His slack jowls quivered, his cheeks flaming with the rage he wasn't holding in check. He shook his fist in the air as if to make his point clearer.

"This is not the Dark Ages. What kind of contract." Back stiff, she faced the man who'd sired her. He was mean-spirited and meant nothing to her. No familial feelings had ever existed between them.

"A written agreement, signed and notarized, promising you will marry Charles Robertson. In this matter, you'll do as I tell you." He moved forward in his chair as if this would accentuate what he said.

"I will never say the words and in the end, it is up to me." Head high and fiercely determined, Storm faced her opponent. "Real fathers, real men don't betroth their daughters any more. It's archaic." So angry, her body shook with rage and the tempest brewing inside.

"It's my choice. I am your father and this marriage will be in your best interest. I have only your feelings at heart." His voice had regained a slight measure of calm, but his eyes had darkened.

"You have no feelings or a heart. Look what you did to my mother, your wife. She's in her grave now, because of you."

A few shattered seconds passed as Storm considered her biological father. A man who had despised her the second he knew she was not the male heir he'd coveted. More than anything, she needed to discover the truth about why he'd decided to sell her off like an animal to the highest bidder. "Why?"

His ensuing grin sent chills down her spine. "I can do whatever I want with you. It's time you were out of my home. You should have a husband who can control your impulsiveness. And children to keep you in the home."

"I'll leave." Her nerves snapped, and she tried to hold on to her fast-rising temper. Ravyn, her older sister, would give her a home. Storm had funds, one thousand pounds, her father didn't know about. Long ago, her survival instincts had become part of her everyday life, and she'd found a way to hide every extra penny.

"You'll do as I say," Bradford shot back, his temper flaring to life. "This is your fault. I don't have the funds to send you to London and The Duchess, Storm. For the last few years, I've asked you to find a husband, and you've blatantly ignored my wishes. Now, my health is not at its best, and I want to see you taken care of when I can no longer do it."

"To you, I'm a means to an end. I can take care of myself. And when have you ever cared about my well being?" Storm challenged, seeing the angry red splotches on his face. "What is this really about? For the same number of years, you didn't care what I did. Why now?"

Bradford sat up straight, his hands on either side of his chair. "Charles Robertson has offered for you when no one else will have anything to do with you. You are wild, impulsive and have no manners. You've frightened away all the men who might have shown interest. I've had it with you and your willfulness. I will see you wed before I die."

Storm watched her father rub his fingers up and down his breastbone. She understood the signs of his failing health. That much he hadn't lied about. "The state of your health is nothing new."

"I care now, Storm. You cannot continue to run around the countryside doing whatever only God knows." His voice was raspy, the color of his face growing white as death. "You're a woman who has past her twentieth year. All this time you have refused to listen to my requests. I gave you ample opportunities to find a husband for yourself. Since you have failed, I found one for you."

Storm pressed her mouth together, ready to defy her father again. "Bradford," she began, loathe to call the man in front of her, Father. "We have talked about this matter on numerous occasions. My feelings have not changed. I do not want to marry anyone. Ravyn has given you an heir, a male heir. There is nothing more to discuss."

"What Ravyn has done is no concern of yours. Charles wants an heir," Bradford retorted, his voice stronger. "Every girl wants a husband. Your sister Ravyn is happily married. You can be too."

"Not to Charles. I can't stand the man. And, what, can he find no one willing to marry him? Am I surprised? Hardly. He is as mean and as despicable as you, Bradford."

"I will have some respect."

"When you have earned it. If you acted like a father, I would both love and respect you. I am nothing to you, except a way to make money. So tell me, what will you gain from this marriage? I'm beginning to think this affair goes deeper. What have you done?" Storm approached her father. "Despite what you haven't told me, I don't like Charles and I won't marry him."

"It doesn't make any difference if you like Robertson or not. Many successful marriages are made every day between people who don't like each other." Bradford drummed his fingers on the table, his brows drawing together.

"I won't be one of them." Storm closed her eyes for a moment, trying to tamp down the rage threatening to explode. "Bradford, I want you to listen to me," she said, praying her words would reach him and change his stubborn determination to control her. "I loathe Charles and as

I said earlier, I would rather jump off the cliff at hell's edge than wed that man."

"Storm, you must realize by now that a signed contract is binding. I expect you to honor my wishes. I have no apologies. This is expected of you. You are my daughter whether you like it or not."

Strom faced the door, wishing she could run away from this conversation and what it meant to her future, but it was imperative she get to the real reason he was selling her to Charles. She wiped sweaty hands on the red day dress she wore while she paced the length of his study. "It can't be binding," she argued. "You can't do this without my consent and I don't give it."

Bradford sat forward, his forearms on his desk, and his hands clasped tight. "I never told you it was a betrothal contract."

She strode to the desk and rested both hands on the polished surface, knowing her fingerprints there would anger him. "Now we get to the truth. What is it then, the real reason for this travesty?"

He cleared his throat, and she watched his Adam's apple move up then down on his meaty throat. "More of a gentleman's agreement."

"You are not a gentleman. Did you gamble something away, me? Charles is a cheat. You should know that fact."

"I did not gamble with Charles but his father, Henry."

Storm sat on the chair in front of her father's desk in an effort to calm her escalating emotions. "Stop skirting the question, Bradford. Tell me the truth and not one lie."

Bradford grinned again. "A few days ago, Storm, I borrowed some money from Henry to escape a debt. I'd placed too much money on a horse race and lost. I was sure the beast would win."

"But he didn't. Was he a horse from your stables?"

"You told me he was the best. That he would win every race. It's your fault."

The facts became clearer. "You bet on Fiacre. He is not ready to race. When I spoke of him, I spoke of his future. Did you enter him against my wishes?" She held her breath, searching for an inner calm but found nothing remotely similar to tranquility.

Bradford cleared his throat then leaned back, folding his hands in front of him. "Henry wants his money, and I do not have that much. I lost a small fortune. Now he wants me to settle. But the real problem stems back over fifteen years. I've owed him money and interest on what was borrowed."

"Settle?" Storm questioned. "What does that mean?"

"The translation is simple. He gave me a choice, the cash or..."

"Or agree to marry me off to his son," Storm finished, the despicable reality of the situation finally out in the open.

"Yes."

"You hate me that much, Bradford? Surely Mr. Robertson knows how I—no, how every girl in the town feels about his son."

"He doesn't care anymore than I do. Charles has told him how much he adores you and can't live without you. That's enough for Henry, and if I had a son, I would give him whatever he wished for."

"That sounds like obsession, not love. Do you know why Charles left last year?" The hair on the back of her neck stood on end.

"Not really, Henry said, "he was looking for adventure. Quite respectable for a young man."

"He...yes, I suppose it is acceptable for the male to find adventure." She knew what had happened and she'd agreed not to tell anyone, but Charles had forced her best friend and an illegitimate child had resulted from his action. He left to allow things to cool down, but now that he'd returned, he was causing more trouble.

"Tell me if I'm wrong. You have signed an agreement with Henry Robertson that states he will forgive the debt if I marry Charles." Her father was worse than she'd thought. How could a father do that to a daughter?

Bradford grinned. "You are very bright for a girl. It's that or turn the stables over to him."

"Fine," Storm said, "then we will do just that."

"Good."

"We will hand over the stables. He can have them. He won't know what to do with them but that's his problem."

Bradford rose, his body quivering in anger. His hands fisted on the desktop. "You are a selfish bitch just like your mother. The stable and the brewery are all we have. If I turn the horses over to Robertson, I'll have nothing."

"What about the brewery?"

"The funds are controlled by my brother Tenley. I couldn't sell my interest even if I wanted. As the eldest, Tenley controls everything."

"Oh, you might have to sell the house?"

"You would be on the streets."

"I would find some way to support myself. I'm young and smart. I'll be fine." Her bravado was just her way of covering up the real fact. Other than begging on the streets, she didn't know how she'd survive.

Bradford's lips thinned when he glared at her. "You can't do that! I've arranged a fine marriage for you to one of the richest young men in these parts, next to Hadden Johnston."

"Charles is an ogre and the most odious creature I've ever met." Storm knew her arguments were not heard. Bradford's mind was made up, and she'd have to figure some way out of this situation or she was well on her way to becoming Mrs. Charles Robertson.

"If you won't do it to improve yourself and your status in the community then do it for me. I'm bound to honor the contract, and I know you don't want to lose the animals. Your selfishness will dishonor me. I don't think I could live with the shame."

Storm's fingers dug into the armrests on her chair. She tried to keep from screaming at her father. In a tight, controlled voice, she said, "I'm selfish? You accuse me when you fathered so many children on my mother, wishing for a son, that she died in childbirth. How dare you speak of selfishness? I did not gamble all my fortune on a horse and borrow money from Henry Robertson. I will not be bartered so you can pay him the money owed. I don't care if you sell the stable, sell the house, or sell your soul to the devil himself, but I will not marry Charles Robertson."

~ * ~

When anyone asked Storm to keep a secret, her lips were closed tight, but this had gone on far too long. Ella needed to step up and tell the world what Charles had done. But that wasn't going to happen. They were the best of friends but opposite in every way. This time Storm needed someone to listen to her woes. And it was this very difference that always prompted Storm, at every crisis, to turn to Ella for counsel and advice.

Ella Brummel and her new husband Lawrence lived in a plain brick house situated near the center of the village located near Berwick-upon-Tweed. Although Ella had wanted to live closer to Storm, Lawrence insisted they live close to the port where he kept the books for many of the merchants. Ella had confided that she didn't understand why this was so important to Lawrence, but she refused to question her husband. Ella had been grateful Lawrence had accepted the bastard child into his house. In return Ella would give her husband everything his heart desired.

After leaving her father's study, Storm had raced to the stables, saddled her favorite horse, Fiacre, and with hair flying behind her, sped to her best friend's home. Riding into the Brummel's yard, Storm jumped off the horse, and tossed the reins over the hitching post while muttering a few choice phrases, and praying Lawrence wasn't at home. She needed to talk to Ella about the situation her father had put her in, but it was private and she didn't want to hear Lawrence's opinion. She strode to the front door and pushed it open a crack, poking her head in and calling, "Ella? Ella are you home?"

"In the kitchen, Storm."

Her heart racing, Storm closed the front door and strode through the tiny living room into her friend's kitchen.

"What brings you visiting this afternoon?" Ella's voice was cheerful. She bent over and with a large mitten on her hand, opened the oven and brought out a loaf of freshly baked bread. "I didn't expect you today. I thought you were training the new filly at your stables."

Throwing her hands in the air, she said, "Everything has gone awry." Storm was curt and immediately regretted the way she sounded. "Bradford has done something cruel, and I have to talk to someone. I hope this isn't a bad time."

"I'd love to talk with you. Sammy is taking a nap and should be asleep for at least another hour. So out with it. What's on your mind?"

"Way too much and none of it good. I've a problem and it's the biggest I've ever faced."

"So what has Bradford done?" Ella's smile faded. She took her friend's hands in hers and led her to a chair. "Sit and I'll slice some bread and pour us a cup of tea."

Until Charles had forced Ella, she'd always thought a cup of tea would solve the world's problems. But Storm was too upset to sit. Instead she paced the length of the kitchen then back. With a reluctant sigh, she gave up and pulled out a chair. "What I need is a glass of wine or a shot of the best scotch you have, not a cup of tea."

Ella's eyebrows disappeared into her fringe of bangs. "Bloody hell, Storm, what could be so bad? You know I don't judge and there has been a number of times we've both indulged but..."

"Bradford."

Despite her concerns, Storm couldn't help but remember other times. Mostly the anxiety had come from Ella. But this time she was shocked when Ella rose and went to the sideboard where she pulled out a bottle of scotch and poured her a drink.

"Here you go. Now let's have some girl talk. Tell me what your father has done to upset you this much."

"He sold me." Storm told her friend. "He bartered me and signed a contract with Henry Robertson, selling me into marriage to Charles."

Ella hissed in a lungful of air. "Doesn't he know what Charles is capable of? If he did, he couldn't have done anything so despicable. Didn't you tell him what he did to me?"

"You swore me to secrecy. Besides, Bradford doesn't care about me, only himself. He would tell me that you had wanted it, and Charles couldn't refuse you or your advances."

"That much we both know is true. But why? This seems so sudden."

"It's a long story." Storm downed the scotch in a gulp, grimacing at the fire shooting through her insides. She slapped the glass on the table and poured herself another drink. "It seems Bradford entered one of our horses and bet on him, but the stallion wasn't ready. He wasn't old enough to race." Storm finished the tale, tears sliding down her cheeks. "And he did it to pay off another debt plus interest he accrued years ago."

"Well that's your father. I don't think he will ever change. He's a selfish man, but to betroth you to that scum of the earth, Charles Robertson." Ella paused, then, "You need to tell him."

"No." He wouldn't believe me and even if he thought there was a grain of truth in the story about you and Charles, his wishes would still come first on his agenda. I'm a female and can be used in any way he pleases. He's proved many times what he thinks of women."

Ella gazed out the window for a moment, sucking her bottom lip beneath her teeth. "You know, Storm," she began, "he has a point. Not with Charles Robertson but with someone else. Wouldn't you like to be married and have children?"

"Not really...maybe if I loved that someone."

"You are wed to your horses and now you are about to lose them. What will you do? How will you take care of yourself?"

"I have thought about that very thing. I will go to London then on to America. Ravyn will take me in and give me a home."

"That would be running and that's not you. Honey, this is your home. I understand you're afraid, but I know you and you are determined and courageous. I've never seen you hide from adversity. You stand up and fight."

Ella was her supporter, but could she reveal Ella's secret to the world? No, she could not but maybe Ella could. "You said earlier that I should tell Bradford what happened to you. Did you mean it?"

Ella's face drained of color but she stiffened. "Yes, Lawrence knows the truth, but I don't believe he wants the entire village to learn of it. Telling your father would be a wild card."

"Charles would be dishonored, and his father would know him for the reprobate he is."

"Yes, yes..."

Looking at Ella's face, the lines of worry and despair etched across her forehead, Storm understood the secret had to be kept. She could not infringe on Ella's happiness. "I'll figure out another way around this. No matter what Bradford says or does, I won't marry Charles."

"I'm asking too much. I'm just as selfish as your father."

"No, you are not. You have your family to think about, and they should come first. I feel better now just talking to you."

This time Ella poured herself a shot and Storm her third. They both downed the drink in one gulp. After a huge sigh, she said, "You have to tell Bradford everything. I will speak to Lawrence and if anyone would understand, he would. He's told me more than once how mean and despicable Charles is when he drinks. He would abuse you and cheat on you. Nothing in this world is worth that kind of pain. Your life would be a miserable one, and I won't have my dearest friend undergoing a lifetime of sorrow and misery."

"I can't do that. I won't lower myself to discuss something so...so private with him. Even if I did, he wouldn't believe me. As I said before, he wouldn't care. The debt is all important to him."

"But Storm you have no choice."

"No," Storm repeated. "When you told me about what Charles had done to you, you made me give my word I wouldn't speak of it to anyone. I feel like I betrayed you just thinking about telling Bradford. I don't know what Bradford would do with the information. Even if he went straight to Charles, you know the man would deny it, and I know who Bradford would believe. "

"What are you going to do?"

"I don't know yet," Storm said. "I thought maybe you had a better plan than running to London or the United States."

"You know," Ella said, tapping her glass on the table, slanting her gaze to the ceiling then back to Storm. "I just might."

Storm inhaled a breath of air, her nerves shattering while she waited for Ella's idea.

"What you need is to marry someone, and I'm not telling you that because I've found wedded bliss with Lawrence. You need to do this before Charles returns from his hunting trip. When will he be back?"

"I have no idea but that's not the answer to my problem. I don't want to marry anyone. I just want to go on running the stables."

"You and I both know that won't be possible, not unless you can find the money to pay back the debt and the only way to do that is to marry the wealthiest man in this part of the country."

Ella rose and for several minutes paced the length of her kitchen. She halted in midstride, her eyes lighting with excitement. "I've got it. You can marry Hadden Johnston.

Storm leaned back in her chair and laughed until tears ran down her eyes. "That's the most foolish idea I've ever heard. Hadden doesn't want to marry any more than I do. Besides he's always gone. He sails with his merchant ships. We see him in town every six months or so."

"Don't you see? That's perfect. He would be at sea, and you would be home in the stables doing what you love. You'd never stomp on each other's toes." She clapped her hands together. "What do you think?"

"Really? You're serious about this aren't you? You've lost your mind, is what I think."

"This calls for another drink." Ella sat down and poured them each another shot of Scotch. "My dearest friend, he's not only the answer to your problem, he's the perfect answer."

"At this rate I'm not going to be able to ride home." Storm downed her drink anyway then set the small glass on the table.

"Fiacre knows the way home."

"I might have to rely on that. Your scheme while worthy has too many flaws. Mr. Johnston is not going to suddenly ask me to marry him. Why on earth would he want too?"

"Well that is exactly what we are going to have to figure out."

"You are aware that every girl of marriageable age is after him. I don't stand a chance. And besides no one has received so much as an invitation to a dance, much less a wedding ring."

"That doesn't matter." Ella slanted her a huge grin. "It just doesn't make any difference what so ever. We can figure out some way to pique his interest."

"Ella," Storm said as if speaking to a stubborn child. "Hadden Johnston does not want to get married and neither do I."

"I understand all that. It's what makes this plan so flawless. The two of you could come up with some kind of agreement. You know, a marriage of convenience." She put a finger to her lips. "He doesn't want all that female attention, and you need someone to pay your debt. It's a bargain neither of you can deny."

"You've gone crazy, Ella. He would never agree to something so insane. He would never agree to this devil's bargain."

"He might, if we, if you laid out your plan in a way he couldn't refuse." Her eyes sparkled to life in a way Storm had never seen them.

"Ella, no."

"Storm, yes. All we have to do is figure out how to lay out our plan so Hadden Johnston is in agreement. After we do that, you can go to him and present the idea."

"Idea? It's more like a proposition which doesn't sound so good. I refuse to blackmail him."

Ella planted her hands on her hips and glared at Storm. "Would you please stop seeing something bad in every thought I have. I'm trying to help you out of a terrible place and I never said blackmail."

"I know you are," Storm gave her best friend a huge hug, "and I appreciate you more than I can ever say. But Ella, this idea or proposition is so ridiculous I can't take it seriously."

"I really think you should, or you're going to find yourself walking down the aisle with Charles Robertson before you have time to blink an eye. Now I know you're adamant that you won't do it, but I think in this matter Bradford has the upper hand."

"I know I would lose everything. But wouldn't that be better than a life with Charles?" Storm inhaled a deep breath.

"Do you want to live in poverty?"

"No, but The Duchess or Ravyn would take me in."

"You wouldn't have your horses," Ella countered.

"Better than having Charles for a husband. I've got some serious thinking on my plate. So what if I did talk to the elusive Mr. Johnston? And he agreed. What then? That still isn't going to solve the problem of paying Henry back. We would still lose the stables, so what's the point?"

Ella paused for a moment, looking a bit sheepish, then said, "I think after a woman gets married, her debts become her husband's responsibility, so Mr. Johnston would probably be legally bound to pay Mr. Robertson."

"Ella!" Storm was stunned by her friend's despicable plan. "That's horrid. I can't believe you'd think this let alone suggest it. I would never do that to Hadden Johnston. I don't even know the man, except from doing business with him, and he's never been anything but honest and polite with me. I couldn't possibly deceive him like that."

Ella waved a dismissive hand. "Nonsense. We'd figure out some way to pay him back."

"How?"

"I don't know. Let him have your best racing stallion and all of that horse's colts to do with as he pleases. He could keep them for himself to ride or he could train them to race."

Storm's eyes narrowed as she thought about all of the possibilities. "You might be on to something. I don't think he'd want to ride. I've heard he doesn't like horses, but racing them. If the horse wins, I could have the debt paid off in no time, and I wouldn't lose the stables and my beloved horses either."

"Right," Ella nodded excitedly. "Everybody wins. You get to keep the stables and you're safe from Charles Robertson, and Hadden Johnston saves a fortune. And, you can also use the shipping contract he has with the Graham brewery to further cement the deal."

"Well, in the first place he hasn't lost anything. So that brings me back to the beginning. Why don't I just go to Mr. Johnston with the proposition that he pay off my debt and receive the winnings from the races and the colts that are sired and see what he says? If he accepts, there is no reason for marriage."

"Because that won't save you from Charles," Ella countered. "You know what that man is like. He's crazy-insane. If Henry thinks Charles wants you, he won't give up. What you need is protection only a man like Hadden Johnston can give you. No, you need to marry Mr. Johnston."

"Well, I still don't think Mr. Johnston will agree to something quite so preposterous. How on earth would I go about approaching him?"

"Play on his sympathies. You just said the two of you have a good business relationship, which means he likes you. Tell him about the deal you're willing to offer him, and if he argues, confess you're being threatened by Charles and your father. But don't call your father, Bradford. That will not do at all. Hadden despises Charles, so he'll most likely take pity on you."

"Why does Mr. Johnston hate Charles?"

"Ah, a couple of years ago a cousin of his came to visit and there was some trouble between Mr. Hadden and Charles over her."

"Indeed, Charles asked her to go buggy riding. Hadden allowed her to go, but something must have happened, because afterward, Mr. Johnston challenged Charles to a duel. Of course that's no longer legal, but Charles agreed then turned and fired at Mr. Johnston before the count of ten. Charles missed and Mr. Johnston was gentleman enough to shoot him in the arm when he could have killed him."

"I remember. Did the Robertson's press charges?"

"And have Charles' cowardice come to light? No, they didn't. But there were enough people in attendance that the truth could not be hidden for long."

"Knowing what I know now, I hate to think what Charles might have said or done during that buggy ride," Ella said.

"Anyway, knowing how he feels about Charles, if you tell him you're being forced into marriage with him, he just might agree to help."

"Or he could kick me out."

"You have nothing to lose. The worst he can do is say no."

"If he told me no, I would just be back where I am now. I really don't want to leave my home and my friends or my sisters. What if he laughs in my face?"

"He won't." Ella pushed away from the counter and gave Storm a reassuring hug. "After all, he can't be all bad. He did challenge Charles to a duel, and he didn't kill him when he had the chance."

Cast adrift after fleeing the home of Jokul, the ice demon, Atantsi, a firestarter, grew to womanhood as she moved through time to keep the demon from finding her. Though stubborn and courageous, she was ill prepared to use powers she had not been taught. Her first sight of the intoxicating Carr McKenna left her breathless, and her second encounter gave her hope for a future she never thought she had.

A playboy, a second son and a shifter, a man who thought his life would be carefree, Carr McKenna was shocked to discover the woman he'd paid as an escort is a firestarter who is running for her life. He is the leader of all the McKennas around the world and that he has multiple powers. His passion for Margo and the need to defend her might cost him his life as well as hers.

Sweet Talkin' Sugar
Book Four in the McKenna Clan Series

Lyonesse McKenna, was dreaming or was she? From the instant Lyn saw Deacon McClain across a black jack table in a crowed Las Vegas casino the unmistakable attraction sent Lyn's senses flying into overdrive. Her family of shapeshifters believed in soul mates. She'd always been skeptical yet she couldn't help but question the way her heart sped when he looked at her.

When Deacon appeared in Las Vegas he knew his first job was to save Lyn from a Sea Demon, but the next order of business was to convince her he would someday mean more to her than she'd ever expected. But her stubborn nature and unbendable spirit consumed Deacon...and he had to chase away all the demons real and imagined in order to win her heart.

Sweet Talkin' Sugar
Book Five in the McKenna Clan Series

Lyonesse McKenna, was dreaming or was she? From the instant Lyn saw

Deacon McClain across a black jack table in a crowed Las Vegas casino the unmistakable attraction sent Lyn's senses flying into overdrive. Her family of shapeshiters believed in soul mates. She'd always been sceptical yet she couldn't help but question the way her heart sped when he looked at her.

When Deacon appeared in Las Vegas he knew his first job was to save Lyn from a Sea Demon, but the next order of business was to convince her he would someday mean more to her than she'd ever expected. But her stubborn nature and unbendable spirit consumed Deacon...and he had to chase away all the demons real and imagined in order to win her heart.

Dakota's Bride
The first book in the Lakota/Pinkerton Series

When Emma St. John received her brother's letter imploring her to escape her stepfather's vengeful scheme and to trust Dakota Barringer with her life, she was willing to chance it. But the handsome, brooding riverboat owner Emma found in Natchez a danger of another kind. For Emma soon found herself surrendering to an unrelenting desire.

Raised by the Sioux when his parents were killed, Dakota had been betrayed once before by a white woman. He wasn't about to trust another, especially one claiming that her stepfather, a powerful U.S. senator, had framed her as a murderess. But he couldn't let Emma's intoxicating effect on him. Now Dakota would risk his very life to protect the innocent beauty who had seduced him with her tender love.

My Angel
The second book in the Lakota/Pinkerton Series

A BEAUTY IN BUCKSKINS
When her father decided to send her to a finishing school back East, Angela Chamberlain refused to be confined to stuffy drawing rooms.

Instead, the daring spitfire who could shoot like a man and ride like the wind longed for a life of adventure and romance—and she knew exactly who could give it to her. Devil Blackmoor was a hired gun with a dangerous reputation. But Angela was willing to go to the ends of the earth to capture the handsome devil's heart.

A DEVIL IN DISGUISE
He'd come to America looking for excitement, but Devil Blackmoor got more than he bargained for when he encountered a beautiful rebel who answered his kisses with a wild innocence that touched his very soul. Yet standing between them were more obstacles than either ever dreamed. For Devil had strapped on a gun for the wrong man. And that made Angela his enemy. Now he'll have to choose between his duty and the woman he loves more than life.

The Locket
The third book in the Lakota/Pinkerton Series

The year is 1894. Seeking revenge for crimes against his family, Misha Petrovich follows a path that leads straight to Ariel Cameron's boarding house in Mist Harbor, Oregon. A family heirloom in Ariel's possession leads Misha to believe she is guilty. The locket has been handed down to the oldest girl in the Petrovich family for generations. Ariel is innocent of wrong doing, but her father is not. Misha is torn by his feelings for Ariel and his need for restitution against her father. Knowing that the relationship between them is fragile, Misha does everything in his power to protect Ariel's father. His efforts are to no avail when her father is shot. Ariel comes to realize Misha's steadfast courage and determination to protect her and her father despite what has happened to his family. Ariel's love and devotion heals Misha's heart.

The Talisman
The fourth book in the Lakota/Pinkerton Series

Running from a marriage that lasted one night, Dr. Moriah McKeown discovers the land she has settled on is coveted by determined and lawless men. Yet the proud young woman who once vowed never to abandon her home has second thoughts when her adopted children are threatened. Her only recourse is to enlist the aid of a dark, dangerous gun for hire.

Haunted by the past and a betrayal he will never forgive, Ian Civanovich uses his fast gun and his reckless courage to forget the faithlessness of a woman in his past. He will trust no female—nor will he rest until the threat hovering over Moriah McKeown is put to rest.

Forever His
The fifth book in the Lakota/Pinkerton Series

Struggling to come to terms with the part she played in Jacob St. John's death, Etta Barringer resigns from Pinkerton Agency and seeks peace and solace in a Rocky Mountain Cabin.

Jacob has vowed to discover the reason Etta has betrayed him, sold him out to his enemy and left him for dead.

Isolated in their cabin, they discover their love for each other and learn to trust. But the trust is shattered when Jacob learns she is married to his sworn enemy; the man who left him in the desert to die.

Allura's Secret
Twelve Dancing Princesses Book One

Allura McClellan is horrified by her father's decision to take out an ad in the Times awarding her to the man strong enough and smart enough to win her hand and uncover her secrets. She's an intelligent young woman who takes great delight in the freedom allotted to her by her father. She's well aware that marriage would effectively curtail the adventures she's shared with her sisters and cousins.

Hunter Gray is nothing like the other men who've arrived to vie for Allura's hand in marriage and everything that goes along with it.

However, he is the first to refuse to concede defeat and pursue her despite her attempts to disguise her true appearance. It's her temperament that is of more concern to him than her looks. Hunter has worked all his life with the hope of someday owning his own land. Now that it looks like there's a very real possibility that everything he's ever wanted is within reach nothing is going to deter him – including Miss Allura's disagreeable disposition.

Amorica's Wager
Twelve Dancing Princesses Book Two

Amorica Hepburn was sent to London to find a husband. Finding a man was the last item on her agenda. With her two cousins, Amorica wagers she can dissuade her suitor before the others. Despite her efforts she discovers a chemistry that cannot be denied. Suddenly she is the arrogant man's wife, pledged to a marriage neither desire. But swept off to his ancestral home above the Dover cliffs and into his strong embrace, Amorica is soon possessed by a raging passion for the husband she had vowed to despise…

Damian Andrews couldn't afford to trust the emerald-eyed spitfire who happened upon his secret. Amorica's hatred of all men of his kind only inflames the war that rages between them. Still, he cannot control the intense desire his stubborn bride inspires, or make her surrender to his will until he has conquered the headstrong beauty on the battlefield of love…

Ravyn's Marriage of Inconvenience
Twelve Dancing Princesses Book Three

A REGAL BEAUTY
When The Duchess decides to wed her to a wastrel and a fop, Ravyn Graham takes matters into her own hands and declares her engagement to another man. Instead of fessing up and telling her great aunt what she has done, she goes through with the pretense. Aric Lakeland is the bastard son

of an earl and has a dangerous reputation. But Ravyn is willing to do most anything to keep The Duchess from discovering the lie.

A DEVIL-MAY-CARE SMUGGLER
He'd bought land in America, looking to put down roots and end his life of adventure, but Aric Lakeland got more than he bargained for when he encountered a beautiful heiress who made a promise she didn't want to keep. But the promise could not be undone and standing between them were more obstacles than either ever dreamed. Aric had made plans to spend the rest of his life in America and that was at odds with Ravyn's plan of living in England and running her father's estate. Now, he'll have to choose between his dreams and the woman he loves more than life.

Christel's Sunrise
Twelve Dancing Princesses Book Four

He Made Her An Offer...

Life has thrown Christel McClellan some experiences that could have devastated a less determined woman. Beautiful, self-assured and fiercely independent, she is trying to forget the loss of her stillborn child. But is the child alive?

She Couldn't Deny...

Life is carefree for Ryder MacLaren who loves to see what is on the other side of the sunrise. Laird of Clan MacLaren, he is wealthy, handsome and happily unencumbered...until stunning Christel McClellan enters his life. When he hears her story, he believes the child she thought dead has been sold to a wealthy buyer.

Storm's Passion
Twelve Dancing Princesses Book Five

SHE MADE A PROPOSAL...

Life strikes Storm Graham a shattering blow when she learns her father has bartered her to a man she detests. Storm is beautiful, self–assured and fiercely independent, and refuses to be a pawn in her father's schemes, yet she can find no way out of this bargain made in hell. Going on the offensive she asks the wealthiest man on the eastern coast of England to marry her, never believing she might fall in love.

HE TRIED TO REFUSE...

For Hadden Johnston life has provided everything he ever wanted, including a sanctuary for homeless children. He is wealthy, handsome and happily unencumbered...until stunning Storm Graham marches into his life and proposes a marriage of convenience. Yet this type of marriage to a woman who inflames his senses is far from acceptable. If he's going to be tied down, he will move heaven and earth to have this woman warming his bed.

Gotta Have Fayth
Twelve Dancing Princesses Book Six

A regal beauty with raven hair and piercing blue eyes, Fayth Graham is unwilling to parade herself in front of the wealthy Lords of England during the season. Seeking a means to dissuade any man wishing to wed her, she seeks a way to ruin herself for marriage. When she unexpectedly meets a man with sparkling gray eyes and an infectious grin, she decides this is the man who will keep her from agreeing to obey.

He returned from six months at sea, looking for a few nights of pleasure with a willing lass, but Jarret Kinsley got more than he bargained for when he met a beautiful debutant who responded to his kisses with a wild innocence that touched his heart. Yet the obstacles looming between them might rip them apart. Both had vowed never to marry, so when consequences of their dalliances got in the way, Jarret would have to choose between the life he's always desired and the woman he loves more than life.

Ella's Pleasure
Twelve Dancing Princesses Book Seven

A WHISPER OF PLEASURE

Ella Hepburn was an auburn haired debutant from the harsh Scottish coastline—a wild innocent to be seduced and tamed. A spirited beauty, she captivated Drake Montgomerie's jaded heart—while succumbing to the smoldering desire she felt for her unyielding suitor.

A WHISPER OF DANGER

In Drake Montgomerie's glittering world of money and privilege, young Ella discovered passion and desire could overcome everything she'd been taught to resist—entangling Drake, the heir apparent, in a lethal coil of aristocratic family intrigue. But grave peril would only nurse the sparks of a love that knew no limits and a magnificent ecstasy that would not be denied.

Eveleen's Seduction
Twelve Dancing Princesses Book Eight

A WHISPER OF SEDUCTION

A brutal attack on Eveleen Hepburn's cherished island off the Scottish coastline leaves her shattered and bewildered. Learning a man she once trusted can kill as easily as he can breathe even though the deed saves her life, creates questions that need answers. An innocent beauty, she enchants Logan Maxwell's cynical heart—giving in to the raging passion she feels for her mysterious suitor.

A WHISPER OF INTRIGUE

In Logan's Maxwell's world of espionage and privilege, young Eveleen discovers truths about herself she never expected, and a need for passion and love can overcome all her fears if she learns to accept certain truths. She finds herself entangled in a lethal battle for land that was once owned by French nobility, taken from them during the revolution and sold to Maxwell. But grave peril would unleash the flames of love that simmers, creating a magical union that cannot be refuted.

Tavia's Deception
Twelve Dancing Princesses Book Nine

WHISPERS OF DECEPTION

When her father decides to send her to London for her season, Tavia Hepburn resolves to see the world instead. The raven haired beauty decides to disguise herself as a lad and find employment on a ship bound for Barcelona as a cabin boy. But she never bargains on finding passion and love to a red haired sea captain who rescues her from certain death.

WHISPERS OF MURDER

For James Macmurra, the world is black and white until he meets a young debutante, who turns his world upside down. He's unable to deny Tavia's intoxicating effect on him. In a match tense with obstacles, unwillingness to divulge secrets, and unforeseen peril, irresistible desire and passion grows into undeniable love. James would risk his life to shelter and protect the innocent debutante who seduces him with her sweet love.

Twelve Days to Love

When Archer Steele shows up at Calanthe Durand's failing plantation with an alligator over his shoulder, Cali thinks she's never seen a more handsome man. During the war she had to defend herself and her servants from both union and confederate soldiers. Independent and self-sufficient, she vows to never marry.

But Archer Steele has different ideas. The first time Archer sees Cali in town, he feels an instant attraction. He decides he will do everything and anything to convince the beautiful Miss Durand he is worthy of her love. During the weeks leading up to Christmas, he gives her twelve gifts in hopes she will fall in love with him. Yet they are faced with challenges they must overcome before Cali can commit to a marriage.

Door to Heaven

Jessica Lawrence is the stepdaughter of a woman born in the twentieth century transported back in time to the year 1868. An acclaimed suffragette, she raises Jessica to believe in the equality of women. Jess Law believes everything she was taught, and when the time is right she becomes a private investigator. Courageous and impetuous, Jess finds danger in her quest to save all women from white slavery. Her passionate mission results in a wedding to Roc Newman, a man she knows can steal her heart...

Roc can't trust the sapphire-eyed spitfire who invades his home in search of secret papers and knocks him flat with her karate moves. Jessica's refusal to obey his wishes serves to inflame the war between them. Still, he cannot control the intense desire his reluctant bride inspires, or make her surrender her independence, until he has conquered the headstrong beauty on the battlefield of love...

Rebel Heart

HER REBEL SPIRIT DEFIED HIS OUTSIDERS SOUL... She was velvet and silk, eyes the color of a summer storm and amber hair. Victoria

DeMontville, because of a promise and a codicil to her father's will, was forced to marry one man to protect her from another. She hated Cameron Savage with a fierce passion. But to hold on to her genetic research and find a cure for the deadly Signe virus, she must pretend to love the enemy at her door, come with weapons of fire to melt her icy heart...

HIS OUTSIDERS TOUCH IGNITED RAGING PASSIONS... He wore a mask, disguised as the Phantom, a true legend come to life. Even as war and debate over new genetic research engulfed them all, he would find his greatest adversary in the beauty who'd branded him an outsider and barbarian, the woman he was born to possess, his soul mate.

Safari Moon

Solo St. John, a wildlife photographer, is preparing for a trip to Alaska. Suddenly, Solo finds women of all sorts invading his privacy, his home and his office, all cooing nonsense words and blatantly throwing themselves at him. Solo doesn't know why, and he has no idea how to rid himself of the persistent women. He finally decides to beg a favor of his best buddy Nyssa Harrington.

In love with Solo for the past ten years and knowing he doesn't return her feelings Nyssa doesn't want to talk to Solo. She knows if she accepts his phone call, she will not be able to resist the temptation to hope again.

Straight to Heaven

Running from demons, Alexandra McMurdie stumbles into Forbidden Ground where up is down and elements of nature are contested. Though a strong independent woman in the twenty-first century' she is unprepared for life in the 1800s. Her first site of the formidable James Lawrence makes her heart skip a beat, giving her cause to reconsider her desperate need to find a way home.

Born with a silver spoon, James' life was torn apart during the War Between the States. Moving west he vows to put the life he once knew in the past. When he discovers a half-frozen woman near Gold Hill, his heart begins to thaw. His love for Alexandra and his need to keep her from a man who has pursued her through time might cost him his life as well as hers.

A Valentine's Anthology

The Lending Library-a fantasy by Christie L. Kraemer

Faeries try to fit into the human world when the forest where they make their home is destroyed by a mysterious enemy.

Chasing Rainbows-a contemporary romance by Genene Valleau

An eccentric aunt, an inventive uncle, a mother who wears poodle skirts, and a brother who wears pearls provide a hilarious backdrop for the courtship of a young woman who yearns for a "normal" family.

The Gift-an historical romance by Christine Young

A man and a woman on opposite sides of the Civil War get a second chance at love after one final battle returns soldiers to their war-torn homes to rebuild their lives.

A St. Patrick's Day Tale
by
Christine Young, C. L. Kraemer, Genene Valleau

Tumble through time…

…to Ireland in 1817, when tensions are high between Protestants and Catholics and faey people guide the fate of villagers. A lovely Catholic lass stumbles upon the weakly ritual fisticuffing between Irish lads. She falls into the lap of a handsome young Protestant. Family ties, grudges, and two conniving faeries threaten their budding love. But the faeries outsmart themselves when they hijack a time machine that has mysteriously appeared in their forest and are whisked to…

…Eugene, Oregon in the 20th century, amid a property feud between the local faeries and night elves. The conniving faeries from Olde Ireland try to stir up more mischief. However, a warrior gnome convinces the magic folk to control their own destiny, and forces the intruding faeries to take refuge in the time machine again, spinning their way toward…

…A modern day castle in western Oregon. An eccentric inventor is determined to reclaim his wayward time machine and save his beloved wife from her latest misadventure. If only they can travel safely past the black hole…

a May Day Anthology
by
Christine Young, C. L. Kraemer, Rosemary Indra, Genene Valleau

Highland Miracle -- Christine Young

HURTLED THROUGH TIME, Sean Michael Sterling, landed in the midst of a May Day celebration he didn't understand, assuming the role of Laird Sterling.
ILLIGITAMATE CHILD OF NOBILITY, Reagan Douglas searches for a way out of her half brother's house.

Defying the Odds -- C.L. Kraemer

The night elves on the hill aren't happy without their magic. They concoct a plan to punish those who were involved in the act that rendered them almost human. Meanwhile, Uther, the rogue night elf, has returned to woo the Librarian to be his eternal mate.

Love in Bloom -- Rosemary Indra

When childhood friends reunite it takes two fairies and a matchmaking daughter to help them admit their true love for each other.

No More Poodle Skirts -- Genie Gabriel

After drifting for years in the innocent age of the 1950s, a woman struggles to join today's world by finding a career and a new love, with some help from her zany family.

Once Upon a Christmas Moon
by
Christine Young, C. L. Kraemer, Genene Valleau

TWELVE DAYS TO LOVE

When Archer Steele shows up at Calanthe Durand's failing plantation with an alligator over his shoulder, Cali thinks she's never seen a more handsome man. During the war she had to defend herself and her servants from both union and confederate soldiers. Independent and self-sufficient, she vows to never marry. But Archer Steele has different ideas. The first time Archer sees Cali in town, he feels an instant attraction. He decides he will do everything and anything to convince the beautiful Miss Durand he is worthy of her love. During the weeks leading up to Christmas, he gives her twelve gifts in hopes she will fall in love with him.

BOOTS AND BLADES

An ancient evil from the old country has arrived in the high desert of Oregon. Gnome children are vanishing then re-appearing, showing various stages of traumatization. Tiamoon, warrior gnome, will put her skills to use alongside Killian, a handsome warrior, also in need of a cause.

CHRISTMAS PAWSIBILITIES

With their world destroyed and their space ship malfunctioning, the dogizens of Planet Canid have little choice but to crash land on Earth. They face tortuous experiments at the hands of the Geeks in Green...or they can trust an eccentric inventor and his zany family to deliver the Canine Queen's puppies and help them celebrate new lives.